MS. MONEY BAGS

LADY BILLIONAIRE SWEET ROMANCE

DARCI BALOGH

KNOWHERE MEDIA

For all the ladies who have lessened themselves to lift up someone else or given up their dreams and think they may never come true.
This Lady Billionaire series is for you.
All of my books are for you.
Find yourself, name what you want, and make it happen.
You are worth it.

CHAPTER 1

*L*orna Presley Monroe lifted the slender wine glass to her lips and took a sip. The Chardonnay was crisp, cold, and it rushed across her palate leaving traces of flavor that many people found delicious, but to her tasted like hair spray.

She concentrated to keep from wrinkling her nose in disdain as the bitterness filled her mouth. This was, after all, the best Chardonnay made in Italy. A guest of a renowned vineyard, she was being served by the owner himself, Conteggio Domenico Bolsena. He was a Count whose ancestry reached so far back through time in the Umbrian wine region that he was as much a part of this country as the rolling hills and sparkling lakes. Nobody could ask for a better wine drinking experience than this one.

The Count, that's what she called him since his name was so much to pronounce, controlled half of the province in Italy where her family's business interests were looking to expand into eco-tourism. They needed his cooperation and blessing to move through the mountains of red tape associated with such things. She could not wrinkle her pretty little nose at his wine selection. It cost too much. The nose, not the wine.

Lorna, known as Presley to both her friends and enemies, delicately took a pale round cracker from the lavish charcuterie board in front of her and nibbled the edge. She had managed to eat next to nothing today despite the constant spread of cured meats and cheeses that seemed ever ready here at the Count's grand estate, Villa Pallotta. One cracker wouldn't kill her.

As the cracker snapped between her teeth she sighed inwardly. Though bland, it was lightly salted and crispy and the mere act of chewing on it awakened food cravings that should have been successfully suppressed by her Garcinia supplement. She doused the urge to eat quickly with a healthy sip of hair spray wine.

"You like, Ms. Monroe?" the Count asked eagerly.

She nodded, doing her best to put off the correct mixture of politeness and boredom. "It's very nice," she said. "And, please, call me Presley." The Count beamed.

Presley hated being called Ms. Monroe. It reminded her of her mother. And she was definitely not her mother.

Presley put a lot of stock in names. She believed it mattered what people called you in life. A name could make or break a company, a product, and a person. She had always dismissed her first name, Lorna. That was her great-grandmother's name. Given to her only to appease her father, Malcom Peter Monroe II, a billionaire businessman who was known to his friends and family as 'Mack'. To the public all across the world he was known as 'Mr. Money Bags'. Her middle name, and chosen moniker, was also given to her by her father. For his love of Elvis, obviously.

Presley had suffered a brief stint as Lorna Presley Monroe-Calhurst in her early twenties when she had made the huge mistake of marrying Lawrence Calhurst. That had not lasted. Not at all. The marriage had been a disastrous three months in real life, though closer to two years on paper.

Larry had swept her off her feet during her last year of college with gross displays of romanticism and a charming smile that she learned, after they married, was a device he liked to use on many women. Many, many women. Young and stupid, she had taken the bait. It still irritated her that she could have ever considered marrying someone who went by the name 'Larry'. Thank goodness for pre-nups.

Her short time as a Calhurst was what she referred to as her rebellious stage. The one and only time she veered from the narrow path her father, Mack, had laid out for her since she was a little girl.

"You're the oldest, Presley," he had told her throughout her life. "I've built an empire for you and your sister and brother. And you..." here he would always lay his massive hand on her shoulder and smile. "You were built to be in charge."

And take charge she did.

In fact, Presley had taken charge as CEO of Mack Industries since her father's part-time retirement two years ago.

Mack was a huge, broad man with a booming voice and a reputation for taking over his competition by the strength of his personality alone. He had a strong jaw, sandy blonde hair, which started turning white in his early forties, and a larger than life presence that had not faded as he aged. Unfortunately, though his personality remained in tact, his heart had weakened over the years. Too many late night meetings and down to the wire stock takeovers had taken their toll on his health. And after one too many scary doctor visits he had been delegated to the back seat of Mack Industries by their long time family practitioner, Dr. Zalman.

Mack handed Presley the keys to his legacy, literally, in an over the top congratulatory party her mother threw to celebrate the transition. He shook her hand and smiled for the cameras and gave her full control of the real estate holdings, the hotels, the portfolios of stock investments, various other construction and industrial businesses, and the chain stores that had started it all, Mack Extras. The specialized convenience stores with the kitchy name were owned and operated throughout the United States, Europe, and most recently Asia. All of this had been put under Presley's exclusive command.

Her father built his billion-dollar empire from humble beginnings. He invested all of his life savings into purchasing a convenience store located in the lobby of a popular hotel in Santa Barbara. The first Mack Extras store. He had focused on providing high end convenience items to hotel patrons. Nothing tacky. Only the best of the best snacks, toiletries, clothing, books and entertainment were sold at Mack Extras. The first one had caught on and became a second and a third, then he had moved into purchasing the hotels and nearby real estate. The rest, as they say, was history.

Presley had watched him work his way up in the world since she was a little girl. Unlike her younger sister and brother, she could actually remember the 'good old days' when they only owned a few shops and lived in a one story ranch style house. She and her sister, Veronica, had shared a bedroom and their mother had made dinner in the small, narrow kitchen. She was a terrible cook.

Those days were long over. Thankfully.

The Monroe's lifestyle was significantly and forever changed through Mack's business prowess. They owned nothing but sprawling mansions, too many to remember sometimes, in the most beautiful corners of the world. Their mother hadn't cooked a meal in over 30 years. The initial struggle to succeed was over. The Monroe family had made the Forbes list of American billionaires for more than ten years and Presley had the reins. She kept a tight grip on those reins and vowed every day to protect and improve the fortune her father had worked so hard to obtain.

"Would you like more wine...Presley?" The Count hesitated slightly when he used her first name. He tipped the wine bottle toward her half empty glass.

She shook her head, "No, thank you." His smile stopped, but only for an instant. Presley politely reassured him, "It's delicious. I'm simply a little tired from my trip."

"Of course, of course," the Count was filled with contrition for not recognizing her fatigue, counterfeit as it was.

Presley had arrived from New York mid-morning. Traveling on a private jet was not nearly as fatiguing as flying on a commercial airline. Mack Industries jets were equipped with comfortable seating, King sized beds, luxury bathrooms, and full kitchens complete with a chef and staff. Using jet lag as an excuse to avoid offending people who she wanted to do business with was a standard tactic and almost never failed.

The wine tasting room at Villa Pallotta was in the basement, cool and dark. Lit with massive candles as big around as tree trunks resting on tall iron stands, and rustic iron electric chandeliers placed strategically from the 15-foot high ceilings, it was not dim. The lighting gave it an almost glimmering feeling, as if they were under water instead of under ground. The walls were made of stacked clay bricks, likely handmade and hundreds of years old, if not thousands. The floors were clay tile, lain in a swirling pattern so they gave the illusion that one was walking on waves in a stylized ocean.

They were seated in massive high backed chairs at a heavy wood table that had to have been more than a century old, full of nicks and knife marks, and black burn spots, but polished to a dull shine. Light classical music surrounded the small party seated around the antique wooden table.

The party included the Count, but not the Countess who had remained upstairs to oversee dinner preparations. The Count's nephew was in attendance, as was the Winery captain, and the CFO of the Count's affairs. Representing Mack Industries was Presley, her personal assistant Jaxson, and the president of Mack Industries Hotels European division, Drew Beeker, who had arrived from London just after Presley landed. A few quiet yet efficient waiters and waitresses hovered around the perimeter, monitoring the food, fetching whatever the Count requested, and whisking away used items.

It was all very pleasant for a wine tasting party, but this was not a party. It was a business meeting. One that Presley could not quite wrap her head around, which was irritating.

Mack Industries had always been about elegance and glamour in their hotels and the Mack Extras stores. But eco-tourism was beyond Presley's experience and she didn't know why they were kicking off this project with a meeting in a wine cellar. They weren't in the market for another vineyard, not after the mess her mother had made of their vineyard in France.

When her father had called her late last night and insisted she attend this meeting in person, Presley had had questions. A lot of questions. Mack had promised to fill her in on the details before she sat down with the Count and his people. Yet, here she was, sipping her least favorite type of wine and searching for excuses to stall.

Presley glanced at Jaxson, who was usually able to read her mind. He was jotting notes down by hand with a stylus on his tablet. A slight wrinkle of her brow caught his attention and he responded with a barely perceptible shake of his head. Presley did not keep her cell phone on her while in business meetings and relied on Jaxson to inform her of any urgent messages. He knew she was awaiting further instructions from Mack, but Jaxson's negative response to her unspoken question told her that her father had not yet been in touch.

"If you'll excuse me," Presley stood, which triggered all of the men at the table to stand. This chivalrous move never failed to please her. "I would like to take a short break and use the restroom."

"Of course, of course," the Count agreed wholeheartedly. "Please take your time. A small walk around the grounds may refresh you." He spread his arms wide to encompass everyone at the table. "We will all take a small break and I will check with the Countess to see when dinner will be served."

In the bathroom Presley surveyed her reflection in the full-length mirror. She smoothed her hair. She was back to blonde after a few years as a redhead. She'd gone just above shoulder with her length at the suggestion of her hairdresser, Phillip, and the ever style conscious Jaxson. Her straight, thick hair ended in a flirty blunt cut right at her collarbones. The look suited her, she thought. Lightened her up.

She pulled a red matte lipstick from her Chanel clutch and leaned into the mirror, reapplying and dabbing with a tissue to soften the lines. Running a shining red manicured fingertip carefully under her eyes, she wiped away any tiny smudges of makeup that may have occurred during the wine tasting.

This close to the mirror she took a moment to glance over her face. Small wrinkles had begun to form at the corners of her eyes and lips when she turned 30, and increased exponentially at 34 when she took over as CEO. Presley wasn't one to waste too much time worrying about plastic surgery. Not anymore at least. Besides, her nose looked perfect, a gift she had given herself after her divorce in her 20's. And her eyes were still that crisp Monroe blue, inherited from her father.

Presley pulled away from the mirror and smoothed her houndstooth pencil skirt. She had chosen a plain black long sleeve knit top to go with it and liked the total look. The black was a nice contrast to her blonde tresses, plus it made her eyes pop. And she had on a new pair of Manolo Blahnick pointed toe pumps, which she liked. Very much.

"Presentable," she said, giving her reflection a brief nod.

She wondered what time it was. Without benefit of her cell phone she was at a loss and wished she would have grabbed it from Jaxson's safe keeping before she came to the bathroom. Not being on 100% sure footing when it came to business, or life, made Presley tense. Mack's special blend of part-time retirement did not always include keeping her up to speed on certain dealings. And not knowing gave Presley twinges of anxiety. She didn't like it.

"Come on, Dad," she muttered to herself as she stepped back into the wide, empty hall. She wanted to give her father as much time as possible to get in touch before heading back to the meeting, so she decided to take the Count's advice and go for a quick stroll outside. Get some fresh air.

Turning right instead of left when she emerged from the bathroom, Presley followed the hall as it sloped up and up until she found a heavy wooden door that led onto a terra cotta patio looking over rolling hills of vineyards. She stepped into the sunshine and immediately wished she had shoved her sunglasses into her clutch. Coming from the cool darkness of the wine cellar, the glorious mid-afternoon sun was positively blinding.

Presley squinted, trying to see her surroundings. Her eyes watered fiercely and she instinctively raised her clutch to her forehead in an attempt to shade them. They refused to open more than the tiniest slit in the too bright day as she stepped onto the smooth tiled patio. This move turned out to be a mistake.

Her brand new pointed toe pumps slipped on the smooth tile and she lost her balance. Reaching blindly for what should have been a handrail along the edge of the patio to steady herself, Presley found something slender and solid to grip. It was definitely cool iron in her hand, but as she leaned her weight on it for support, it swung away from her unexpectedly. Her eyes streaming tears of protest and refusing to open, Presley stumbled forward. She lunged one foot in front of her, arms flailing to each side in panic, but her foot did not come down on terra cotta patio, or any kind of solid surface.

Air.

Her foot found nothing but thin air.

Presley felt her body careening through that thin air towards an unknown abyss. For one terrifying moment she remembered that the Count's mansion had at least four stories and she let out a frightened shriek.

homp!
Presley landed on a solid warmth that cradled her body perfectly.

No. Not landed. Not exactly.

"Whoa, there," a man's voice sounded in her ear.

Muscled arms were wrapped under her back and knees. They pulled her against what felt like a man's chest. His clothing was heavy and rough, and Presley smelled freshly cut wood and dark spices emanating from him. Her eyes still filled with irritated tears, she blinked madly, but could see nothing. Feet kicking wildly in dissent she pushed away from the unknown person who was holding her.

"Let me go," she commanded.

But the stranger did not obey. He held her like a she was a bride and he was carrying her over the landing on their wedding night. She imagined that this dirty, sweaty, landscape laborer was getting muddy handprints all over her clothes. Not to mention plotting on copping a feel as he did. She pushed harder on his chest, but his arms held her in a vice grip.

"Hang on a second," the voice growled.

Presley was no longer falling, but she was still mid-air and being manhandled by God knew who. Her rescuer/kidnapper was moving far too slowly. She felt his breath on the side of her face and heard the scuffing of his feet.

"Put me down," she insisted. Louder this time. She was prepared to scream bloody murder if this Neanderthal didn't release her at once.

"Gladly," the voice said, and she felt her body lower until her bottom rested on a hard surface. The arms disappeared and Presley kicked in the direction she thought they had moved, hoping to keep them away.

"What do you think you were doing?" She spat the question in the general direction where she could hear sounds of someone catching their breath. He had placed her on some kind of patio furniture from the feel of it. Presley rubbed the tears out of her eyes with a scowl.

"Um…catching you?" he responded.

Though his voice was masculine and not entirely unpleasant, she assumed he was uneducated. Blue collar. Obviously slow witted. Presley blinked up at him, he was only a blurry blob of blue and brown hovering over her. Her eyes were still watery and had barely adjusted to the sunlight.

"Who are you?" she demanded to know.

There was a moment's hesitation before he answered with, "You're welcome."

She huffed air out of her lungs. Honestly. The nerve of some people. A thought occurred to her and she began to madly feel around the patio chair and the tiles at her feet.

"What's the matter?" the smart aleck asked.

"My purse," she snapped. Presley watched the blob of blue and brown move away.

"It fell into the shrubs. I'll get it," he called out to her from what must be the edge of the patio.

Presley didn't respond. Her eyes were finally adjusting to the light and she took a few moments to inspect her shoes for scuffing and her clothes for muddy handprints.

"Here you go," the man was back. His jeans and clunky brown work boots moved into her peripheral vision as he shoved her clutch under her nose.

She snatched it away from him and looked up, ready to give him a piece of her mind. But at the sight of him, words failed her.

His jeans and work boots were labor ready, for sure, but dirty and sweaty he was not. He was tall and lean like a swimmer, but with more hair. Much more hair. In fact, he had a tumble of thick, dark, curly hair that almost reached his shoulders and a short, semi-unkempt beard. Topping his jeans was a denim shirt, no tie, and a dark brown corduroy sport jacket.

Denim on denim, Presley wasn't sure she approved.

Yet, somehow, on him it worked. In many ways he was quite handsome and his overall demeanor was not one of a random field worker, so her defenses lowered. He must work for the winery. Winery guys always had that earthy, tousled look about them. Almost like an architect, but not quite as put together.

"Are you all right?" he asked. His expression did hold concern, but with an equal amount of amusement.

"I'm glad you think this is funny," Presley said as she stood, waving away his hand when he reached out to offer assistance.

"No, it's not funny. You could have cracked your head open." He gestured with a quick jerk of his head toward the edge of the patio where an iron gate hung open over steep stone steps. She must have grabbed the gate thinking it was a solid handrail.

"Hmmph," Presley half snorted at the shoddiness of the patio's build then shot a grudging look at her rescuer.

He was eyeing her with curiosity. "You're Presley Monroe, aren't you? Mr. Money Bag's daughter?"

The sheer audacity of his questions insulted her senses. Who was this ridiculous person who she had unfortunately allowed to catch her when she fell? She leveled a cold stare at him.

He smirked. "You don't remember me, do you?"

"No, I do not."

"Hobie," he said as he touched his chest, obviously expecting her to recognize his name. He tried again. "Hobie Brent?"

Presley watched with disdain as he tapped his chest again. Did he not realize he was acting like Tarzan? She furrowed her brow and gave him a shake of her head. She didn't know him and, more than that, she didn't want to know him.

He sighed then continued, his original hope defeated. "Hobart Brent. Barcom."

"Barcom?" Presley's eyebrows lifted in surprise. She knew that name. Her father's old partner from the early days of Mack Extras stores had gone on to start Barcom Incorporated. Her father had named Barcom Incorporated as the company he wanted to do a joint venture with involving this whole winery, eco-tourism plan that had been so loosely thrown together. She looked more closely at her rescuer's face.

"We went to school together?" he added.

A vague recollection of a tall, skinny boy who hung out with the band kids came to her. He was the younger brother of Danny Brent. Danny, she remembered. Danny was the dreamy rowing team and basketball star who was two years ahead of her in high school. She definitely remembered him.

Presley peered more closely at the man in front of her.

Tall, lean, dark and handsome. She supposed he could be Danny Brent's little brother. All grown up. "Hobie…" she said slowly, trying to remember. "You moved or something before we graduated?"

A shadow fell over his face and he nodded. Then, changing the subject, "I'm here to meet with you, actually. And Count Bolsena."

She lifted one eyebrow. He was a little late to the meeting, not a good sign. Then she remembered–the meeting! She had lost track of time.

"It's already started, I need to get back," she said as she turned to the door almost forgetting to add, "I'll show you the way."

"Um," he faltered.

She snapped her head back to look at him impatiently. "What?"

"Do you need to freshen up or anything after your accident?"

She scoffed at him. "No, I'm fine. And it wasn't an accident. I just slipped."

Still Hobie hesitated. "Are you sure?"

"I think I know when I need to freshen up or not," she said stiffly. Turning her back on him she finished, "If you want to come with me that's fine. I don't care. But I'm returning to my meeting."

She refused to look back at him, but could hear the shrug in his tone as he said, "Okay, whatever you say." He followed her back inside.

The meeting commenced and Presley took over with the utmost efficiency. She was motivated by the addition of Hobie to their meeting and felt compelled to take over and whip everyone into shape. Feeling exposed after the accident–or tiny slip–that had ended with her falling literally into Hobie's arms, Presley strove to appear as in control and competent as she knew she was. After all, it was Mack Industries who was being asked to put up the bulk of the financing for this misadventure. She wasn't about to stand down if she wasn't sure that it was in the best interest of her family and the shareholders.

Hobie's presence at the table was annoying. His rumpled appearance, casual posture, and easy manner in how he treated the Count, the other executives at the meeting, and even the wait staff was too base for her taste. The man was too unkempt to be in charge of anything, let alone Barcom. She certainly didn't want his influence over this project. In fact, Presley wasn't sure she wanted this project at all. As they drove deeper into the numbers, permits required, marketing plans, and cost versus revenue it became clear to her that this was not a sure thing. What had her father been thinking?

To make matters worse, Jaxson was acting strange. Ever since she returned to the meeting with Hobie on her heels he kept giving her tiny lifts of his eyebrows while she was speaking, or softly clearing his throat and tapping his temple when there was a pause in the discussion. Since he would have gestured to her cell phone in his lap if her father was calling, she ignored these other meaningless signals. She was on a roll and she was not going to pause for anything unless her father called. When she glared at him to stop he didn't return to note taking, but instead glanced nervously around at the Count and the others, including Hobie.

During moments when she was not speaking, which were few and far between, Presley found her eyes drawn to Hobie and his relaxed man posture. He looked like he was ordering a beer at a country music bar, not sipping some of the most expensive wine in Italy while making a multimillion-dollar deal. Once again she was struck by his good looks, despite his course, down home demeanor. She wondered if that was why Jaxson kept looking at him, though Jaxson didn't normally allow attractive men to distract him from the task at hand when he was working.

"What are your thoughts, Drew?" Presley asked her European division president after a long, drawn-out response she had just given to the Count's admission that much of the marketing would be focused on a demographic of people who made less than $100,000 per year. These were not, in her opinion, the kind of people who could spend the kind of money necessary to make the whole thing viable. Presley didn't see how any of this was going to pan out and she expected Drew felt the same. Drew's brows knit together as he studied the numbers on the report in front of him with concern.

"I think there are some real questions about the profitability," Drew responded, though he did not look at her.

Vindicated by Drew's agreement, she shook her head, feigning disappointment as she watched the Count's face fall. She opened her mouth to say that they would put all of this on the back burner for now and wait for some projections that promised more of a return for their money.

"But it's not about profitability," Hobie interjected, stopping her from speaking. He hadn't said anything since he complimented the prosciutto and cheese. All eyes turned from Presley to him. "The meaning behind all of this is to open up this beautiful area to more people. To bring joy. To do it in a way that is sustainable and actually keeps the culture and the natural beauty of the area in tact. To ensure that all of this," he opened his arms and gestured to the ancient, cool wine cellar. "Stays the way it is and is accessible to everyone." He paused again and looked directly at Presley before continuing, "And to remove some of the elitism that surrounds this industry."

Heat rose in Presley's chest. She feared it was going to

enter her cheeks and look like a blush, which it was not. It was fury. She glared at him and opened her mouth to respond when Jaxson's gaze jerked down to her phone in his lap. The movement caught her attention and Jaxson looked at her with meaning. Her father was calling.

Self-editing what she was about to say, Presley replied instead, "That is something we will have to look at. If you will excuse me, I need to take this call." She stood and all of the men followed suit. She was not so charmed this time. Presley snatched her cell phone from Jaxson, answering it as she headed to the restroom for privacy.

"Hi Pumpkin," her father's deep voice resonated confidence.

"Dad, what took you so long to call me?"

"Oh, we've had some dealings with your brother. I couldn't get away."

Presley's stomach dropped. "Pete? What happened?"

"Nothing for you to worry about right now. He's fine and everything is calm. How's the meeting?"

Presley pushed open the restroom door and stepped in, glancing around to make sure she was alone.

"Dad I don't know what you want me to do with this. It's a mess. I mean it's beautiful here and everything, but as far as the numbers go even Drew thinks this is not a money-making proposal. I think it would be a waste of time and resources."

"Look, honey, that's all well and good, but I want this. I don't care if it loses money." The heat that already sat in her chest like a knot, swelled and blocked her throat so she couldn't respond. He was undermining her decision, which always made her feel like she was ten years old. "It's important to an old friend of mine and it's important to me. I want you to make sure it happens."

He was not giving her any wiggle room. Presley looked

distractedly around, hoping for a response that would convince him to change his mind. Her eyes fell on her reflection in the full-length mirror and she gasped in dismay.

The makeup around her eyes had smeared when she'd been blinded by the bright sunshine and teared up outside, leaving huge black circles around her eyes. She looked like a raccoon. Ever since she had returned with Hobie from the patio she had looked like a raccoon. Mortified, she leaned against the wall and listened meekly to her father's demands.

"I want you to do this for me, Pumpkin. I'm counting on you."

"Okay, Dad," was all Presley could say.

CHAPTER 3

The whirring click of his camera calmed him, as it always did. Hobie reframed and pushed the button again. Capturing the deep purples and reds of the Umbrian sunset over the Count's vineyards distracted him, if only momentarily, from the events of the day.

Photography was more than taking pictures for him. Ever since he had picked up a camera as a pre-teen it had helped him focus. Helped him work the kinks out. Helped him forget.

This evening he didn't necessarily want to forget, but he did need to process the situation.

Presley Monroe. He'd known they were going to work together, of course, after his father had told him about Barcom's involvement on this project. But Hobie had not been prepared for what seeing Presley Monroe again would do to him, let alone holding her in his arms when she fell.

Instinctively, Hobie reviewed the images of the sunset on the screen of his camera. They were good. He would move to another spot and get a new angle.

Trudging through the narrow space between two parcels

growing different types of grapes Hobie headed towards a small growth of trees nearby that looked like they'd been growing there since the beginning of time. Gnarled and ancient, twisting out of the ground towards the colorful sky, the old branches and lush leaves would make an interesting foreground.

Making his way over clumps of dirt and grass his mind wandered back to Junior High and High School. Presley and Ronnie Monroe were both in his memories, as was their younger brother, but it was always the images of Presley that shone more brightly than the others.

Beautiful, small, but not in a frail way. She was sharp around the edges even as a girl, so serious, it had always been a kind of feat to get her to laugh. He'd managed a couple of times and had stood frozen, gawking at the brilliance of her smile, not to mention her piercing blue eyes that glittered when she laughed.

Not that she would remember those moments. He didn't blame her, he'd been a mess when he was a kid. Gangly, awkward, shy. Then everything that happened with his family had kind of sent him over the edge.

Hobie shook off the darker memories and framed the sunset from his new vantage point by the trees.

Click-whir-click-whir-click-whir

Presley had grown up since the last time he saw her, that was for sure. She was a beautiful woman, still small, but shapely. And still with those amazing blue eyes.

Hobie grunted his dissatisfaction with the pictures he had just taken and adjusted the f-stop. He shot again.

Click-whir-click-whir-click-whir

"You going to be able to concentrate with her around?" His brother, Danny, had teased him when they heard about the project.

"Why would that be a problem?" Hobie huffed.

Danny laughed and put his hand on Hobie's shoulder. "You never could talk to girls, especially not girls like Presley."

Danny was right. Presley had definitely been more in his crowd than Hobie's. Danny was a jock while Hobie played the saxophone in the band, badly. Danny was older, taller, better looking, more popular. He had been exactly the kind of guy a girl like Presley Monroe dated. But they hadn't dated, probably more because Danny had plenty of interest from the girls in his own class.

"I guess that's good," Hobie muttered to himself.

He paused, his trip down memory lane disrupted by that thought. What did it matter if Danny had ever dated her anyway? Danny was married with kids, besides Hobie was in charge of Barcom and whatever interactions he had with Presley Monroe at this point were based on business, not friendship or anything else.

He sighed, exasperated. Everything about this situation made him uncomfortable. Barcom was Danny's turf, not his. He wasn't sure Barcom should be partnering with Mack Industries at all, but they were. And the first meeting with Presley had gone…well…less than perfect.

The image of Presley stomping back into the meeting with the Count, makeup rings under her eyes from squinting in the sun, made him chuckle. She was still sharp around the edges, sharper than when they were kids. Even in that ludicrous situation she was fierce.

And gorgeous.

And those eyes. No amount of running mascara could dull those eyes.

CHAPTER 4

"It's been positively dreary without you here," Faye announced. Her red silk shirt shimmered in the candlelight, the color a spot on match to her perfectly applied lipstick.

"Really?" Presley didn't believe a word of it. Faye was one of her oldest friends. Besties since childhood, attended the same college, and knew each other's deepest secrets. Presley had never known Faye to live a dreary existence, but she was prone to drama.

"Grace's filming schedule was delayed so she hasn't been here. Ronnie is still in New York, probably working herself to the bone. I didn't have anybody to play with," Faye whined into her martini.

They were enjoying an early dinner at a sleek yet comfortable restaurant in Aspen. Faye kept a house in Aspen and when she was there she spent most of her time skiing, going to various spas, or socializing. Although Faye's version of skiing was more about sipping hot toddies in the lodge near a fireplace and flirting with the occasional snowboarder than actually flying down the slopes. She came from money, a lot of money, and had never worked a day in her life. She did spend a lot of time loudly resenting her friend's desire to do so. Still, Presley knew that Faye was mostly teasing. Underneath her beautiful, well maintained, and costly exterior was a basically nice person with a good sense of humor.

"What about Ruby? Hasn't she been up here planning her big fundraiser?" Presley asked, sipping her own drink, a cosmopolitan.

Ruby ran nonprofits. She was the do-gooder of their group of friends, and her pocketbook reflected that fact. All of them had spent every summer together as kids at a luxury camp for girls near Aspen. They were five total: Presley, her little sister, Veronica who they called Ronnie, Faye, Grace, and Ruby. Their friendship had endured through decades.

Faye let out a sigh. "She's been so wrapped up with the details of her party she hasn't had time to do anything with me. I'll be glad when it's all over this weekend."

They ordered dinner and another cocktail as Presley regaled her friend with her recent difficulties at Mack Industries. Faye tried to stay focused on Presley's complaints surrounding the business side of things, but she kept returning to her favorite, and Presley's least favorite, part of the whole subject, Hobie.

"I haven't seen him around anywhere for years," Faye said. "What does he look like now?"

Presley rolled her eyes. "He looks like a degenerate architect. Even his name sounds like a surfer dude who's spent too much time baking in the sun."

Faye's well defined eyebrows lifted with interest and she cooed, "That sounds delicious."

"He's not delicious. He's ridiculous."

Just how ridiculous was not something Presley wanted to relive over dinner. She wanted to forget about her recent entanglement with him, which had begun with her awkward fall and ended with her looking like a macabre clown trying to conduct a powerful business meeting. Forgetting the second time they had encountered each other at her offices in New York a few days later was preferable, too.

He had shown up in his standard issue brown sport coat and jeans. Presley wondered if he owned any other clothing, but checked herself before she asked him out loud. He had brought Barcom's CFO, a wild haired elderly woman named Mary Collins who kept asking for water and had a thick cough. The two of them had monopolized Presley's morning and then, right when they had been getting to a place where she thought they could wrap all of this up and hand everything over to her team so she wouldn't have to think about it on her trip to Aspen, Hobie's cell phone buzzed with a text. And he stopped everything to read it.

Presley had been astounded at the blatant disrespect for her time, let alone her team's time. After looking at his phone, Hobie's admittedly ruggedly handsome face turned ashen and he had excused himself–excused himself! Stunned by his rudeness, Presley and her team had forged ahead with the phlegmy Mary, but hadn't been able to come to terms. The memory of it still made Presley angry. She took another sip of her cosmopolitan to quell the feeling.

Faye was halfway through her second martini and looking openly relaxed. "I always thought Hobie was handsome."

"No, you're thinking of his brother, Danny."

"Am I?"

Presley nodded confidently. "You must be."

Faye looked off into the middle distance and pondered that assertion. Then she shook her head coyly and turned her grey eyes back to Presley. "No, I remember both of them. Hobie was always aloof, you know, secretive and morose in a tall, lean, delicious kind of way."

Presley pursed her lips in mild disgust. "I don't remember that at all."

"Of course, Danny was gorgeous as well. It's too bad what's happened to him."

Presley's eyebrows pinched together, uncertain to what Faye was referring. "What are you talking about?"

Faye's expression changed into pity, obviously sorry for Danny, but also sorry for Presley for not knowing about it. She leaned in closer so others around them wouldn't hear and, in a stage whisper caused by her martinis, said, "He's got cancer. In his brain I think." Taken aback by this news, Presley made a sympathetic sound. Faye continued, "Poor thing. He has a family, you know. A wife and two kids. And he's been running Barcom since the day he graduated from college, practically. His father wasn't able to keep up the pace so Danny took over."

A queer emptiness entered Presley's stomach, replacing the annoyed anger at Hobie that had previously settled there. "I didn't know," was all she could think to say.

Faye patted her hand like she was precious, yet impossibly simple. "Of course you didn't know. How could you know?" She waved her other hand in the air to signal to the waiter she desired a third martini. "That's why Hobie's back from Asia…or Africa, maybe. I'm not sure where he's been."

The waiter brought Faye her martini and another cosmopolitan for Presley. She waved it away. She was already going to have to spend extra time running tomorrow to burn off this night out. Faye didn't have a problem eating and drinking to her heart's content without it ever changing her lithe figure, but Presley's genes were not that forgiving.

Her mind clicked through all of this new information. Hobie hadn't been in charge long, which might explain his complete lack of business decorum. And general decorum. Maybe she could use that to her advantage. Get the best terms for Mack Industries. Between Mary Collins as their CFO and a green Hobie in charge it shouldn't be a problem. Considering this new information she was actually glad they hadn't gotten everything determined in New York before she left.

Presley felt the familiar surge of excitement she always had when she figured out the power play in a business deal. She hadn't sat at the knee of Mack Monroe for years watching him do business without learning anything. Not that she was glad Danny Brent had brain cancer, that was a terrible thing to be sure, but as far as what that meant for her dealings with Hobie she saw light at the end of the tunnel. She wanted more information and who else knew more than anyone about everything? Why, her good friend, Faye, of course.

"Hobie's been out of the country for a while?" she asked nonchalantly.

Faye grinned at her slyly. "I see your little brain working. What are you cooking up?"

"Nothing, I'm only curious."

"Oh," Faye swished her hand in the air as if shooing away all suspicions, "You're only curious." She giggled and tasted her new martini. Presley waited patiently. One thing she knew about Faye was that she would spill the beans on almost anything once she'd had a few martinis. Finally, she began, "I think he's been in Asia most recently. But he spent a long time in Africa before that. He might have even gone to school there, you know, after he left Jessup."

Jessup Academy was the prep school Presley and Faye had attended through graduation. Some memories of the Brent brothers were returning to Presley as Faye spoke.

"Why did he leave Jessup? Danny didn't," Presley asked.

Faye's eyes widened with shock at how much her friend

really didn't keep track of other people's lives. "Honestly, Presley, you don't remember?"

"No, I don't remember."

"Their mother died," Faye declared, shaking her head with dismay. "It was sad. You really don't remember?"

Presley thought back to high school and all of its turmoil. There were boys and clothes and her own mother to deal with, let alone trying to get good grades in that hyper competitive school. As much as she had crushed on Danny Brent, his little brother had not been on her radar.

"I remember Danny graduating, because I remember his senior stunt," she offered.

"Yes, but Danny was two years ahead of us. Hobie left before graduation."

"Well, I remember that much," Presley dismissed Faye's concern over her lack of recollection. "I just didn't remember why."

Faye readjusted in her seat, leaning back and taking in the scenery of other well to do patrons at the restaurant. Dining out contributed significantly to the interactions of the upper class who lived in Aspen. Faye saw someone she knew enter and gave them a polite nod and smile before continuing, "Their mother got very sick and Hobie left school to be with her. I think she had cancer, too. That's sad, isn't it?"

"That is sad," Presley agreed. She wasn't completely cold hearted to such things.

"Oh, that's right," Faye said, more to herself than to Presley. "That's what he's been doing with his time. He runs some research project or nonprofit or something that has to do with the cancer his mother died from." Faye's eyes teared up at the thought of it, "How sweet. Isn't that sweet?"

Presley wouldn't go as far as to call Hobie Brent "sweet". Still, it explained his general inability to impress her with his negotiating skills. And maybe it explained him being distracted. She was sorry that he'd lost his mother and sorry that Danny was sick, but ultimately none of that was anything she could solve or worry about. She could handle this whole deal better knowing that Hobie would rather be somewhere else doing something else. She would just take over and make it easy on him. And if Mack Industries came out ahead in the deal then so be it.

"I bet Ruby knows what the name of it is," Faye was still rambling on.

"The name of what?"

"Hobie's nonprofit research group."

"Oh," Presley picked up the menu. They hadn't even ordered yet.

"She should be here by the time we get dessert," Faye continued. "And Ronnie and Grace better be here by Wednesday, I've reserved the spa for us to rejuvenate and get gorgeous."

Presley agreed. She looked forward to spending a spa day with her friends, but she already felt rejuvenated now that she knew what to do about Hobie Brent.

CHAPTER 5

Faye's red high heels clicked satisfactorily across the marble in her expansive foyer. She loved the sound of fine shoes on marble, it reminded her of her mother.

Still a little tipsy from her martini laced dinner with Presley, she focused on walking as gracefully as possible as she headed towards the study.

"I'll need some black coffee, Basil," she told her butler as she breezed by his stoic form. "I have a phone call scheduled with Mr. Tanner.

Mr. Ezekial Tanner was another relic from her mother and father's time. Even though he had invited Faye to call him Ezekial, she couldn't bring herself to call him anything other than Mr. Tanner, like her parents always had. He had been her father's financial advisor and was put fully in charge of all of her family's wealth when her father passed away. Naturally, after her mother passed just a few years ago it was Faye who he insisted on speaking with on a regular basis.

She sighed as she entered the study and flipped on the

lights. It was so unspeakably dreary in this room, but her mother had insisted on leaving it the way her father had kept it. And even though, technically, today Faye owned the study, the mansion, and the entire estate, she could not bring herself to redecorate this room either.

Wood everywhere the eye could see. Or books. The rich brown hand hewn irreplaceable mahogany paneling gleamed from floor to ceiling. Its impressive veneer was only interrupted by a handful of massive oil paintings by her father's favorite masters and, of course, one full wall of built in shelves that were stuffed with her father's books.

"You will read all of these one day, Faye," her father used to tell her when she came to visit him in his study.

Faye remembered a moment when she was seven years old peering up at what seemed like a 100 mile high tower of books, her father standing next to her with his hands clasped behind his back, and thinking to herself, "I doubt it."

This was the first times she could recall contradicting her father. Of course, she hadn't said it out loud. Standing dutifully in her Robin's egg blue dress, she distinctly remembered the color, and white tea gloves she had insisted on wearing even though they weren't going to tea, Faye had determined that whatever was in that huge stack of books couldn't be as much fun as wearing pretty clothes and getting her blonde tresses primped and curled.

Her first contradiction had also been her last. Not too many months after that moment her father had passed away. Heart attack. Too much brandy not enough exercise. Faye had never quite shaken the childhood guilt she felt for not wanting to live up to his expectations.

She sat down at his heavy desk and ran her hand along its shining polished surface. African Blackwood, normally reserved for making musical instruments, but used by expert woodworkers to build this one of a kind desk. Her father had fallen in love with the wood when he received a specialty made chess set using the same material. Powerful and elegant the desk was a heavy reminder of the kind of man her father had been. Part of the reason Faye couldn't bring herself to redecorate this room was the presence of this desk.

A maid carried in a silver tray carrying a small silver thermal carafe and one of her favorite cups, the blue Ginori Iris mug. She placed the tray down on a slender buffet that was set against the wall, not on the desk. Never on the desk.

As the girl poured her coffee she asked, "Can I get you anything else, ma'am?"

"No, thank you, but you can stop calling me 'ma'am'," Faye answered, taking the offered cup.

The girl's eyes widened with apology and a twinge of fear, but she didn't stammer when she answered, "Yes...as you wish."

Faye scowled as the girl scurried out the door. She hated being mean to the staff, but she also hated being reminded of her age. Lately it seemed that she was doing absolutely nothing with her life except getting older.

Faye leaned back in her father's leather chair and glared at the slim lines of the executive phone sitting on his desk. Three lines, all land lines, led to that phone. None of them were lit up. She sipped her coffee and let her gaze slip up the wall of books.

Maybe he had been right. Maybe she would have a more interesting life if she had applied herself and read all of those books like he had wanted. Maybe if her father hadn't died she would have been more interested in business and finance, like Presley.

She grinned. Her dinner with Presley had been interesting. That whole business with Hobie Brent and Barcom had really gotten under Presley's skin. Oh, she tried to act like she wasn't pumping Faye for information, but if anyone knew anything about pumping for information it was Faye. She was an expert on reading people and retaining important details of their lives and if she went on her intuition alone, ignoring all of Presley's false bravado, she would lay odds that Hobie was causing problems in Ms. Monroe's heart, not just her business meetings.

"I'll have to ask Ronnie about it," Faye said out loud. A nugget of excitement popped into her chest and she spoke out loud again, as if making a deal with herself, "There is nothing more fun than a spark of romance."

It would be good for Presley to loosen up a little and have an affair. She was so tightly wound all of the time, jetting here and there, signing contracts, heading up meetings with stuffy old businessmen. Faye firmly believed that it was a waste of a vibrant woman's life not to have a handsome fellow on her arm, at least every now and then.

Just then one of the lines lit up on the executive phone and Faye was brought back to the present and her own meeting with a stuffy old businessman.

Moments later Basil's voice came from the phone's speaker, "Mr. Tanner is on line one for you, Madame."

Faye rolled her eyes. How was it that Basil got away with calling her Madame, she wasn't sure. Probably because he was indispensable and it was a slightly better term than 'ma'am'.

"Thank you, Basil," she said. She pressed the blinking Line 1 button and picked up the receiver, cooing into it as she did, "Hello, Mr. Tanner. How have you been?"

CHAPTER 6

*A*romatic candles scented the warm, inviting space. Lilly's, a chic spa that had taken over most of Aspen's high end customers almost a decade ago was all shining wood surfaces and soft, white pillows with occasional mirrors reflecting glittering candlelight. Soothing piano music filled the air, but not so loud that it intruded on their conversation. The five friends were well into the chocolate pedicure segment their spa day, which included rich, chocolate scented buttery cremes being rubbed into their feet and calves before their toenails were painted.

Ronnie had gotten in from New York late the night before. She had wrapped up the management of her spring line of handbags and accessories then hopped on the family jet with Mack, who was also on his way to Aspen for Ruby's big fundraising gala. Grace had arrived in town earlier in the afternoon, the filming for her latest movie finally complete and looking forward to some much needed relaxation. And Ruby had been in and around Aspen all along, though neither Presley nor Faye had gotten to see her until she showed up the morning of spa day.

"Do you have any of the sea salt chocolates?" Grace asked one of the Lilly's staff members, a young woman who was walking to each of them offering fine chocolate from a small silver tray as a snack.

"Yes, ma'am," the girl said as she indicated which of the elaborately molded shining chocolates were of the sea salt variety.

Grace took one with a small frown. She popped it into her mouth and leaned back into the pedicure chair, which was lined up against one wall of the room with four other chairs, all inhabited by her friends. She sighed, depressed, "I hate being a 'ma'am'."

Still in earshot, the girl blushed at the comment and lowered her gaze so she wouldn't accidentally catch Grace's eye. Ruby occupied the last pedicure chair and was the last to be offered a chocolate. She smiled with true warmth at the girl, reassuring her that Grace's complaint wasn't to be taken seriously.

"It's a badge of honor, Grace. Nothing to be ashamed of," Faye answered lightly. This was a funny comment coming from Faye, who had gotten more procedures done than any of them, including Grace who was a movie star.

"Would you truly rather be called 'Miss'?" Presley asked, her voice low and relaxed as the pedicurist expertly massaged the bottom of her feet. Her love of high heels did a number on her feet, but if you wanted to be beautiful, you had to pay the price. "I think I would take it as an insult now."

"You're right. I don't want to be a 'miss' anymore, but they do get the best parts. My agent has been pitching me a lot of step-mother and old witch roles lately."

Ronnie laughed. Ronnie was always laughing, it was her way of moving through the world, to make a joke of it. A bouncing brunette with a short sassy haircut, the Monroe blue eyes, and a wide, easy smile, Presley's little sister was the life of the party.

"Maybe you could embrace it, you know? Start putting curses on people," Ronnie giggled her suggestion.

Grace, who was all glamour with long, black hair, luminescent skin, perfect bone structure, and gorgeous green eyes, slid a sideways glance at Ronnie. Though Presley was pretty sure she was feigning annoyance, it was sometimes difficult to tell with Grace's superior acting skills.

"I say we focus on becoming cougars and find us some adorable snowboarders to take to the party," Faye suggested. "Oh, wait, are you still with Sampson or have you two called it off again?" She directed this question at Ruby who was leaning back in her seat with her eyes closed.

Faye was referring to Bill Sampson, Ruby's on again, off again boyfriend of several years. Ruby opened one deep brown eye, her full lips screwing into a disappointed smile. "We're off…for good this time." Murmurs of condolences rose from their little group. Ruby shook them off. "No, it's all good. I called it off. He's just never going to grow up and I've got things to do in life, you know?" They all murmured in agreement.

"It's snowing," Presley noted. Big fat flakes of wet spring snow were tumbling past the grand picture window in the front of the spa. A fire crackled on the far end of the room and she was glad for its cheery warmth. She was also glad she had dressed cozy for their spa day. She had gone for her full Aspen look which included jeans, a soft, loose sweater knit from nubby oatmeal colored yarn, a favorite pair of low heeled brown leather boots that were as soft as butter, and a dark green leather bomber jacket. It was a casual look for her, but this was Aspen. People wore huge fuzzy boots with fur pom-poms here, after all. But even more than being casual, the outfit, which currently waited neatly hung up in the massage room while she donned a thick Lilly's spa robe and slippers, was warm. She would need warm when she stepped back outside.

"I love spring snow in the Rockies," Ronnie said dreamily.

"So back to the question at hand, who is everyone taking to Ruby's party?" Faye asked.

"I'm going with Pete," Ronnie answered.

Faye blinked at her. "He's your brother."

"I know," Ronnie grinned. "We both needed a date."

Faye sighed in mock frustration and looked at Grace, "What about you?"

"Oh, um, well," Grace hemmed and hawed just a little too much as they all waited patiently. "Syd said he would come with me. He'll be here by this weekend."

Ruby perked up. "Syd Masters? The director?"

Grace nodded. Whenever Grace worked on a film she inevitably got involved with the director, a producer, or a leading man. On her most recent film the leading man was gay in real life so she had apparently gravitated to the director.

"And what about you?" Faye asked Presley.

Presley hesitated. She didn't have an answer. She hadn't even thought about taking a date.

Ronnie chuckled, "You look like a deer in the headlights, Pres."

"Don't let her pressure you," Ruby chimed in. "You don't need to take a date. I'm not going to have a date."

"Yeah," Presley responded. "Ruby doesn't have a date, why do I need one?"

"Well, technically Ruby is throwing the event. So she'll be working," Grace said.

"I could give you a job to do," Ruby offered.

Presley started to respond when Faye interrupted, "Do

not give her a job. She works too much already. You all work too much. That's part of the problem."

"Who are you going with?" Ruby asked Faye, turning the table on their friend.

Faye smiled serenely. "I have a number of different men I can choose from. I will take the youngest and hottest from among them."

After their mani-pedis they were led into the next area where they had facials. Since each woman's skin was unique, Lilly's gave them each a different concoction of the organic, plant based creams and exfoliants to address their individual needs. Presley crunched on a celery stick from the snack tray provided and watched as they slathered a deep hydrating cream over Ruby's soft, brown skin. Presley had requested the wrinkle diminishing facial. Sometimes she worried that working so much was aging her before her time. Then she worried that she was worrying about it. She sighed lightly, it was a vicious circle.

It was more difficult to chat during the facials since they had to keep their mouths still. While Presley sat there with the anti-wrinkle facial hardening on her face, her eyes closed and weighted down by cool gel packs made to reduce puffiness, she let the sensations take over. The light piano music tickled her ears, the deeply aromatic scents of the facials and nearby candles filled her lungs, and she ran a fingertip along the smooth surface of her newly painted nails. She was completely, utterly relaxed, thinking about nothing, worried about nothing.

And that's when an unexpected thought drifted through her mind. Why didn't she have a date for the big fundraiser event?

Why had the thought of bringing a date not occurred to her? The thought of going out on a date at all hadn't popped into her head in...what...years? That was a little pathetic.

Wasn't it? Her other friends were keen on finding romantic partners, even if they didn't keep them for long. Even Ronnie had thought to arrange to go with Pete. Why hadn't Presley thought of that? It was as if the thought of partnering with anybody was foreign to her brain. She'd been alone for so long. And she'd been working on running a billion dollar company. That was nothing to sneeze at, she reminded herself. She could make Jaxson come with her as a date. No, that would be silly. Plus she would have to pay him for his time, which felt sleazy.

They moved on to the hot stone massages, where flat, smooth basalt stones were oiled until they were a deep ebony color then heated and used by the masseuse in 90 minutes of delectable deep tissue massage. Presley focused on thoroughly enjoying the experience. Her masseuse was a huge man of Native Hawaiian descent named Akoni. Akoni had magic hands and he hummed quietly as he worked, a deep baritone humming that added to the calm vibe in the room. Even as Akoni worked his magic through the muscles of her legs, arms, neck and back, Presley couldn't shake the thought that she had been overlooking something important.

Sure, her early marriage and subsequent divorce had left a sour taste in her mouth towards relationships. But her marriage to Larry the cheater had ended over a decade ago. And she had had minimal romantic relationships since. As Akoni pressed the warm stones into her back muscles and pulled them expertly down the sides of her spine, Presley counted her romances in her mind.

Larry the cheater, that was the first serious relationship she'd ever had. So that was one. Then there had been Jean Luc, her rebound relationship. That was two. Then there had been a long dry spell until just before she turned 30 when she dated Grant for almost a year. And her last relationship had been nearly two years long in duration, with Spencer. That was four total. Only four?

Presley was surprised at this revelation. Of course she'd had an occasional date here and there that never turned into anything long term. But four? That was pathetic.

And, another thing she realized while under the spell of Akoni and her hot stone massage, none of her relationships had lasted more than just a few years. Even her marriage. What did that say about her? Whatever it said, she didn't think it said anything good.

When her 90 minutes was up Presley felt as limp as a rag doll and about as brain dead as one, too. She stayed flat on her back on the firm, yet comfortable, massage table as Akoni readied himself to step out of the room so she could get dressed.

"Akoni?" she asked.

"Yes?" He paused politely, his giant frame dressed in a tightly fit white cotton T-shirt and clean white slacks.

"Are you married?" He paused, a strange look on his face, and it became clear to her that she needed to clarify her question. "I mean, I was just thinking that I'm not married and wondering why I'm not at least dating someone. And I was wondering if you are…married…or dating someone." Akoni looked pained, like she had just pinched him. "No! Not like that," she tried to explain. "Not that I'm asking if you want to date me…or get married." Why couldn't she stop talking? "I'm just asking in general. In general, I'm wondering who in this world is married or dating. And you were the first person I saw," she ended this drawn out embarrassing ramble in a kind of whimper.

Akoni's features broke into a wide, brilliant smile. "Yes, I am married, Ms. Monroe. Six years of pure happiness."

"Great," Presley said with extra enthusiasm. "That's wonderful."

"If you'll excuse me," Akoni bowed slightly as he stepped out of the door.

Presley called after him, "Of course. Thank you…for the massage…and the humming. It was very nice."

Afterward, the five women had a late lunch of organic delicacies in Lilly's dining area before getting dressed in their street clothes and heading into the snowy afternoon. The fat, wet snow had accumulated to almost two inches and the whole town had that fresh, uniquely Colorado feeling. The feeling that even though it was snowing, the sun was about to burst through the clouds and turn the world into a wonderland.

Rather than stay to have their hair and makeup done by the Lilly experts, Presley and the others opted to go home and make it an early evening. Massages, facials, and mani-pedis were more exhausting than one might think. Having her muscles kneaded until they were sore tended to make Presley feel a little under the weather. Probably due to the release of stress and toxins, or so she was told.

When they stepped outside of the warm protective walls of the spa onto the sidewalk, wet snowflakes fell thick in the air. They smacked Presley in the face, melting immediately against her newly beautified cheeks and lips. Squinting into the snow, Presley zipped up the front of her leather jacket and wrapped the dark orange wool scarf she had worn with it around her head. She hadn't brought a hat, but her Lexus SUV was parked around the corner of the building. She didn't mind a little snow in her hair. Lilly's had valet service available, but she and Ronnie hadn't seen the need when they arrived earlier in the day.

"Where is your car?" Faye asked with concern as she moved toward Andrew, her driver. He had already jumped out of her Lincoln and was holding the back door open.

Grace and Ruby were close on her heels. Faye had picked them up on the way to Lilly's.

"It's just around the corner. We can wa–" Presley was cut off abruptly when the hand she was waving toward the parking lot smacked a passerby hurrying through the snow. He was tall and she couldn't see his face because he was bundled up against the cold. "Oh!" she exclaimed.

"Excuse me," the man said and something about the sound of his voice made her pause. She looked at him, slightly stunned, as fat snowflakes pummeled her face. He hesitated, too, then asked, "Presley?"

CHAPTER 7

*P*resley grimaced. Standing in front of her on the sidewalk, wrapped in a horrible faded green lumberjack coat with a plain brown wool hat pulled down to his eyebrows, tiny curls of his dark hair escaping from underneath, was Hobie Brent.

He smiled as his recognition grew. As he smiled she saw the hint of dimples she hadn't noticed before, and a glimpse of his more handsome older brother in his looks. A tiny shiver went through her and before she knew what was happening she found herself smiling back.

"Hobie," she said.

The snow was an ever moving veil that made him seem like a mirage that would disappear in a few moments with the next gust of wind. In the grey light of the afternoon, his dark eyes shone warmly and Presley could not think of one thing to say. He glanced at Ronnie, who still stood next to her, then to Faye, Grace, and Ruby who were all frozen in their tracks halfway to Faye's waiting car. They were wondering who he was, no doubt.

"Were you heading this way?" Hobie gestured in the direction of the parking lot.

Presley nodded, "Yes."

"May I?" he asked. He stepped to the side and slightly behind her as if he was escorting her onto a dance floor.

How was she supposed to answer that? It would be impolite to refuse.

"We're going to our car," Ronnie interjected. She stuck out a gloved hand. "Ronnie, I'm Presley's sister."

Hobie nodded and smiled, shaking her hand with his own mittened hand. Presley scowled. Her hands were freezing. She hadn't brought any gloves. She glanced at Faye and the others. All three were exchanging looks. The kind of looks they gave each other whenever one of them met an attractive man. She rolled her eyes at them, but didn't have time to do anything else, because Hobie was escorting her and her younger sister to their car.

As he chatted Ronnie up, Presley wondered what in the world Hobie was doing in Aspen and questioning her luck at running into him like this. As soon as these thoughts crossed her mind they were at her SUV and she realized Ronnie was speaking to her.

"What?" Presley asked, squinting at Ronnie through the falling snow.

"We can give him a ride, can't we?" Ronnie asked.

A ride? Presley's eyes narrowed.

"Oh, no, don't worry about it. I'll call for a car," Hobie dismissed the idea.

"Don't be silly," Ronnie kept talking, ignoring her big sister's scowl. "It's snowing like crazy. We'll just drop you off."

Hobie looked at Presley for approval, innately understanding the need for agreement between the two sisters.

Presley had no choice but to go along. She motioned for

him to get in the back seat. A few minutes later she inexplicably found herself driving through a snowstorm with Ronnie talking animatedly in the front passenger seat to a politely pleasant Hobie in the back.

The Monroe estate was a beautiful mountain property, hidden in the forest about 20 minutes outside of the city of Aspen. Ronnie put the address Hobie gave her where he was headed into the GPS and it came up as being a few miles past their place. Visions of a dilapidated cabin with no running water and only a wood stove for heat came to Presley's mind when she thought about where Hobie might be staying. That wasn't completely fair. He was not a man without any means, she simply didn't think Barcom or the Brent family were quite on par with her own.

She glanced in her rear view mirror and caught his eye. He was listening to Ronnie chatter on and on about Ruby's fundraiser, but his eyes caught hers in the mirror and held them. For an instant Presley experienced the same tiny shiver she had earlier when he first recognized her in the street. He smiled at her in the mirror and, once again, she smiled back. But only for a moment before turning her attention back to the increasingly perilous road.

What was wrong with her? She must still be overly anxious about not having a date to the party. Ridiculous. Partly because she was Presley Monroe and she did not require an escort to go anywhere. Ever. And partly because what she should be doing was focusing on the worsening driving conditions.

The heavy, wet snow had built up quickly and thanks to the late afternoon dip in temperature it was freezing and creating slick spots. She slowed the SUV and double checked that the four wheel drive was engaged. It was.

"Is everything all right?" Hobie interrupted Ronnie's one

sided conversation about her latest purse designs to ask Presley the question.

She glanced in the mirror to see concern in his eyes. He must have noticed tension in hers as she drove.

Ronnie looked at Presley then to Hobie then back to Presley and finally out the windshield where apparently she was just discovering the bad weather.

"Is it slippery?" Ronnie asked.

As if in response to her question the back end of the vehicle slipped just slightly before Presley could correct it by moving more into the center of the road. The roads in this area weren't wide and the higher you went up the mountain, the more twisting and turning they became. It made for wonderfully private estates, but did not make an easy drive in bad weather.

Presley cursed under her breath. Why hadn't they just had Trevor, the chauffeur on duty, drive them today? It had seemed a lark for them to run off on their own, like they were teenagers escaping undetected from their parents. Not so fun anymore.

The smooth running engine of the Lexus SUV roared as Presley slowly maneuvered it over a mound of icy snow that had built up on the edge of an extra tight hairpin turn.

"Careful," Ronnie said.

"I am being careful," Presley snapped at her.

All conversation ceased.

Presley stared straight ahead, her eyes trained on the road and any possible issues as she made her way at a snail's pace. They had never turned on music, since Ronnie and Hobie had been talking, and the sound of the windshield wipers sliding back and forth, removing each fresh blanket of thick snowfall as they did, was the only sound in the car. Presley half expected Hobie to start telling her how to drive from the back seat. He was a man, after all.

"I have a suggestion," he said.

Tension returned to her recently massaged body. It reemerged in her arms first, probably from gripping the steering wheel, then continued into her neck and shoulders. If she had felt comfortable taking a hand off the steering wheel, she would have flung it around in the air and scolded both him and Ronnie to be quiet while she drove.

"Why don't you just go to your place and I'll call our driver to get me from there. I don't want to make you go out of your way in this weather," Hobie said.

Ronnie gave her a sideways look. Presley considered his suggestion, but didn't want to admit defeat.

"It's fine. I can do it," she said with determination.

"I'm sure you can," Hobie said. Something in his voice made her shoot a quick look into the rear view mirror. She found him watching her in the reflection, his eyes concerned yet calm. "I insist," he told her.

In truth, she was relieved. But she would never admit that to anyone. When they reached the Monroe estate's drive, she maneuvered the SUV carefully around the slippery curve. The weather had created a rather perilous icy spot, but after that their way was fairly clear. Trevor met them at the eight car garage with a large umbrella to first escort the Monroe sisters and guest to the house then take care of the car.

All hope of getting rid of Hobie was lost when they were greeted by their father, instead of the butler, at the door. He pulled the great door open and boomed at them immediately.

"What were you two doing out driving around in this weather?"

"We were at the spa, Dad, remember?" Ronnie laughed off his displeasure easily. That didn't work for Presley. Their father's disapproval twisted like a small knot in her gut.

Mack Monroe stood firm in his conviction that his adult

daughters had somehow done something wrong and his expression did not change from its agitated state until he noticed Hobie walking in behind them. He went from vexed and worried to surprised, then pleased.

"Well, Hobie, I didn't know you were coming," Mack's voice raised a notch with pleasure. His strong features broke into a wide smile as he stepped forward and shook Hobie's hand.

"Yes, it was a surprise to all of us," Hobie said, returning the older man's smile and handshake with equal warmth. "Your daughters were kind enough to offer me a ride. I let my driver know he should come here to pick me up."

"Nonsense, you're staying for dinner," Mack announced.

The knot in Presley's gut twisted tighter. This was not how she had envisioned the rest of her day, babysitting a business guest. She felt a nudge in her ribs and turned her head to Ronnie, who was poking her with her elbow, her eyes full of mischief.

"What?" Presley whispered.

Ronnie didn't answer, just lifted her brows in a 'you know what I mean' look and giggled. Presley sighed and shook her head to dismiss any thoughts Ronnie was having of being entertained by this…this interloper. Not only had her pre-spa tension returned in her neck and shoulders, but a throbbing pain had settled in over her left eye. She reached up and rubbed the spot with her fingertips, closing her eyes as she did.

"I don't want to intrude," Hobie said. Presley opened her eyes and shot him a look. He was talking to her father, but glancing at her.

"It's not an intrusion at all. Simon will tell the cook we have a guest for dinner," Mack said as he gave a quick nod to their butler who tipped his head forward in understanding.

Mack put his big hand on the back of Hobie's shoulder and led him toward the front den, adding, "I insist."

"Shall I have baths drawn for you, ladies?" Simon asked the sisters.

"Oh, I would love a bath before dinner," Ronnie said agreeably. "I feel a little sticky from the spa. Are you coming upstairs, too?" she asked Presley.

Presley was still watching her father and Hobie as they walked away. What were they going to talk about? She didn't understand why her father had been so pleased to see him anyway. Since when were they chummy? And what could they possibly have to talk about except their family's joint venture?

"Ma'am?" Simon stood waiting patiently for an answer.

Presley looked at him then glanced up the massive front stairway. Built from heavy curved logs polished to shining perfection it led up to her rooms, to a warm, lavender infused bath. She looked back at the rapidly diminishing backs of her father and Hobie. She sighed, knowing what she had to do.

"Not right now, Simon. I'll join father and our guest first." She gave Ronnie a wan smile and headed toward the door where Mack had just shown Hobie into the front den.

CHAPTER 8

It became painfully clear to Presley during the impromptu meeting in the front den that she was losing control of the Barcom joint venture. Her father, for reasons that she found difficult to comprehend, seemed completely taken with Hobie Brent. He kept saying odd little phrases to him. Things like "my boy" and "a chip off the ol' block", all while slapping him on the back in camaraderie. As if Mack was a coach and Hobie was his new all star player. Or something.

Hobie, for his part, kept coming back to sustainability studies and the complications of global tourism. After removing his horrible hat and coat he didn't cut quite the rumpled figure he had at their first meeting. Or maybe she was getting used to the way he looked.

He was dressed in jeans and a sleek charcoal grey zip pullover. His hair was mussed from wearing his hat and looked better for it. Curlier.

She couldn't deny that he was an attractive man. Though she wondered if it wasn't his passionate responses to her father's questions that were making him more appealing. Passionate men were more attractive in her opinion.

"That's the truth of it, Mack," Hobie was saying. "If we want to retain the beauty and draw of the area over time we must address sustainability. I have a few people on staff who are experts in managing tourism. We can keep the environment protected and offer the community benefits as well. I would like to see a few specialists like them permanently on staff at Villa Pallotta."

Wait. Was he seriously suggesting adding two more full time salaries into the mix? She could barely believe what she was hearing.

Presley listened to Hobie describe what was akin to a fantasy world of utopian green companies who never crossed the line, always recycled, left zero carbon footprint, and helped save the world. In other words, a never-never land that wasn't possible if you wanted to make money.

She waited for her father to rip into Hobie, figuring it would be better if he did it and not her, since she would still have to face Hobie at future meetings. But the butt chewing about how making a profit had to come over everything else or there wouldn't be a company to run never came.

Presley sat and listened and sipped lemon water, the sweet smelling lotion from her massage making her feel oily and tired, but her father just laughed and agreed with Hobie. He never let loose with one of his Mr. Money Bags confident conversation takeovers that had made him famous, and billions of dollars, over the years.

The longer she listened the more the conversation between her father and Hobie grated on her nerves. The way Mack was latching onto this second son of the second rate Barcom empire in a much too chummy way made her uneasy. Presley tried to remember the last time Mack had spoken so freely to her about sustainable business practices and the ecology. It had never happened.

What really irked her was that he was treating Hobie like she wished he would treat her little brother. Mack had rarely, if ever, buddied around with Pete like this, at least not since Pete had grown taller than their father at the age of 16. This whole meeting rubbed her the wrong way.

"I don't want to be a killjoy," she interjected suddenly. This wasn't true. In a very big way Presley was in the mood to be a killjoy. "But I don't know that I agree."

Both of the men stopped talking and looked at her, almost like she had just walked into the room. This made her even more prickly.

"You don't?" Hobie did not appear to be crushed, but he did seem…disappointed.

Presley stood to her full 5'7" and wished she was wearing her customary heels rather than the low heeled boots she had worn to the spa. She flipped her hair the tiniest bit, like a thoroughbred horse feeling antsy before a big race. The desire to take the reins of this little get together had been bubbling inside of her since she had walked through the door of the den. Her father's soft approach to the whole thing had thrown her off, but that didn't mean Presley would step aside and let this project becoming a money losing venture. She had her family's empire and her personal reputation to protect.

Leveling her gaze directly on Hobie, she said, "We have minuscule margins on this as it is. Two more salaries? Two?" She looked to Mack for emphasis and then back to Hobie. "I don't suppose these environmental experts come cheap, do they?

"No, they don't," Hobie admitted.

Presley scoffed before jutting her chin out the way she

did when she felt stubborn, when she had decided enough was enough. "It's not happening. Not unless you can justify the cost with more than just your," she fluttered her newly manicured hand at him while she looked for the right word. There. She found it. "Your *fantasy* of saving the world."

Hobie studied her with no reaction. Not anger, not offense, nothing, just an even gaze from his deep brown eyes. Her father, on the other hand, the infamous Mack Monroe, Mr. Money Bags himself, flushed red.

"Presley," her father said, his chin jutting out. She had inherited that look from him. "There's no reason to be rude."

Stung by this rebuke, heat rose in her cheeks. Her mortification was compounded by the fact that Hobie was witnessing the whole thing.

As for Hobie, his attention switched between Presley and Mack, but he didn't seem uncomfortable by the father daughter power struggle playing out in front of him. He remained calm while Mack stalked to a rustic sideboard and refreshed his scotch and Presley glared down into her glass, equally infuriated and embarrassed.

When it was apparent that the air in the room was not going to clear by itself, Hobie spoke up, looking at Presley first, "Your concerns about cost are valid."

He probably meant this to be helpful, but Presley's hackles rose regardless. She didn't need his validation. She knew she was right.

"And I think we can address all of those concerns," Hobie continued, either not noticing she was ticked off or not caring. He turned his irritatingly positive commentary toward Mack, "This can be a touchy subject, Mack, but I'm not afraid to dive into the conversation." His gaze flicked back to Presley and she swore there was a twinkle of amusement in his eyes. "Even if the water's cold."

He held her attention with his look, barely raising one eyebrow, the corners of his mouth lifting into a friendly grin. Presley was flung back in time to high school and the informal way both Brent boys had treated their classmates, her included. Before she could think to control her response, she answered his smile with one of her own. It was a smile of co-conspirators and it came as a complete surprise to her as it spread across her face. A different, more demure, heat filled her cheeks and for an instant she forgot that she was upset. In fact, she forgot what she had been talking about at all.

Hobie took control of the conversation, masterfully guiding both her and Mack through the murky waters of their shared need to control and bringing them to a mellow center place. A place where all three of them could discuss the different ways sustainable tourism could be worked realistically into their Italian wine country tourism business.

He did it deftly, almost like the slight of hand a magician used to pull off astonishing tricks. So light was his touch on their conversation and interlaced with such good-humored commentary that Presley barely noticed she had lost control of the situation again.

When she did notice that she and Mack were both laughing at a story Hobie was telling about his time helping care for baby elephants in Kenya instead of talking about business, she didn't know how to feel about it. It seemed they had fallen under some kind of spell that Hobie cast as naturally as he breathed. As much as she wanted to believe he had some ulterior motive for distracting her from their joint venture, she wasn't sure he was actually being calculating.

Hobie's demeanor felt genuine. It felt fun. And those qualities had somehow spilled over into her and her father's interaction, making Presley realize something. Something painful. She and her father's relationship wasn't always this relaxed. It wasn't always fun or friendly. Very often they spoke only of business and money, leaving the more light hearted interactions for him and Ronnie.

She tried to remember the last time her father had paid this close attention to an amusing anecdotal story she told, his blue eyes merry, a deep chuckle forming in his chest even before she was finished speaking. She couldn't remember. And if she was being honest, she couldn't remember the last time she had tried to tell an anecdotal story to him or anyone.

Presley mulled this realization over during dinner as she pushed her lobster rigatoni around with her fork. Ronnie had joined them after her luxurious bath upstairs. She sparkled with new makeup, her dark hair freshly blown straight, and a smart black blouse over jeans.

"How long did you stay in Seoul?" Ronnie was grilling Hobie on all of his world travels. It turned out after his mother's death in his late teens, he had spent several years traveling throughout Asia and Africa, just like Faye had thought. What Faye hadn't known was that he had done manual labor for money along the way and backpacked for much of the time, leaving behind the high end lifestyle he had grown up around. This type of gritty realism appealed to Ronnie.

"Almost two years," Hobie said. "I got a job working on a fishing boat. It was a charity case, really. I didn't know anything about fishing. I think they just felt sorry for the bumbling American teenager who didn't know the language." He laughed at the memory, a deep, warm laugh.

Ronnie laughed brightly, a little too brightly. Ronnie was flirting, that was pretty obvious. She was a much bigger flirt than Presley, always had been. Bothered by her overbearing happiness, Presley's brow pinched into a tiny scowl.

Sitting next to her younger sister at the long dining room table Presley looked tired and worn out. Her sweater was bulky and droopy after her long day, her blonde hair was still mussed and stringy from the spa oils, and she hadn't put a speck of fresh makeup on since they got home.

Since she had realized that her relationship with her father was probably stagnant and perhaps even superficial she had grown more and more morose. Being the oldest, Presley had always assumed a certain camaraderie with her father, a bond that was unique and special. With the certainty of that connection faltering, even momentarily, her confidence was thrown off. And she didn't like being thrown off.

"This storm is going to get worse before it gets better," Mack said, his attention turned toward the massive floor to ceiling windows in the dining room that looked out over a Colorado mountain scene. Fat snowflakes continued to fall and blanket the pines in a thick layer of snow, the kind that pulled the branches lower and lower with its weight.

"I appreciate you having me for dinner, this was delicious," Hobie said as he made to stand. "But I should probably call for my ride. I don't want to make him drive through this stuff if it's getting worse."

"Nonsense," Mack dismissed this idea with a wave of his big hand, motioning Hobie to sit back down at the table. "You'll stay here tonight."

"Yes, do!" Ronnie said with delight.

Hobie lowered back into is seat slowly and looked at Presley as she was the only one who hadn't expressed her desire for him to stay. There was a good reason for that. She didn't want him to stay. She didn't want to entertain a guest. All she wanted to do was go upstairs and take a long, hot bath in her soaker tub with its private view of the snowy pine trees outside, and ponder what she had realized about her relationship with her father.

Hobie waited for her response, but Presley could only offer him a weak smile.

"We'd be glad to have you," she lied.

Hobie smiled and thanked them all for their hospitality, but in his eyes she could tell that he suspected her invitation to stay was not completely sincere.

CHAPTER 9

*H*obie had to hand it to them, the Monroe's were a fascinating bunch. From Ronnie's easy laughter and lively conversation to Mack Monroe's infamous charisma which simultaneously flattered and controlled to Presley's cool aloofness that occasionally fell away and revealed her lighter side…or her darker control issues.

Fascinating.

Considering he had only had dinner with part of the Monroe clan, Hobie wondered what it was like when they all got together.

"Like lighting a match at a fireworks stand," he said out loud.

He was alone in one of the guest rooms of the Monroe estate, watching the snow come down hard. The room windows were large as was the room, so large the sound of his voice echoed through the space.

Shirtless, in a pair of pajama bottoms the Monroe's butler, Simon, had brought to him, Hobie was too restless to go to sleep. The events of the day kept rolling through his mind. His plans of going home early from his office in town had been thrown off, first by the storm moving in, then by running into Presley.

That moment of recognition they had shared on the sidewalk replayed in his mind's eye. With the snow falling thick around her face he had thought for a moment that she was something out of a dream and blurted her name out without thinking. Then when she smiled at him and said his name... well...it had taken his breath away.

A buzzing noise from the dresser brought him back to the present. His cell phone. It was his Dad.

"Hey, Dad," Hobie answered.

"Hi son, Trevor tells me you're stuck somewhere because of the snow?"

"I'm at the Monroe's house. They gave me a ride back from town and fed me dinner."

"Ah, you're at Mack's place then?"

"Yes, I'm just gonna stay here and Trevor will give me a lift in the morning when the roads are more clear."

"Good, good," his Dad answered, his voice tired.

A pang of concern hit Hobie's heart. Though his father and Mack Monroe had been business partners much of their early years and were the same age, his father had always seemed older. Not to say he wasn't intelligent, because Hobie was certain his father was one of the smartest men he had ever known. Wise, too, which wasn't always as easy to come by as smarts. He simply didn't have Mack Monroe's physical presence and Hobie often worried about his health. Especially since Danny had been stricken with cancer.

Suddenly Hobie felt the urge to reassure his Dad. He didn't want his father to have any qualms about him taking over. He would do everything in his power to run Barcom Industries with as much professionalism as Danny always did.

"We had a really good meeting this afternoon, too," Hobie offered.

"Did you?"

Hobie gave a short update of what they had gone over during the meeting, leaving out the family drama that he had witnessed playing out between Presley and Mack. He also left out how sexy Presley looked with her mussed up hair and how she had smelled like chocolate.

"Sounds like you're on top of things, son," the senior Brent told him amiably.

"I'm trying, Dad."

"You're doing a great job for Barcom and for your brother, Hobie. Just a great job." Hobie smiled at the encouragement. "Well, you'd better get to bed. Sleep well, son, and we'll see you tomorrow."

"Thanks, Dad, you sleep well, too."

He hung up the phone and climbed into the King sized bed where he still had a good view out the window to watch the snow. Ever since his Mom had gotten sick his Dad had told him and Danny to 'sleep well' instead of good night. Over the years Hobie had come to realize that 'sleep well' was his father's stand in phrase for 'I love you'.

He sighed. His father and his brother were counting on him, probably more than they ever had before, and he couldn't let them down. He would do his best to focus on Barcom's interests instead of getting distracted by his interactions with Presley. All business. That was the key.

Hobie turned over and pulled the luxurious bedding over his bare chest and shoulders. Maybe he would renew his focus on something other than Presley by taking his camera out into the fresh snow at sunrise.

CHAPTER 10

Sometime while they slept the snow stopped falling, leaving behind a breathtaking winterscape. When the sun peeked over the horizon in the morning, the light spread across this wonderland, sparkling like so many diamonds, creating a heavenly blanket for every tree, stone, and pinecone in the area.

Presley requested coffee in her room at 5:30 am. She had always been an early riser, it was one of the reasons she got so much accomplished every day. The rigatoni she had forced down the night before had congealed with the chocolate soufflé they had for dessert and made her feel bloated. So she had requested black coffee, two hard boiled eggs, and a glass of lemon water to be her morning repast. And to be ready for its delivery, she got up at 4:30 to use the treadmill in the small gym off of her room.

After her run and some light stretching, she took a cool shower and dressed in a warm pair of black winter leggings, an olive tunic, and a deep red sweater with rippled edges and long sleeves that fell well past her fingertips. Certain that nobody else in the house was awake, Presley set up her laptop at a table she sometimes used as her desk in her room and poured a cup of coffee. The table was situated against a wall of windows that gave her a magnificent view of the morning sunrise while she leaned back in her chair and breathed in the magic aroma of Kona coffee from Hawaii.

She took a sip of the full bodied coffee and sighed. A wonderful way to start her morning. She would finish her coffee then wade through the mountains of emails she no doubt had since she'd been virtually offline since yesterday morning. Jaxson was scheduled to be at the house at 8:00 am so they could get some work done. She didn't want to fall too far behind even though her trip to Aspen was supposed to be a semi-vacation.

Just as she was about to take her second sip, Presley saw something in the glittering morning snow. Something, or someone, was moving awkwardly towards the trees on the side of the estate. She wondered why any staff would be out in the snow heading into the woods. Leaning closer to the window she recognized the green jacket and ugly brown hat. It wasn't one of the staff, it was Hobie.

What was Hobie Brent doing bumbling about in the woods on their estate? The roads couldn't possibly be cleared enough for him to go to his place. Was he planning on hiking out?

She didn't know and she didn't care, but the more she watched the green and brown figure slowly making its way into the pine trees, the more her curiosity wouldn't let her focus on her emails. Finally, she sighed, and shut her laptop.

"I better see what he's up to," she mumbled to herself. Then she called for her warmest snow parka and boots and tromped downstairs muttering about what a distraction Hobie was turning into. She slid into her pale pink opalescent quilted snowsuit with the pink fur trim, which she normally used for skiing or snowboarding and shoved her feet into her pink fur lined Uggs. Finally, because the sun was coming up and the reflection off of the newly fallen snow was bound to be blinding, she grabbed her Ray Bans and pushed them into her snow pants pocket before heading outside.

Trudging through the fresh 10-inch snowfall and wrapped snugly in her thermo protective snowsuit, Presley was plenty warm. She was also a little out of breath by the time she made it to the edge of the cleared side yard that was lined by the forest where Hobie's form was fast disappearing.

"Excuse me," she called out. He didn't hear her. She tried again, this time waving her arms in the air above her head. "Excuse me!"

There was always a soft silence the morning after a heavy snow in the Rocky Mountains. The muffling acoustics of the snow, the fact that all of the animals and people nearby were still tucked away staying warm and cozy, made it especially quiet. No cars nearby. No sounds of life.

Presley's shout pierced the silence and brought the Hobie form to a stop. She squinted through the trees as the form turned to look at her. She waved her arms over her head again. The form lifted one arm in acknowledgement.

She called out to him, "Where are you going?" The Hobie form lifted his hand to his ear indicating he hadn't heard her question. Presley cupped her bare hands to her mouth, she had forgotten her gloves, and shouted, "Where are you going?"

The Hobie form hesitated then turned and started making its way back through the woods, apparently to get close enough to hear what she was saying. Presley stepped into the edge of the wooded area to meet him. As she did, she brushed against the branches of a young pine tree causing clumps of snow to slide off of its needles and plop into the drifts of snow on the ground. The loss of this extra weight made the branches spring upward and this motion caused more branches above to lose their snow covering in the same way. This chain reaction created a small blizzard above, around, and in front of Presley, the lighter snow swirling in great, glittering clouds into the air. Her view of the Hobie form was temporarily blotted out and she made a small sound of surprise as the cold snow hit her cheeks and lips.

When she made it through to the other side of the snow flurry area Hobie was only about 20 feet away. He was standing completely still watching her emerge from the cold clouds of bothersome snow with a curious look on his face.

Presley stopped at the sight of him. Something was different. Still in his green coat and brown hat with his long curls peeking out from underneath, Hobie looked the same, yet somehow his outfit wasn't as off putting as it had been when she first saw it. It wasn't ugly, but simply rugged. He looked masculine and strong standing under the majestic pine trees, ankle deep in fresh fallen snow, unshaven. He wore a pair of worn, fingerless black gloves and was holding a professional looking camera attached to a thick beaded strap hanging around his neck.

"You look like a furry, pink, abominable snowman...or woman, rather," he said, grinning.

A surprised laugh escaped her. "A what?"

Hobie tipped his head, reminiscent of the way a cowboy might tip his hat towards a lady, "Or, I should say, a *beautiful*, furry, pink, abominable snow woman."

She laughed again, a coquettish laugh that surprised her as she heard it dance across the drifts of snow.

Hobie's grin widened into a dimpled smile and his eyes twinkled. He kept on, "Do you mind?" He lifted the camera as he asked. He wanted to take her picture.

"Oh, I don't know," Presley's hands fluttered towards her

face to wipe some of the snowflakes that had landed and melted there.

"No," Hobie reached out one hand to stop her. "Just like you are. You look perfect."

He raised his eyebrows with the unasked question and after a moment of hesitation, Presley nodded. Hobie immediately lifted his camera and aimed its wide, bulbous lens at her. The camera clicked and whirred several times before Presley could even think to smile. She looked directly into the lens, turning her chin to the left and down so her best side was showing, just like she had been directed by their company photographer during all of the photo shoots she'd been to over the years, and smiled.

Hobie lowered his camera.

Presley's smile dropped. "What?"

"You don't have to smile at me," Hobie said.

"Oh," she didn't know how to take that. Glancing at her immediate surroundings she became confused. "What should I smile at?"

"You don't have to smile at anything," he said with a chuckle. Seeing her confusion he continued, "You don't have to think about what you're doing with your face is all. Just be relaxed."

"Oh," Presley said, as if she understood, which she didn't. She took a deep breath and exhaled. "Relaxed, got it." She shook her shoulders and arms like a boxer about to head into the ring then looked at Hobie again. He still hadn't raised his camera up.

"What are you doing?" he asked.

"I'm relaxing," she said. She motioned for him to lift his camera and take a picture. "Go ahead, I'm ready." Hobie didn't laugh out loud, but a laugh definitely flickered through his eyes. "Take your picture," she instructed him, wanting to get it over with.

He looked away from her, considering what to say. His eyes skimmed the morning sunshine twinkling across the snow in the trees.

"Why don't you look at the snow," he suggested.

"The snow?"

Hobie nodded, more sure of his idea, "Don't look at me and don't try to smile, just look at the snow."

Presley glanced around them. There was snow, literally, everywhere. Uncertainty surged through her and she stiffened.

"You don't have to think about anything," Hobie's voice grabbed her attention again and she turned to him.

He was watching her reaction with kind eyes and a gentle smile, but it was his voice that wrapped around her and held her in a daze. Their surroundings changed him, that was for certain. Being outdoors under the towering pines gave him an air of power and control, but it was his voice that affected her. The sound of it entered her body and let the uncomfortable stiffness slip away, yet kept her completely still. A strange, new, tenderness moved through her heart and she was captivated by the feeling, unable to tear her eyes from his.

They looked at each other for a long moment. He waiting for her to decide what to do. She wondering why she was unable to think straight while under the spell of his gaze.

The rising sun saved them at last. Sunshine broke through more of the snow covered branches from the East and shone its glorious light across them. The glittering snow intensified. Some of the tiniest flakes still danced magically in the air around them from when she had moved through the trees and caused the small blizzard.

Hobie's eyes lit up as he watched the light. He looked at her with new intensity. "See that? Look at the snow now."

Presley did look and she could see exactly what he saw. A

fairy like world around them. The brisk cold forgotten, everything forgotten, Presley took in all of its beauty. The graceful curves of the drifting snow, the dark contrast of wet pine trunks, the deep green needles holding great mounds of sparkling white snow, the smell of snow and pine blending and filling her with a sense of possibility.

She heard the clicking of the camera, but it was as if the sound was coming from far away. He must be taking pictures of the beautiful sunrise through the trees, because it was truly something to behold. For those few minutes, Presley was lost. Not lost in a way that caused her fear or anxiety, but lost in the way she used to lose herself in a book or while she was swimming in the ocean. Lost in the moment.

She realized the clicking had stopped and she turned to look at him. That strange look had returned to his face. The same one that he'd had when she walked through the tiny blizzard of snow. Presley didn't have words for him. They had shared this enchanting moment and she didn't know how to move on from it.

His face broke into a wide smile, dimples galore. Keeping one hand on his camera, he gestured with the other hand, sweeping his whole arm gallantly to the side and asked, "Would you like to go on a walk with me?"

CHAPTER 11

Hobie wasn't just a hobbyist. Apparently he had taken quite seriously to photography in high school.

"It helped me cope," he told her when she asked what drew him to it.

They had been walking for quite a while, talking a little and picking their way through heavier areas of snow while Hobie paused to snap pictures here and there. Apparently he had won awards at the art shows in their school and had been paid for his pictures since his late teens. Apparently photography was part of the reason he traveled so extensively. And, apparently, he hadn't just been paid by his family's business partners or small obscure magazines, but by real time serious publications like National Geographic and Time. This was news to Presley.

"I had no idea," she said.

Hobie looked at her sideways and smirked, "You weren't really paying much attention to the likes of me in high school."

"What is that supposed to mean?" Presley stopped

walking and pulled back her pink fur trimmed hood to look at him better. All of this hiking had made her too warm inside her snowsuit anyway. The fresh cold air felt good.

Hobie stopped, too, taking advantage of the moment to peer into the trees. He shrugged and said matter of factly, "You had your popular girl thing to do."

"My what?"

Hobie lifted his camera and focused on something in the pine tree. The camera started clicking. Presley looked at what he was aiming at, expecting to see some particularly artful blob of snow. Instead, she was surprised to see a blue bird with a white face and stomach and what looked like a tiny black mask across its eyes.

The bird cocked its head at the clicking. Hobie stopped taking pictures and lowered his camera. He kept his eyes trained on the bird for such a long moment Presley turned her attention to him instead of the bird.

"Are y–" she started.

"Shhh," Hobie raised his free hand to quiet her.

She had just been shushed. Stunned would have been the correct word to describe her at that moment. Incensed would be another one. She pursed her lips together and took in a deep breath in order to tell Mr. Hobie Brent, successful photographer or not, that she did not 'shhh' for anyone.

Keeaa! Keeaa! Keeaa!

A sharp screeching call came out of the blue bird. The sound was so loud and unexpected in the silent morning that Presley gave a surprised little hop and yelped. The bird flitted away, its blue feathers spraying snow from the branch down onto them. Or, more specifically, onto Presley's face. She was startled again, but this time the cold spray of snow made her laugh out loud. The camera clicked and as soon as she wiped the snow from her eyes she saw that Hobie had been aiming the lens at her.

He grinned and said, "I think you scared him." Her previous annoyance with him melted away.

"I scared him?" Presley tried to regain her composure, which was easier said than done.

"I think any kind of noise is going to bother them in this environment. It's so quiet." He took in their surroundings with contentment.

She was curious about Hobie. He had a general air of satisfaction about him that wasn't grandiose or pompous, but more…what was the word? Sensible.

"Are you what would be considered a nature photographer?" she asked.

"I wouldn't say that, exactly."

"But you like nature," she prodded.

He indicated their surroundings with his hand. "Who doesn't like nature?"

An involuntary image of Faye crossed Presley's mind and she was about to tell Hobie that she knew someone who was not a fan of nature, when he eyed something interesting in the middle distance and moved towards it. She followed, watching him as he strode confidently through the snowy wilderness. She used his footprints in the deeper drifts as stepping stones of a sort, trying to keep her Uggs from getting too wet.

"So running Barcom has never really been your main interest," she stated. It was more of an observation than a question.

He stopped and turned to look at her, taking her in, maybe sizing her up and trying to determine why she had asked the question. Then, with a small shrug, he turned his attention back to his camera and answered her question without looking her in the eye.

"No, it's never been my main interest. Or my interest at all."

Surprised at his candor, she didn't know how to respond and a tiny kernel of guilt sat in her stomach, as if she was the one who had forced him into working in his family business instead of wandering the world being a photographer.

"Sorry." It was all she could think of to say.

Still studying his camera, he raised his eyebrows in amusement and when he lifted his eyes to hers they were smiling. "There are worse things. It's kind of like being a vegan cowboy."

Presley wasn't sure she had heard him correctly. "A vegan cowboy?"

Hobie nodded and took the lens off, intermittently talking and blowing lint off of the internal workings of the device. "I lived in a village once in Vietnam where one of the families owned a small herd of cattle. The oldest son was in charge of taking the cows out in the day to graze and he cared for the calves. His whole life was to work and keep them healthy. He really loved those cows." Hobie clicked the lens back into place and gave her his full attention. "It was horrible for him. He cried like a baby every time they sold a calf. His brothers would have to almost carry him home he would be so broken up. He refused to eat their beef, then any beef, then he refused to eat any meat or dairy or eggs at all. He was just too broken up about it."

Presley waited, but Hobie didn't continue.

"What happened?" she asked.

"Oh, he ate rice and vegetables and tofu. He was fine," Hobie reassured her.

"No," she shook her head. "What did he do about selling the cattle? Did he stop doing it?"

He cocked his head. "No, he didn't stop doing it."

"Why not?"

Hobie paused as if waiting for her to come to the answer on her own. When she didn't he seemed neither surprised nor disappointed, but there was a resigned tone in his voice when he answered, "His whole family depended on those cattle. Not only that, but the village needed them, too. He had to keep raising and selling cattle for market. He didn't have a choice."

The kernel of guilt she'd felt for Hobie expanded into a knot of sadness for the unknown vegan cowboy in Vietnam.

He turned his attention to the daylight that shone brightly through the trees and was warming the spring snow to its melting point.

"We should get back, it's almost nine," he said.

Presley was brought out of her melancholy by the mention of the time. "Nine?" Then with some alarm, "I had a meeting at eight."

CHAPTER 12

*T*heir return to the house was mostly quiet. Cheerful chirping of birds interrupted the silence occasionally as the cold of early morning quickly disappeared under the bright Colorado mountain sun. She wondered what kind of birds they were, because they were definitely not the blue bird with the raucous screeching call that had shocked her earlier.

As she walked she kept envisioning a Vietnamese man dressed in old West cowboy clothes and a worn straw hat sitting in the middle of a green meadow weeping bitterly as his cattle were led away. She couldn't get the strange story out of her mind.

Hobie stopped often to take more pictures, but Presley forged ahead because she had already lost so much of her morning in the snowy woods with him. She got to the house first and found Jaxson waiting impatiently.

Though he would never say anything to her, his lips were pressed together in disapproval and he fluttered around with an air of uptight concern. His long pale fingers fiddled with the black and white striped tie he had stylishly paired with a grey cashmere sweater vest over a tight, white business shirt.

"Thank goodness, I was wondering if we should send someone to…" Jaxson's voice trailed off as he spotted Hobie emerging behind her. Hobie followed her footsteps back into the house and Jaxson gave her a look of astonished bewilderment before catching himself.

"I'm fine," Presley said brusquely, trying to pretend she just hadn't been wandering around in the winter morning with a tall, dark stranger for hours. "I just need to change."

Jaxson nodded, lips still tight. His eyes flicked up and down her pink snowsuit.

"You don't want to wear that?" he asked.

For a personal assistant he could be a little snarky.

Changed and back to work in the corner library where they would be out of the main comings and goings of the house, yet still have a good view of the front drive, Presley and Jaxson got down to work. He had several reports for her to review that he had marked with small 'sign here' yellow sticky notes where she needed to initial her approval.

"And here are the most pressing emails I've printed them for you," Jaxson said crisply as he laid a small stack of papers on the desk in front of her. He didn't like it when she got off schedule. Normally she didn't either.

From her position at the desk she could see out the front windows and the arrival of a deep burgundy four wheel drive caught her attention. She picked up the emails and pretended to look through them as she watched Hobie step outside to greet the driver with a handshake. He waved toward the front door where she imagined her father was seeing him off, then climbed into the vehicle and it drove away.

In the pit of her stomach, in the darkest part of the center of her body, disappointment trembled. A quiet whisper of misery, which came so unexpectedly that Presley put her hand on her stomach as if she could quell it.

She wondered at the feeling and tried to push it aside. But it would not be told what to do, and for a few long moments Presley stared blankly at the emails in one hand while the other pressed firmly against her abdomen. When she looked up, Jaxson was staring at her. His competence at reading her in an instant told him there was something afoot, while his strict adherence to protocol kept him from saying it out loud.

Presley opened her mouth to deny whatever his suspicions were, when her cell phone beeped with a text.

Was that who I thought it was? The text bubble asked. It was from Faye.

At nearly 10 o'clock in the morning, Faye had probably just woken up. Presley didn't answer. She didn't like to encourage Faye texting her during the work day. Things could get out of hand if her friend thought she had enough time to have text conversations. A few minutes later, a new message bubble appeared.

So which one of you has dibs on him?

She was referring to Hobie, of course. And wondering if a sisterly rivalry had erupted. The quivering misery in Presley's stomach surged into a sharp pang of hot jealousy wrapped up in irritation. She answered quickly tapping the message onto her phone as Jaxson looked on. He tried to cover his annoyance at the interruption by clearing his throat.

Neither of us put dibs on him. We are not children. Presley responded.

Well I think you should, because Ronnie already has a date. He seemed like a fine candidate to escort you to Ruby's party. Faye answered.

That thought had not actually crossed Presley's mind. She

didn't want to give Faye the idea that she was considering it, but in truth it wasn't the worst idea she'd ever heard. He was, after all, pretty good looking. He might clean up well.

I don't need a date. She typed.

He was very handsome. Faye ignored her.

Did you see what he was wearing? Presley added a sarcastic smirk emoji for emphasis.

You could dress him. In fact that sounds like a fun project! Faye added her own emoji, the one with the pounding heart eyes.

Jaxson cleared his throat again. Presley put her phone face down on the desk so she wouldn't see any more of Faye's texts and tried to focus on the printed emails in front of her.

One was from her New York office, something about new building regulations. One was from their offices in Chicago regarding the reports she had just signed off on. One was from the Count inviting her to meet with him and the Countess in New York when they arrived in a few weeks.

Again, Presley's focus waned. Her mind flew back to the winery, the patio, the way Hobie had caught her and carried her to the patio chair. The strange feeling in the pit of her stomach fluttered and climbed up into her chest. It really had been a long time since she'd been on a date.

Presley leaned over the emails and jotted down a few words of response to each one of the print outs. How much would the renovation delays cost? The reports for Chicago were approved, plans should move forward. And, yes, she would be delighted to join the Count and Countess in New York. She handed Jaxson the emails for him to respond appropriately. He took them, studying her with a keen eye.

"I want to meet with Hobie Brent tomorrow," she said suddenly.

Jaxson paused momentarily before reminding her, "You have a lunch scheduled with Ms. Clemonte and the others."

"Keep that, but rearrange whatever else I have so that I

can meet with Mr. Brent. He has proposed some changes in staff that I want to talk to him about." Presley didn't look at Jaxson as she spoke. She turned to her computer and clicked importantly on her mouse, indicating her directive was complete.

"Of course," Jaxson said.

Presley swore she could hear a twinge of amusement in his voice, but because her excitement at the prospect of seeing Hobie again would be too obvious if she dared look at Jaxson, she avoided eye contact and couldn't be sure.

PRESLEY JOINED her father and Ronnie for a late lunch. They settled into the casual dining room situated at the rear of the house. The room they all referred to as the sunroom. Three full walls of glass showed off the view of the entire back of the estate, which was complete with a well manicured rustic styled lawn edged by wooded slopes and a wide natural meadow that was visited often by deer and elk. A wood stove, large pine table with comfortable pine chairs, and dark red rug on the wide planked hardwood floors mimicked the feeling of a log cabin without lacking any modern luxuries.

"You went on a walk in the woods with him?" Ronnie asked, her eyes sparkling with delight.

"Yes, I walk in the woods sometimes," Presley answered.

Ronnie coughed out a laugh, "Since when?"

Presley ignored her younger sister's teasing and looked over the lunch fare being served. Some sort of Mexican fusion. She took a single Mahi Mahi taco and a spoon full of pico de gallo.

"Did you come to any conclusions on this walk?" her father asked.

"No, not yet," Presley hesitated to tell him that they

hadn't talked about business at all. "We're meeting tomorrow morning about the whole sustainability engineers or experts or whatever that nonsense he was talking about yesterday was." She popped a piece of Mahi Mahi into her mouth.

Her father looked up at her from his plate where he'd been concentrating on getting a stuffed shrimp stuck onto his fork. He furrowed his heavy brow at her and asked rather sharply, "Why do you call it nonsense?"

Presley was surprised by the question and by the tone of his voice. She glanced at Ronnie, who was looking at her with similar surprise. Presley swallowed and put her fork down on her plate.

"It's nonsense because added expenses like that will eat into profits and make the whole thing unpalatable to our shareholders," she said, trying to maintain the fine line she had walked for years, the one between being a CEO and being a daughter.

Mack Monroe's blue eyes flashed. He didn't like her answer, that was obvious. What astounded her sensibilities was why? What was his connection to this project? To Barcom? To going along with the do-gooder dreams of someone like Hobie?

Tension filled the room, but Presley did not look away. She wanted to know what was going on. This joint venture was a strange animal, her interactions with Hobie weren't normal, not for her anyway, and her father was acting bizarre. Mack Monroe was not approaching this project in his normal businesslike manner. There was something personal going on.

"Dad, I–" she started.

"Everyone can relax, I'm home!" Pete called out as he entered the sunroom.

"Pete!" Ronnie exclaimed, happy for their brother's arrival

and, no doubt, his ability to distract Presley and their father from having an argument.

"Hey, sistas," Pete greeted Ronnie and Presley as he swung his long legs into one of the pine chairs. He nodded at their father with a grin, "Pops."

"Pete," Mack said, shifting his attention to his youngest child and only son. He forced a smile.

Maybe it was because he was the youngest, the boy, taller, louder, more flippant and irreverent, or just more likely to say something shockingly funny, but Pete was usually the center of attention wherever he went. Especially in their home.

He was good looking with dark hair, the Monroe blue eyes, and the same square, masculine features of their father. His personality, however, had come directly from their mother. Unable to take anything seriously, always up for a good party, concerned with comfort and enjoyment, Pete sometimes took his celebrations to the extreme.

"What's up, fam?" Pete reached for a plate and dug into a pile of homemade tortilla chips that were still warm from the oven, pouring a scoop of hot queso over them.

"Where is your mother?" Mack asked, looking toward the door expectantly.

"She's still in Denver. She's meeting some Cherry Creek ladies for lunch then they'll come up."

"Ah," disappointment shadowed Mack's face momentarily. It bothered Presley to see it. Her mother rarely did what was expected and Presley felt a keen stab of regret for Mack whenever his wife chose their social circle over him. Married over 40 years, though, she guessed they had to be doing something right.

"I was afraid you weren't going to make it," Ronnie told Pete. He had a history of not going along with plans.

Pete pretended to gasp at the idea. "What? Stand you up?

Never." He winked at Ronnie, making her giggle. "When is this big party anyway?"

"Saturday," Ronnie and Presley answered at the same time.

Pete lifted his eyebrows. "You guys excited about it or something?"

"Yes," Ronnie said.

"Not really," Presley said.

"Who are you going with? Mom and Dad?" Pete asked Presley with a sarcastic smile.

She scowled at him.

"She can come with us if she likes," her father retorted. He was trying to sound supportive, but in the eyes of her little brother Presley knew the idea of going with their parents was lame.

"I think she should go with Hobie," Ronnie chimed in.

Pete chuckled, "What is a Hobie?"

"You remember Hobie Brent. Tall, quiet guy. He was in Presley's class," Ronnie said.

Pete crunched on some tortilla chips as he thought about Ronnie's description. Then his face lit up with recognition. "Hobie? Right. I remember him. Wasn't he a rower or something?"

"No, that was his brother, Danny," Presley corrected him.

"Oh…" Pete studied her for a few moments. "So, you're dating Hobie Brent now?"

"No!"

"We have business dealings with Barcom, his family's corporation," Mack explained. "If you kept up on what we were doing you would know." By 'we' he meant Mack Industries, a continual sore point between father and son.

Pete was not much of a businessman. If he was suited for any job in Mack Industries it would have been as a salesman. Presley had always thought Pete would be a great salesman.

However, his lack of interest and dedication combined with continued financial support from his parents meant Pete was not, and had never been, significantly involved with Mack Industries.

"Right," Pete lowered his gaze to his plate and picked up another cheese covered tortilla chip. The mood he had lifted when he arrived was fast dropping to the earth again.

"Are you romantically interested in Hobie, Pumpkin?" Mack asked abruptly.

Presley met her father's quizzical look with as much indifference as she could muster, though she could feel heat rising up her neck.

"No, Dad, not at all," she responded, looking down at her taco so he wouldn't see her blush.

Her father grunted his approval of her response and went back to stabbing the shrimp on his plate. Presley stole a glance at her siblings who were exchanging amused glances at her discomfort over the subject.

Great, that was all she needed. Her unruly sister and brother teasing her about Hobie while she was trying to handle the joint venture and her father's strange interest in it at the same time.

CHAPTER 13

*R*onnie closed her laptop and rubbed her eyes. The strain of reviewing all of the images her assistant had sent her from New York was giving her blurry vision. Best to get some sleep and review them again in the morning.

"Want some company?" The question came at the same time her bedroom door swung open and Pete stepped in. He held up a bottle of wine and two glasses while wiggling his eyebrows up and down. "I come bearing gifts."

Ronnie smiled and motioned her little brother to take a seat at one of the comfy chairs set up near the windows. It had been a long day, but it would be nice to catch up with Pete in private.

"So what's new in your world, sis?" Pete poured two generous glasses of Merlot as she settled into the chair opposite him, tucking her feet up underneath her like a teenager.

"Oh, you know, the usual. Big line coming out, running short on time, working day and night and getting an ulcer hoping it's a hit."

"Mmm," Pete grunted as he handed Ronnie her glass and took a healthy sip out of his. "Sounds awful."

Ronnie laughed and shrugged, "Well, it's stressful for sure, but in the end it will be gratifying." Pete grimaced and Ronnie felt the need to defend herself. "It's not all that bad."

"What isn't that bad?"

"Working for a living. You should try it." She grinned at her little brother and took a sip of wine.

"No, thank you."

"You might like it, you know. It's challenging. I love the people I work with and there's something really..." she searched for a word, but could only come up with the one, "...*gratifying* about it."

Pete rolled his eyes at her jokingly. "You already said that." Ronnie took a deep breath, ready to argue her point, but before she could say more Pete held up his palm to stop her. "Blah, blah, blah, Ron. I don't want to hear about work or how much I'm missing out on. I get enough of that from Dad. Tell me what else is going on with you. For real."

Ronnie slowly close her mouth as she tried to redirect her thoughts. For real? A few long moments went by as she clicked off everything she was currently doing that she could talk about, but it was all work.

"It's that bad, is it?" Pete asked with a pained look on his face. He sighed dramatically. "No wonder you needed me to be your date to Ruby's thing."

Ronnie smacked his arm with the back of her hand, "Shut up. You needed a date, too."

"Tut-tut, I did not *need* a date."

Ronnie frowned. "Am I that pathetic?"

Pete looked at her with pity. He took another gulp of wine and poured some more as his glass was almost empty.

"Not exactly pathetic. You guys are just too wrapped up in work," he said.

"Us guys? You mean me and Presley?" A surge of sisterly competition went through her and she scoffed, "I'm not as bad as Presley."

"No?" he was amused.

Ronnie scowled. Presley was the workaholic of the sisters, not her. Presley had always been more serious and driven than she was. She was the fun sister. The artsy sister. The one who liked to laugh.

Determined to make her point Ronnie argued, "My work is creative, hers is all that old men in suits stuff. Boring."

"You live in New York City and you can't tell me anything you're doing except sewing together purses…or whatever it is that you do." He grinned, a lock of his jet black hair flopping boyishly in front of his eyes. "Who's the boring one?"

"Presley lives in New York, too, remember?"

Pete grunted. "She lives in the boardroom, like Dad."

Ronnie didn't have an immediate response. She sipped her wine thoughtfully. The interaction between Presley and their father earlier at lunch ran through her mind. They were so much alike, the two of them. Bull headed and controlling.

She smiled, remembering Presley's reaction to their Dad asking if she was romantically interested in Hobie. The smile turned into a chuckle.

"What?" Pete wanted in on the joke.

"Did you see her face when Dad asked if she was interested in Hobie?"

Pete grinned, "Yeah, what was up with that? She must be into the guy for Dad to notice."

Ronnie sighed with empathy. "I think she is, but she'll never admit it."

Pete leaned back in his chair and took another drink, nodding in agreement. He peered at her quizzically, "Is he a good guy? This Hobie?"

"I think so. I remember him from school. Faye only has nice things to say about him."

Pete dismissed this comment with a shake of his head. "Faye. What does Faye know?"

Ronnie laughed. "More than you would think, actually."

They sat in amiable silence, drinking their wine and looking out at the moonlit snow. The storm clouds from the day before were completely gone and the moon shone bright over the forest outside.

Ronnie thought about her big sister. Presley tried so hard to keep everything under control, especially her feelings. She was a good sister and a brilliant businesswoman, just so pent up.

She glanced at Pete who was the exact opposite of pent up. He lounged casually in the chair, comfortable in his skin, in his life. It was funny how different Presley and Pete were and, yet, the three of them worked well as siblings. Like three peas in a pod. Very different peas, but still happily sharing a pod.

Turning her attention back to the moonlight and snow, Ronnie mused, "It would be nice for her to find someone."

Pete, still gazing at the view, grunted in agreement. "Yes, yes it would."

CHAPTER 14

The next morning Presley could not for the life of her decide what to wear.

She had a huge closet. A walk in closet that was the size of a normal sized bedroom. Fit for a queen.

Every inch of her closet was covered top to bottom with the latest fashions made by the best designers and tailored to fit her perfectly. And yet, as she stood in her plush coral bathrobe and pure white wool slippers trying to pick an outfit on this auspicious morning, she came up blank.

Jaxson had scheduled her meeting with Hobie at 9 o'clock-in the morning-which she realized she had requested but seemed at this moment to be some kind of sick joke on her personal assistant's part. What had he been thinking? How could she possibly get up, work out, take a shower and get properly dressed and drive to Aspen to meet by 9:00 am? She had felt nearly brain dead all morning while trying to get through her normal routine.

"Jaxson!" Presley called to him from her closet.

He was settled in her bedroom sitting area working on

flight plans for her trip back to New York, waiting for her to finish bathing and dressing.

"Yes?" Jaxson popped his head into her closet.

She turned to him, flustered. "I need your help."

Thankfully style was right up Jaxson's alley. In addition to being organized, professional, and intelligent, when it came to putting together attractive, fashionable clothing, Jaxson really shone.

"Oh, dear," he said as he took in her state of indecision. "What are you going for in this meeting?"

"You know, the normal. Powerful, intelligent, in charge," she answered.

Jaxson hesitated, the top of his nose pinched together in an almost imperceptible wince.

"What?" Presley asked.

"Are you sure that's what you're going for?"

"What else would I be going for?"

Jaxson winced again, this time more openly. His voice lifted a full octave with his question, "Are you sure you don't want to go for something more…sexy?"

Presley's eyes widened. "Why would I want to look… sexy?" The last word stumbled on her lips.

Jaxson raised one well groomed eyebrow and said, "If you don't know then I'm not sure I can explain it to you."

Presley had to laugh, which was a release and she felt a little better. For a few seconds. Then her shoulders dropped and she let out a huge sigh.

"I don't know what to do, Jaxson," she admitted. "I'm having a mental block or something."

Jaxson tsk-tsked and took her hands in his. "You're about to have a one-on-one meeting with a gorgeous cookie. Move over Jon Snow, you know what I mean?" Jaxson flipped his head back like he was a cheerleader. Presley laughed again. "It's totally natural for you to want to look sexy. But you're fighting your urges and that, Ms. Presley, is making you freeze up like a deer in headlights."

He was right. Absolutely right.

She looked past Jaxson into her reflection in one of the full-length mirrors and answered slowly, "So…you're saying I need to give in to my urges?" Just saying it made her spine quiver a little.

Jaxson turned so they were both facing the mirror. He looked her reflection in the eyes. "I'm saying it would do no harm for you to give into your urge to dress a little spicy, and it will probably unfreeze your deer brain."

"Right. Got it," is what she said, but the quiver of uncertainty did not leave her completely. It moved into the bottom of her stomach where it stayed while they picked out her clothes.

When Presley entered the small, chic office building in the business center of Aspen, she felt strong. She wore a tight black cashmere turtleneck tucked into a mid-calf, well fitted, cotton twill camel colored skirt that kicked out into a flirty flare mid-thigh. Knee high slouchy black suede boots and a silky leopard print scarf to tie back her blonde tresses at the nape of her neck gave the whole look a fun feel, without being overly sexual or, heaven forbid, tacky.

The right clothes helped Presley feel less quivery and the looks she was getting from the other people in the office building assured her that she looked good. Either that or they already knew who she was. Sometimes her Monroe name preceded her, especially in smaller communities like Aspen. Either way she had regained her normal confidence and wasn't nervous at all about seeing Hobie again for this meeting.

Until she saw him.

As his executive assistant ushered her into his office she smiled at him and he was the one who appeared frozen in place like a deer in headlights. He had stood up from the wide, retro desk at the center of the room to greet her, but his greeting slowed to a full stop when he saw her.

He was in jeans, a burgundy button up shirt, and dark brown corduroy sport coat with patches on the elbows. Again. Or maybe this was the same sport coat she had seen before, that was entirely possible. It would be very like him to have only one sport coat.

Still, the sight of him in his rumpled architect look, which she knew was actually a world traveling photographer look, brought back the tiny quiver in her stomach and turned it into a wave of butterflies.

He finally broke free of whatever had caught his tongue and said, "Presley."

"Hobie, good morning," she answered, glad she was capable of saying more than just his name. She could handle this. She just needed to focus on the business at hand and try to ignore that dark curly hair of his and the way his eyes twinkled when he talked.

"It's good to see you," he smiled at her and came around his desk to shake her hand.

Presley seized up, terrified he would feel the tremble in her fingers. When he took her hand in his, warmth moved up her arm and across her shoulders. She couldn't stop looking at his dimples showing under an impressive five o'clock shadow. She took in a deep breath to keep herself calm and was overwhelmed by the smell of his cologne. Black pepper and birch. Intoxicating.

He offered her a seat and she took it gladly, smoothing her tight skirt as she sat and tucking her booted toes demurely under the chair. Instead of going back to his side of the desk, the power side, Hobie pulled the other chair near hers and sat down. They were now facing each other.

To keep from blushing at this pointed attention, Presley

looked around his office. It was modest compared to her offices that were scattered around the world at Mack Industries epicenters, but it was nice. Decorated 50's retro, Madmen style, with an extra touch of luxury, it suited him.

"This is a nice space," she said.

He smiled and she could not avoid looking at him. Jaxson was right, Hobie was a gorgeous cookie.

"How are you today?" he asked. It was a normal superficial question, but something in the way he said things made her think he was truly interested.

Presley squirmed a bit under his unwavering attention, but managed a coy smile of her own. "I'm well, thank you." He held her gaze for a few more moments before she was compelled by her more sensible side to get down to business. "I would like to go over what you brought up the other day with my father."

A flicker of what might have been disappointment moved through his eyes, but was gone too fast to tell for certain.

"The sustainability aspect?" he asked.

"Yes, the sustainability aspect. I don't know enough about it to make a clear decision and I thought..." she motioned to him and her hand got so close to his leg she could feel the heat of his body with her palm. Presley swallowed and focused. "Who better to talk to about it than you? Since you have such a passion for the subject."

"I do," he agreed, eyeing her respectfully. Carefully.

As she gazed into his deep brown eyes Presley's heart skipped a beat and she lost track of what she had planned to say. She didn't respond. Mild dizziness washed over her and she realized she had also forgotten to breathe.

"Would you like some coffee?" he asked. Before she could answer he hopped up from his chair and moved past her, brushing his hand across her knee as he did. The electrical current that shot through her leg at his touch surprised her.

"I don't need any coffee," she blurted out, standing up as well. The feelings she was having made her want to rush out of the door, maybe escape to the ladies room. Instead she turned calmly toward Hobie who was at the far end of the office at a bar where an elaborate stainless steel coffee machine perched on a marble countertop.

"I can do more than coffee," Hobie answered cheerfully. He inspected the touch screen on the machine. "I can do cappuccino, espresso, lattes...machiattos?"

"Really?" She grinned. The idea of Hobie, international photographer, rumpled architect lookalike, head of Barcom Incorporated, making a cappuccino in his office struck her as funny.

He grinned back. "I have a wide set of skills."

Again, the butterflies. Presley suppressed a giggle. She didn't giggle in business meetings. But a drink might be a nice distraction. "A machiatto, please."

Hobie lifted one eyebrow, "You like a challenge, don't you?"

"Don't you?"

He raised a bottle full of amber liquid from the marble counter and asked with a flourish, "How about a *caramel* machiatto?"

This time she did giggle, which only encouraged him. She watched as he showed off making her a drink with exaggerated gestures as if he was a great chef hard at work. When it was done, he handed it to her with a half bow.

"Why, thank you, kind sir," she said, and immediately felt silly.

With a flirtatious look, he answered, "You're very welcome." Their fingers touched as she took the steaming cup from him and that same electricity she had felt before shot through her body.

As he made himself a drink, a cappuccino, Presley sipped

hers and watched. She didn't sit back down in her chair. She found that she liked being this close to Hobie, watching him expertly manipulate the coffee machine, chatting lightly about his thoughts on eco-tourism.

"I see how you could be swayed by some of these ideas," she told him. "But I am not sure about pouring money into something that could be, most likely is, just the most recent fad idea."

"I don't think it's a fad. It's the way the world is moving. And you will be shocked at what sustainability in business does for the bottom line over time. There may be a cost up front, but the end result will save us money. A lot of money."

Presley paused. Could what he said be true? He certainly sounded convinced. "You really have done your homework on this, haven't you?" she asked.

"Well, I'm not an expert," he admitted. He turned back to her with his cappuccino in his hand and lifted it in her direction, "But I do know an expert that might be able to change your mind."

A jingling sound, like keys smacking together, came from behind Presley. Her back was to the door and Hobie's attention shifted from her to something behind her. His expression shifted too, from flirty to surprised horror. He lowered his drink and made a move as if to lunge forward and grab her, but before he could, a powerful weight hit Presley in the center of her back. She lurched towards Hobie, her caramel macchiato erupting out of its cup and into the air.

CHAPTER 15

*H*obie caught her, but not before the caramel macchiato, cooled by its trip through the air, landed all over both of them.

"Rocky!" Hobie called out as another heavy push hit Presley. This time directly on her bottom.

"Oh!" she exclaimed as she was shoved even further into Hobie's arms.

"Rocky, stop it," Hobie said with authority.

Presley's full body was now pressed into Hobie's, his arms wrapped around her. She felt him lift her into the air, but not before whoever Rocky was goosed her.

"Oh!" She exclaimed again, though this time the sound was muffled into Hobie's chest. Her feet dangled as he moved her unceremoniously to his side, placing her back on the ground and stepping forward to intercede with whatever beast was attacking her from behind.

As soon as he let go of her, the air cooled the caramel macchiato, which had splashed over her face and soaked into her clothes. With one hand still holding the empty cup

Presley wiped macchiato from her eyes with the other so she could see what was going on.

"Sit," Hobie commanded.

"What?" Presley's vision was blurred and she couldn't open her eyes all the way because of the stinging.

"Not you," Hobie answered. "Him."

As the room came back into focus, Presley could make out a brown and white blob bouncing in front of Hobie. She squinted and wiped her eyes again.

"Rocky, sit…good boy," Hobie said.

Her eyes scrunched closed, Presley sniffed. Her nose was running. Either that or macchiato had actually gone up her nose during the chaos.

"Here, let me get you some tissues. Stay," Hobie commanded.

Presley assumed he was talking to what could only be a dog. He had better not be telling her to stay. A few moments later she felt him take the empty cup from her hand and press some napkins into her palm. She used them to mop up her eyes and face.

"I'm so sorry, he lacks some basic manners, but he's a good dog…usually," Hobie said.

Presley still couldn't see clearly, but she didn't have to see him to hear the amusement in his tone. She squinted at the brown and white blob that was slowly turning from a blurry form into the shape of a large dog. She could hear it panting and whining impatiently. She was still too shocked and incensed to speak.

After a particularly guttural whine from the dog blob named Rocky, Hobie said, "You be quiet. Look what you did to the nice lady." Another whine sounded then Hobie was standing directly in front of her. She knew this because she could sense his presence, not because she could smell his cologne. The enticing peppery smell of his cologne was overwhelmed by the sickening sweet scent of caramel macchiato. She blew her nose into the napkins.

"Here, these are wet," he pressed more napkins into her hands that he had dampened with warm water. She used them to wipe her eyes and was finally able to see again...unfortunately.

The front of her camel colored skirt was blotchy with dark brown stains and her chest was soaked. The wet fabric was now so chilly and damp against her skin that she had to pull it away using her fingertips and hold it there so it could dry. Presley could only imagine what she looked like after being showered with the sticky sweet drink.

Hobie mopped macchiato off of his chin and neck. Stains showed on his burgundy shirt and she assumed the drink had also spilled onto his dark brown sport coat. Though, honestly, she couldn't see any. So the rumply old coat had one selling point after all.

The perpetrator of this entire debacle sat eagerly nearby. A large mixed breed dog with a long snout, fat black nose, big brown eyes, floppy ears, and a long brown and white coat, panted happily at them. This must be Rocky.

"Presley, meet my dog, Rocky," Hobie said, still in good humor over this whole event.

"Rocky," she said, not quite as amused as he was.

At the sound of his name the dog lunged towards her again, intent on greeting her with some kind of sloppy dog kiss no doubt. Hobie stepped forward and grabbed him by his collar just in time, saving her from another friendly pounce. He made the dog sit and looked at her apologetically.

"He's not normally like this. He must like you," he said.

Presley was about to quip a sarcastic remark when she was distracted by how close Hobie was standing. Holding her tight black turtleneck away from her chest, her hands almost brushed his torso. He was looking down at her…no, actually, he was gazing down at her. His eyes wandered slowly over her lips, her cheeks, her temple. A glimmer of more than just amusement shone in his eyes and Presley's words caught in her throat, the electrifying feeling she had previously felt at his touch shivered through her body just from his look. Her lips parted slightly and she tilted her face up to him, unable to look away and captivated suddenly by the idea of kissing him.

Hobie's hand reached toward her cheek, but did not brush it. Instead, he dabbed at her temple with his napkin and said softly, "You have some in your hair."

"I'm sorry, I lost him after our run," a woman's voice sounded from the open doorway of the office. Rocky jumped up with delight and bounded to greet whoever it was.

Hobie pulled away from Presley almost as if he had been caught doing something he wasn't supposed to be doing. When she took in the woman standing in the door she thought she knew why.

Petite, perfectly tanned, long jet-black hair pulled up into a ponytail, the woman was stunning. Dressed in purple and white tie dye leggings and sports bra straight from Lululemon's athleisure line, there was no doubt she had a perfect body. Somewhere in her late twenties with gorgeous green eyes and the glow of recent exercise illuminating her skin, the sight of her set off Presley's jealousy hackles immediately. She reminded Presley of Megan Fox from the Transformer movies. Every man's dream girl. Presley glanced at Hobie's sheepish expression. Probably Hobie's dream girl, too.

"I'm sorry, we were on our run and he took off when we came into the building," the woman, more like girl in Presley's opinion, said. Even her voice was beautiful. Sultry. Not too nasal or high pitched. Had she said 'we'?

"Presley, this is Megan," Hobie said.

Presley blinked at him dumbly. "Megan?"

He nodded and motioned the sexy young thing into the room with them. "Megan Adams, she's the eco-tourism expert I was telling you about. Well, one of them."

Megan? Seriously?

Megan sashayed into the room like she owned the place stopping at Hobie's side and ruffling Rocky's fluffy head. The dog ate it up and Presley's heart sank as she watched Hobie react similarly.

"Megan, this is Presley Monroe," Hobie continued.

"Oh, wow, I'm honored," Megan reached out and shook Presley's hand like she was some relic of a bygone era that needed to be treated gently. An antique.

Presley only nodded and tried not to scowl. She couldn't stop noticing how close Megan and Hobie were standing and how the dog sat neatly between them as if they were their own little family.

Finally she thought of something to say, "You were on a run with…Rocky?"

Again, at the sound of his name, Rocky lunged toward her to acknowledge the moment with a leap of joy onto her chest. This time Megan grabbed his collar and brought him back down to a sitting position.

"Hey, boy, calm down," Megan said. She flashed a beautiful smile at Presley. "Yes, he has a lot of energy so I take him with me when I run."

Hobie chuckled, "Technically he's my dog, but we all know his heart belongs to Megan."

That was it. Presley understood the situation perfectly. Megan was not just an employee of Barcom Inc. who specialized in eco-tourism, she was Hobie's girlfriend. Or he wanted her to be, which was even more of a bitter pill.

Another infuriating thought occurred to her. He was using the joint venture with Mack Industries to get into this young woman's pants. And he was using her, Presley, to facilitate this sordid plan by trying to convince her to hire little Miss Megan Tie Dye.

Anger boiled up inside Presley. She could barely keep her polite smile plastered to her face as Megan went on and on about some of the sustainability concepts she had been working on. Hobie looked on with interest, but Presley knew exactly what he was interested in, and it wasn't saving the trees, or the Count's precious little Umbrian village, or the climate.

Despite the fact that Presley had drying macchiato in her hair, the meeting continued…with Megan. Presley did all she could to look both regal and youthful, appropriately interested and in charge, in essence unaffected by the younger, prettier, less macchiato stained woman in the room. Though she may have appeared interested to the other two, inside Presley was not focusing at all.

Right when she though she could not stand it any longer Hobie's desk phone buzzed and he picked it up. As his executive assistant spoke on the other end the color drained from his face and his expression hardened. Presley noticed instantly and Megan soon after. The younger woman's voice trailed off as they waited for him to finish his phone call. From the look on his face Presley was expecting him to take charge and tell his assistant what to do.

Instead he merely said, "Okay, thank you."

He hung up and when he looked at Presley he wasn't really looking at her at all. It was an unsettling feeling. His jaw worked with emotion and his eyes, though intense, were not focused in any way on her or their meeting. She did feel slightly better when he didn't look at Megan in any significant way either. His mind was elsewhere and Presley wondered what could be wrong. Even Rocky, who had calmed down and fell asleep next to a window, sat up and whined.

"I have to go," he said abruptly. "Excuse me, but I won't make it back any time soon."

And then he left. Just like that. Abandoned Presley alone with his out of control dog and his peppy health nut love interest to do who knew what? No explanation. No conclusions to any of the questions she had raised during this meeting. She had not been this insulted in a long time. Plus the macchiato was turning into a gooey mess on her clothes and felt sticky on her face. It was probably gobbed up in her hair, too.

Needless to say, after he left Presley didn't stay long with Megan. She wasn't in the mood.

Her mood had been killed. Her mood was lying in a mangled heap in the middle of Hobie's office floor, mortally injured with no chance of recovery. And this dead, macchiato stained mood completely ruined her lunch plans.

CHAPTER 16

The room was full of quiet stuffiness broken only by a rhythmic beeping, which came from the monitor hooked up to Danny's IV. Hobie wished he could open a window for some fresh air, but that wasn't an option in a treatment room. He knew that. Still, he couldn't help but desire outside air in this place.

Hobie and his father sat on either side of a hospital bed, watching in silence as the medicine that was killing the cancer also ate away at Danny bit by bit. It was a horrible miracle to witness. The saving of a soul with tiny drops of poison.

"You okay, Dad?" Hobie asked his father, his voice coming out gruffer than he expected, as if he had just woken up from a long nap.

His Dad looked across the sleeping Danny at his youngest son, giving him a quick nod. "I'm fine, son."

He didn't look fine. Not to Hobie at least. He looked tired, thin, stricken. Hobie was reminded once again that this was the second time his father had found himself bedside to a cancer patient. And this time it was his child. A deep blow to someone who had already lost a beloved wife.

Hobie's heart clenched and he switched his attention back to Danny, his big brother. Danny had always been taller than Hobie, stronger, faster, louder, probably smarter, though that was not something Hobie had ever admitted to before, ever since he'd taken over Danny's position at Barcom he had come face to face with that reality. Danny was a better businessman than he would ever be. Of course, none of that mattered in this room.

Danny had lost a lot of weight, his muscles looked like they'd been eaten away, and he was so utterly pale. Hobie wasn't sure he would recognize him if he just saw him sleeping here in this bed and didn't already know it was his brother. His heart clenched again and Hobie stood suddenly from his chair.

"Want some coffee or something, Dad?" he asked as he made to move towards the door.

"I'll get it, son." His Dad stood stiffly. "I need the exercise to stretch out these old bones."

Hobie reluctantly agreed, feeling a little useless as he stood at the window and looked out at a beautiful spring afternoon.

"Good, you're still here…" Danny said from the bed.

Hobie turned around, a little surprised. "You're awake?"

Danny nodded and licked his lips with a dry tongue. "I've been awake."

Hobie sat back down in his chair with a sarcastic grin, "You were fake sleeping until Dad left?"

Danny managed a chuckle and gave his little brother an amused look, "Not exactly."

"How're you feeling?"

Danny brushed off the question with a flick of his hand. "I don't want to talk about that."

"Okay," Hobie looked around the room and back. "So what do you want to talk about while Dad's gone?"

"Barcom."

Hobie scoffed. "You're kidding, right? You want to talk about work right now?"

"I sure as hell don't want to talk about this," Danny gestured towards his IV drip. Hobie understood.

"Okay, Barcom it is." Hobie rubbed his hands on his knees and rocked back and forth in his chair trying to drum up some key points from all of the business meetings he'd been in the past week.

Danny watched him for a while then coughed out a laugh. "Jeez, Hobie, it's not a test. Just tell me what's going on."

"I can't come up with a short list just like that. There's a lot going on."

"Okay, how's Dad's pet project going? With Mack Industries."

Presley's face as he dabbed caramel macchiato out of her hair flashed through Hobie's mind. He squirmed a little in the chair. "It's going okay."

Danny's eyes grew stern. "Okay? That's all you've got?"

"Better than okay, it's going well…pretty good."

"Pretty good?"

Hobie searched for something more to say. "I introduced Megan to Presley Monroe and I think she's warming up to the eco-friendly side of things."

Danny's eyebrows raised in surprised hope. "Really? That is good."

"Yup," Hobie tried to look more confident than he felt. He actually had no idea how that introduction had panned out. He'd gotten the news about Danny's treatment moving up unexpectedly and rushed out of the room so fast. Then there was the whole Rocky mauling incident. He didn't want to get into the details about that with Danny.

"I figured they would dig in on the extra costs and be impossible to move. Mack Industries doesn't have an especially environmentally friendly record." Danny said as he relaxed back into his pillow.

"Even though Mack's retired he seemed pretty interested in finding out about it when I saw him at their place. But Presley has made it clear it's not their priority," Hobie said.

Danny mulled over this information before responding, "Honestly, I've never understood why Dad insisted on partnering up with Mack after all these years on this thing. I thought it was going to be an uphill battle from the start."

"Did we need their funding?"

Danny shrugged, "It's nice, but we could have done it without them. Maybe it's Dad trying to inject something good into the world. Or at least into Mack Monroe."

Hobie grunted in agreement and the two brothers sat in silence for a few minutes. Hobie's eyes focused on the floor in front of his chair as he thought about checking in with Megan to get her thoughts on her talk with Presley. When he looked up he found Danny watching him with a twinkle in his eyes.

"What?" Hobie asked.

"I'm just thinking about you going head to head with Presley Monroe."

Hobie shifted in his chair. "What about it?"

"I haven't seen her in a long time, but I hear she's something to behold these days. And she's got a reputation."

Hobie paused before asking, "What kind of reputation?"

Danny grinned and Hobie saw his same old big brother in that smile, "I've heard she can be just as ruthless in business as her old man, if not more."

"Ruthless?" He agreed she was confident and demanding, but ruthless? That didn't seem right.

"That might just be sour grapes from her competition,"

Danny offered. "But I suggest you find a way to crack her tough exterior. Otherwise she may outmaneuver you."

Before Hobie could respond the door opened and their Dad stepped in bearing a cup carrier with three steaming drinks.

"I got tea instead of coffee. I hope that's all right," he said. He noticed Danny was awake and exclaimed, "You're up!"

Both charmed by their father's ways, the brothers shared an amused look before Danny answered, "Yes, Dad, I'm up."

CHAPTER 17

"And then, poof, just like that he walks out on me leaving me with that…that…girl." Presley stabbed at her wedge salad with the heavy silver cutlery. She, Ronnie, Faye, Grace, and Ruby were dining at one of their favorite Aspen eateries, La Bleu. Her friends exchanged glances, which did not go unnoticed. She pointed her fork at each of them in turn and said, "And I'm not angry because I'm jealous. I'm angry because he's an inconsiderate, salacious, slob."

Ronnie scoffed lightly, "He is not, Pres. Maybe he had an emergency."

"You weren't there," Presley said hotly. She finally got a piece of crisp iceberg onto her fork and dipped it into the bleu cheese dressing. "His dog practically mauled me!" She popped the lettuce into her mouth and chewed furiously.

"Did it bite you?" Ruby asked. She was the true animal lover of the group. She had two rescue dogs of her own and helped manage the county dog shelter.

"No, it didn't bite me. But it nearly knocked me over. I would have fallen on my butt if he hadn't caught me."

"So he kept you from falling?" Grace asked.

"Yes," Presley could tell they weren't taking any of her ranting as seriously as she wished they would. "I could have been seriously burned, too, you know."

"When your drink splashed all over your face?" Ronnie said with a laugh.

No subject was off limits for Ronnie to crack a joke. Her laughter infected all of them as they envisioned the scene. All except Presley. She stewed over their lack of concern for her well being, letting her knife and fork drop with a clatter onto her plate.

"Now, now," Faye reached over and put a cool hand on Presley's forearm. "You're all right, aren't you? No real harm done, was there?"

"Why are you all defending him?" Presley wanted to know.

"We're not defending him, honey," Grace said. "We just notice that he's gotten to you, that's all."

Presley fumed into her glass of iced tea. Hobie had not *gotten to her*. She did not get *gotten to*.

"Let's talk about something else," Ruby offered.

Grace turned her emerald eyes and attention to Ruby, glad to escape whatever wrath was bubbling up in Presley. Her eyes lit up with an idea, "Tell us everything we need to know about the party."

Ruby happily launched into a detailed report of the fast approaching fundraiser event. The decorations, the guest list, the bands, the food, how she had recently added additional charities like the dog shelter to the auction event that would be taking place. Presley was only half listening. She drank more tea and ignored the rest of her salad, feeling put out at the way her friends seemed to be enjoying her Hobie Brent problem.

"But what will you be wearing, darling?" Faye asked Ruby,

sweeping aside everything except what she considered to be paramount information.

Ruby pointed at Ronnie. "I don't know. She's dressing me."

Ronnie nodded with enthusiasm. "I've got the perfect look picked out for her, too. A delicate balance of non-profit global awareness and high fashion chic. You're going to love it."

"And will you be going with a date?" Faye asked. She directed the question vaguely towards Ruby, but included Presley in her questioning look.

"No, I'm going stag," Ruby admitted, though not unhappily. "I have too many things going on to worry about a date throughout the evening." She looked at Presley cautiously, "How about you?"

Presley arched an eyebrow, ready to launch into another tirade about not wanting or needing a date when Jaxson approached their table. She had asked him to get her early from her lunch so she could catch up on a few items she had ignored in order to make her morning meeting with Hobie.

"Excuse me," Jaxson said politely to the other women.

They all greeted him warmly. Every one of her friends had a personal assistant, but Jaxson was the best known in their group. Possibly because Presley rarely let a day go by without having him join her. They didn't utilize their personal assistants as much as she did because she was the workaholic in their group. Ruby was a close contender, but she also didn't believe in turning her personal assistant into a workaholic so she kept her use of them at a minimum.

"But you haven't finished eating yet," Ronnie motioned to Presley's half finished salad.

"Sit, Jaxson," Faye waved a hand at the waiter to bring another chair. "Surely you don't have to rush away immediately," Faye said to Presley.

Jaxson looked to Presley for approval and she gave him a nod. She would have him check emails for her while she finished her salad. It might be more effort to go against Faye's plan than eat a few more bites of lettuce.

"Do you want anything?" Grace asked Jaxson as he sat down in the newly arrived chair.

"No, thank you."

"Are there any urgent emails?" Presley asked before shoving a chunk of crispy iceberg into her mouth.

Faye gave her an amused smile, "You didn't answer my question, darling."

Presley chewed on her lettuce and returned Faye's look with a less amused one of her own.

"Have you found a date for the party yet?" Faye reiterated, unperturbed that she was annoying her friend.

"You're dead set against going with Hobie?" Ronnie sounded a little disappointed.

Jaxson made a little sound of surprise at the sound of Hobie's name. The whole table turned toward him to see what had caused this small break in their social norms. Presley widened her eyes at her assistant. Why in the world would he react like that at the man's name? Jaxson's attention was held by the tablet in his hand where he had been, until a few moments ago, busily checking Presley's emails.

"What is it?" Presley asked, not sure if she wanted to know—or if she wanted everyone at the table to know.

Jaxson looked up at her from his tablet. For the first time in forever Presley was not able to read his expression. It might be pleasant shock or it might be confused dread. Frozen with indecision, she gave him no instruction, verbal or nonverbal. After a beat Jaxson made an executive decision and lifted the tablet. He turned it so not only Presley could see, but so could her lunch companions.

On the screen an ethereal image of a crystallized forest

buried under a blanket of snow where a beautiful, winter fairy, all pink fuzz and blue eyes, laughed with joy.

It took a few moments for Presley to recognize the setting of the image and the subject. It was her in her pink snowsuit.

"That's you, Presley!" Ruby exclaimed in surprise.

"When did you do a modeling shoot?" Ronnie asked, just as delighted as the rest of her friends seemed to be.

The side of Jaxson's mouth lifted in a knowing smile as Presley looked from the image to him and back again, but he didn't say a word.

"What beautiful pictures," Grace said as Jaxson swept his finger across the image to go to the next one.

"Those are simply magical," Faye added. She was charmed with the pictures. As were they all. Even Presley.

"I–I don't understand," she finally said. "Where did those come from?"

Without blinking Jaxson said, "He sent them to you."

"Hobie?" Presley asked, trying to wrap her mind around what had happened.

"Hobie!?" All of her friends asked, almost in unison.

Jaxson nodded. "They were attached to an email he sent a few minutes ago apologizing for having to cut your meeting short." He gave her another knowing look and, despite the fact that she had been working hard nursing her terrible mood, Presley smiled.

"May I?" Grace reached for the tablet and Jaxson handed it over, avoiding looking directly at Presley so he could pretend not to see if she was displeased with this move.

What was amazing to Presley is that she didn't try to stop him. She didn't do anything. She just sat there in a kind of stunned silence, impressed by Hobie's skill as a photographer and flattered that he had chosen her as a subject. The tiny flutter of excitement that she'd had when going to meet him at his office returned.

"I mean these are really beautiful," Grace said. She had been studying them with her movie industry eye and handed them to Ronnie who was leaning over trying to look at them over her shoulder. "He is very good. And you're beautiful, so that helps," Grace added.

"What I want to know is when and where did you have a photo shoot with him?" Faye asked.

"It wasn't a photo shoot," Presley said. "We were walking by the estate the morning after the storm."

"When he stayed at your place?" Faye asked, her meaning thinly veiled by a faux coy smile.

"It wasn't like that at all," Presley said. The tablet had made its rounds through everyone and reached her. She looked at the images again.

The way Hobie had captured her laughing and the snow glittering as it fell through the air around her after she knocked it off of the branches was so lovely. She couldn't look away, and not because she looked amazing in the pictures. It was something else. Something more personal.

"I don't normally look like this," she said, almost to herself.

"You're beautiful always," Ruby said.

"Thank you, Ruby," Presley said. "But you know what I mean. I'm not a model."

"I think you're just surprised," Ronnie said. "It's not whether or not you're a model that makes a picture. It's what the photographer sees in you."

Presley's stomach tightened. The idea that Hobie saw her like this, as a joyful, beautiful, snow princess, was more than a little thrilling.

"He made you look so beautiful because that's how he sees you," Grace added, her eyes merry and sparkling.

A euphoric sensation rushed through Presley, despite all of her misgivings from this morning. And even though she was certain Hobie and Megan were an item, and she had no interest in dating him or anyone else, she could not keep the smile off of her lips.

CHAPTER 18

"All I'm saying is you should invite him," Faye implored. Her disembodied voice ringing through the interior of Ruby's car. She was driving from her meeting with the band to her meeting with the caterer and her cell phone was linked into her car's audio system. She could turn the volume of Faye's insistent voice up or down at will. Ruby resisted the urge to turn it down.

"Of course I'll invite him," Ruby answered.

"No, I mean really invite him. Make sure he comes."

"Well, I don't know how I can do that, Faye," Ruby responded sharply. She had literally one thousand other details to attend to for her fundraiser, making sure Hobie Brent showed up to the party was not high on her priority list.

"I'm sure you can think of something, darling," Faye insisted.

Ruby flicked her turn signal on and slowed the car. Remaining focused on driving safely while dealing with Faye was not always a simple task.

"Why does it matter so much to you?" Ruby had a sudden

suspicion that Faye was interested in Hobie romantically and her hackles rose at the idea. He was a dish, that was for sure, but anyone with eyes could see that Presley had it bad for him. Faye had no shortage of male companionship while Presley's romantic life had dried up over the years. Maybe she was too hurt from her failed marriage or maybe she was a workaholic. Probably both. Either way, Ruby didn't like the idea of Faye zeroing in on the first man Presley had shown any interest in for years.

"I want him there for Presley," Faye's voice explained. Ruby relaxed. "I think he could be wonderful for her, don't you?"

Ruby smiled at the thought of the perfect and powerful Presley Monroe being swept off her feet by someone like Hobie. Not that there was anything wrong with him, but his casual approach to the world and his globe trotting photography lifestyle would be quite different for the high luxury ultra business Presley.

"Maybe," Ruby cautiously agreed. "But don't you think that should be up to Presley to decide?"

"Of course, of course, but it couldn't hurt for us to make sure they attend the same event every now and then, could it?"

After a few moments of thought, Ruby didn't see the harm and she told Faye she would think about how to ensure Hobie came to the fundraiser. It wasn't until she was halfway through taste testing her caterer's sample hors devours that she had an idea and texted her assistant to put a call into Hobie right away.

Back in her car and heading to a board meeting for the local art center, Ruby's assistant called her with Hobie on the line and soon it was his disembodied voice that filled the interior of her car.

"What can I do for you, Ruby?"

His voice was kind, calm, and deep, with a hint of sensuality, which was quite appealing. Ruby could see why Presley was smitten with him, even if she would never admit it.

"Well, I have a proposition for you," she said. "It involves you and that camera you work such magic with."

"My camera?" He sounded surprised and maybe a little intrigued.

"Yes, your camera. I would like you to use your photography skills on a little charity project…and I have something to offer you in return."

There was a slight pause before Hobie answered, "Okay, I'm interested. What's your proposition?"

CHAPTER 19

The rich and famous were packed into one of Aspen's favorite party venues. Lochwood's was a huge space with that special blend of rustic luxury that was only found high in the Colorado Rockies in this elite playground of a town.

Wood beamed ceilings two stories high, iron chandeliers, and a huge river rock fireplace that covered almost a third of the inside wall complete with a roaring fire contributed to its rustic charm. But that was as far as the rustic element went. Everything else in the space that came into contact with a guest was pure luxury, from the gleaming wide planked hard wood floors to the Ajka crystal to the trays of ornately plated bison or oysters on the half shell.

This was the kind of party where celebrities like Goldie Hawn and Kurt Russell, or Fortune 500 CEOs who normally graced the cover of Forbes Magazine, or monarchs from foreign countries, could be seen. Many of them were present and greeted Presley as she moved through the crowd. Ruby's big fundraiser event was shaping up to be the party of the season. At least the party of the Aspen season.

"Darling, come say hello to Agnus," Presley's mother called out to her over the din of music and conversation.

Agnus Merriweather was one of her mother's oldest friends. One of the oldest people in the room probably. At 92 years of age she was more like an aunt to Presley and her siblings. A bossy, overbearing, dried up old aunt.

Presley smiled at her mother and gave her a little wave, "I'll be there in a minute." She didn't want to stop in her current trajectory through the crowd because she was making headway and anxious to get to her destination, which was Ruby.

Ruby looked stunning and in control. She shimmered in a deep red gown that had a distinctly Bohemian flair while still looking elegant and in charge. Ronnie had indeed done an excellent job dressing her friend for the power party of the year. She was greeting important dignitaries and celebrities while simultaneously directing the wait staff and her assistants, and doing it with style.

Presley wanted to offer Ruby congratulations on a job well done and offer help if she needed it, which she sincerely doubted would be the case. But try as she might to rationalize her motivation, Presley knew she had an ulterior motive for wanting to speak with Ruby.

Presley was aware that the main charity Ruby worked for, the Habernathy Foundation, was the main recipient of the monies that were being raised this evening. She also knew that Ruby's favorite alternate charity, the county dog shelter and its affiliates throughout Colorado, were also on the list that night. What she had just found out, however, was that another charity had popped onto the list for the auction... Hobie's cancer research charity, Suzie's House, named after his late mother.

And while that was all well and good and Presley was glad

to know several charities would be benefiting from tonight's party, what she really wanted to find out was if Hobie was going to be at the party.

She had not heard from him since he emailed her the photos. At first she considered contacting him, which she could do easily under the guise of their mutual project. But she had hesitated to do so. Pushy was not a move she was used to making. Not unless it was a business move, which this definitely was not. After asking for their morning meeting that had turned into a bit of a nightmare, Presley was a little concerned Hobie might take her assertiveness as a sign that she was attracted to him. Which she was. But she did not want him to know that. Especially since he already had a girlfriend.

Letting him know for sure that she was attracted to him might make him think he had an upper hand in negotiations with Mack Industries. That was unacceptable. Though true. Presley was distracted by his good looks and interesting personality as well as flattered by his attention, and could not control her fluttering nerves when he was around, but she would be damned before she gave up control in business dealings or brought Megan or any other eco-friendly gold digger onto her team.

"Ruby," Presley waved at her friend to get her attention. She was just a few groups of guests away from her. Ruby turned and waved back.

Presley had chosen an Aqua silk gown that swept up and over her left shoulder in an elegant drape while leaving her right shoulder completely bare. The narrow skirt flowed from underneath the drape and continued straight to the floor. It had a Grecian vibe that suited her, made her feel a little bit like an ancient goddess. Her golden hair was piled in artful disarray on top of her head and she wore a complete set of aquamarine and diamond jewelry–earrings, necklace, bracelets, and cocktail ring, that Ronnie had given her on her last birthday. She said because they made Presley's eyes shine an electric blue.

The whole look worked and Presley felt well put together, feminine, and maybe just a little romantic. Which is how Jaxson had described her when he assisted her in choosing the dress.

"Do you think it's too plain?" she asked him in her dressing room.

He shook his head no, "It's elegant and chic and a little Cinderella-like...if Cinderella was already rich."

That had made her laugh. Sidling through the last of the crowd, her good humor had been replaced by the ever familiar butterflies she had grown used to experiencing lately.

Ruby's eyes were shining. She positively bloomed under the stress and mayhem of a huge fancy fundraising party.

"How do you like it?" Ruby asked.

"Oh, honey, the party is amazing. It's beautiful in here," Presley praised her sincerely.

"Did you try the bacon chile figs?" Ruby asked, obviously delighted with the food.

"Not yet," Presley responded.

Ruby's forehead pinched in a slight scowl, "Presley you have to eat tonight. There is so much great food here and I want you to have a good time." Ruby looked her friend up and down. "You look gorgeous, but you're getting too thin."

"I didn't think there was such a thing," Faye interjected. She had joined their conversation, a glass of champagne in one hand and a caviar and crème freche tartlet in the other.

"Oh, stop," Ruby scolded them both. "You two need to stop starving yourselves. You're both beautiful."

"I don't starve myself. I'm simply selective," Faye responded, popping the tartlet into her mouth as proof.

"I'm not hungry," Presley said. This wasn't a complete lie. She was a little hungry, but the nerves in her stomach were keeping her from eating.

Ruby gave her a meaningful look and waved one of the waiters with a tray of hors devours over. It was Presley's turn to scowl. There was no way she could eat with her stomach in knots the way it was.

Faye washed her caviar down with some champagne and turned her attention to a different topic, "The prince is here."

"Which prince?" Presley asked.

"*The* prince," Faye said knowingly and Presley thought she knew who she meant, but didn't want to continue talking about it so she stayed quiet.

"Everyone's here," Ruby said with satisfaction.

Presley smiled at her, "Good for you. This will be a huge success for your Foundation."

"I hope so."

"Is Hobie here?" The words came out before Presley could edit them to sound more nonchalant. Both Ruby and Faye turned their heads and looked at her with interest. Another awkward bumbling sentence followed, "I mean, I was just wondering...you know, if he's still up here. Or if he's come back. He was invited, right? And there's his charity on the list," Presley pointed at the sign next to the small stage that was set up with a microphone for the charity auction later, which displayed the list of charities that would be involved. Neither of her friends looked away from her to where she was pointing, but they did give each other knowing sideways glances. "Stop it," Presley said.

"Stop what?" Faye put on her innocent as a lamb face.

"You know," Presley flicked her hand at her friends in

frustration. "Thinking that there's something romantic going on between us."

"With you and Hobie?" Ruby asked, pretending to be shocked.

"I just need to talk to him about work," Presley said, even she knew the argument sounded weak. "And his charity is in the auction, isn't it?" She turned the questioning back towards Ruby.

Ruby took a sip of her drink, nodding and smiling as she did, "Yes it is. He's going to take pictures at the dog shelter tomorrow for me so I told him he should add Suzie's House into the auction. It's a win-win for everyone."

Faye was still studying Presley closely and she was about to say something when Presley's attention was pulled away completely. Hobie entered the grand doorway on the other side of the room. She could see him clear as day because the doorway was positioned at the top of four wide steps that led down into the large room that was the main hub of the party.

Though most of the men were wearing black tie, Hobie had opted for the casual chic of Aspen and wore a black tuxedo shirt with no tie and a black tuxedo jacket, over a pair of blue jeans. This would have normally put Presley off as she felt strongly about men having the capacity to dress properly for the occasion. But with Hobie, once again, she was conflicted.

His thick, curly hair shone in the candlelight and his strong jaw and piercing eyes seemed particularly handsome as he scanned the room with the serious expression of an archer seeking a target. Heat flowed up through Presley's stomach into her chest, making her flush with the thrill of seeing him. Their eyes met and she felt a smile spread across her face. He smiled back and the warmth in her body increased tenfold.

All memories of the horrible macchiato spill and Megan

disappeared as he moved down the steps towards her. All concerns that her friends or family would think she was falling for him were pushed to the back of her mind. Everything else in the room fell away, the people, the music, the chatter. The only sound she could hear was the pounding of her own heart. He was coming straight through the crowd directly to her and Presley found herself smiling so hard her cheeks hurt.

CHAPTER 20

When he arrived by her side her reaction was visceral. The excitement of seeing him continued, but magnified, becoming an ever present tremor that emanated from the center of her body and moved out through her skin in a tingling sensation. It didn't go away the longer they stood next to each other, either. If anything it grew stronger.

Faye and Ruby chatted with Hobie politely and she hoped that she wasn't saying anything too silly. But in all honesty, Presley was unsure of the words coming out of her mouth. Her senses were filled only with Hobie. The tall, dark figure he cut in his tuxedo jacket and jeans. His cologne that she had identified as Huntsmen after describing it to Jaxson. The way his strong hands held a bourbon filled crystal glass, alternately lifting it to his lips to drink or gesturing with it in conversation. The way his eyes twinkled when he laughed and how his laughter, deep and gentle, made her feel content, happy. She couldn't be expected to pay attention to the specifics of the party conversation with his arm brushing hers every time he moved, could she?

She was absolutely overwhelmed by him, especially when he looked at her. In his look was a familiarity that added to her warm, shimmering feeling. They had moved beyond the normal business-like interactions she normally shared with fellow tycoon types. She wouldn't even classify the feeling between them as the chumminess of old school mates. They were in new territory and she found that she didn't know what to do with her hands or where to look if it wasn't into his beautiful brown eyes. The memory of how his arms had felt around her when he caught her at the winery and carried her, practically kicking and screaming, to the patio chair came back to her. Presley blushed.

"...and it increases their adoption rate by nearly a hundred percent!" Ruby was gushing about using professional photographers to take pictures of shelter animals. "So we're very excited about you helping," she said to Hobie.

He smiled and Presley's knees felt weak.

"I'm glad to help. I love dogs," he answered.

"Me too," Presley chimed in. Faye and Ruby looked at her, surprise and amusement all over their faces. Presley gave them a little scowl. "I like dogs," she said defiantly.

Hobie chuckled, giving her an intimate wink, "Rocky certainly liked you. He's a pretty good judge of character."

Faye raised an eyebrow. "Rocky?"

"My dog," Hobie explained. "He was a little excited to meet Presley the other day, kind of knocked her over."

"Oh, really?" Faye pretended she hadn't already heard this story.

"Are you going to be at the shelter fundraiser tomorrow?" Hobie asked Presley. She stumbled on her answer. She hadn't planned on going, but was he asking her? She looked at Ruby for help.

"You were invited," Ruby said graciously. "I'm sure it's on your calendar if you had the time."

"I will make it a point to come," Presley said. She could tell Hobie was pleased and this made her pleased. Maybe the party atmosphere was making her soft, but she really liked the idea of pleasing Hobie.

"I didn't know you were such a fan of dogs," Faye said to Presley with a teasing smile.

It was true, Presley had never owned a dog. Not since she was a child. But she had a good excuse, she had been busy. She liked dogs just as much as any other animal.

"Well…I like them better than cats," she said.

"There are cats at the shelter, too," Ruby reminded her.

Presley scowled again. "Cats are fine, too. I just like dogs better."

Hobie leaned towards her and lifted his bourbon in a mini salute, "Me too."

"Woo hoo, Presley," a female voice rose above the party sounds that surrounded their small group. Unmistakable. Agnus Merriweather's shrill tones reverberated through Presley's eardrums and set her teeth on edge.

"I told you she was over here with her friends." Another voice. Less shrill, more familiar. Presley's mother, Judith.

Hobie stepped to the side, allowing room for the two older women to join them. Much to Presley's disappointment they pushed right in between and separated her from him.

"I've been wanting to talk to you," Agnus said pointedly to Presley. Her frail appearance belied the tenacity that pumped through her blue blood. Agnus reached over and placed a cool, wrinkled hand on Presley's arm gripping it firmly.

"You look beautiful, sweetheart," her mother said as she kissed the air next to Presley's ear.

"You do too," Presley said, and she meant it.

Her mother's fair skin had aged well, which was to say hardly at all. And her hair was raven black, thick and stylishly cut so it just brushed her shoulders. With the best skin and hair products money could buy, not to mention the best makeup and clothes designers at her fingertips, Judith Monroe was a stunning woman even well past middle age.

"Thank you," her mother said sweetly, though her attention had already turned to Hobie standing on her other side. "You must be Hobie Brent," she cooed. "All grown up now I see."

Presley felt her face flush at the flirtatious tone in her mother's voice. She glanced at Faye and Ruby for help in redirecting the conversation, but they were both distracted by an English Duke and Duchess who had approached them to say hello.

"Presley, you're not listening to me," Agnus complained.

Presley swept her eyes down to the tiny yet severe figure of Agnus Merriweather and resigned herself to the conversation. Agnus had been there when Presley was born. She was not to be ignored.

"How are you, Agnus?" Presley asked politely.

"I'm getting nearer to death with every passing moment of the day," Agnus responded bitterly.

The sound of Hobie's deep, warm laughter interrupted them. He had overheard Agnus' comment and he raised his glass to her and grinned.

"Aren't we all, Madame. Aren't we all." It was more of a statement than a question, but he said it with twinkle in his eye and Presley felt Agnus' hand relax where it had been gripping her arm.

The old lady chuckled and said, "Touché". Then, turning her attention back to Presley, she continued, "I want to talk to you about Conteggio."

Presley was surprised, "Count Bolsena?"

"Yes, he's a dear friend of mind and I'm concerned about him."

As Agnus explained her concerns, which amounted to knowing that the Count was not as financially sound as he used to be and that the project Mack Industries and Barcom Inc. were proposing could make or break him, Presley listened with more and more interest. She became so absorbed that she almost forgot Hobie was standing nearby and didn't notice as he moved closer. He was listening to Agnus as well. This information, after all, concerned his family business.

After a few minutes of expressing her thoughts on the matter, Agnus paused and looked at both of them sternly. "You will be discreet with this information, won't you?"

"Of course," they said in unison. Presley glanced sideways at Hobie who was focused intently on Agnus.

"I'm an old woman," she said. "And I don't pretend to know everything about business. But I do know how business can take a wrong turn and ruin someone's life. Destroy everything they've built."

Hobie nodded soberly and Presley did the same, though she wasn't sure what Agnus wanted them to do about the Count's financial failings. They couldn't save him, if that's what she was getting at. They had to keep their own profit top of mind.

Agnus was looking at her directly, a sharp reproach in her eyes, "I am asking that you take his situation into account with your new resort or project or whatever it is you all are working on together."

A stab of embarrassment shot through Presley. Shame for some evil deed that she had not yet done filled her, even though she wasn't completely sure she should feel guilty at all. Some of the guilt came from the way Agnus was looking at her, but some of it came from the fact that Hobie was seeing how Agnus was looking at her. Which was not nice. Not nice at all.

"I didn't...I'm not..." Presley stuttered in an attempt to reassure Agnus she wasn't going to purposefully destroy the Count. Hobie was eyeing her strangely, too. As was her mother, although that could have been for a thousand different reasons. Was everyone under the impression that she was nothing more than a heartless fiend who willingly ruined everyone who did business with her? Her cheeks grew hot under their scrutiny.

"Sorry I'm late," a woman's voice broke Presley's moment of self-consciousness. To her dismay, Megan, a stunning latecomer to their group, shimmied her way in between her and Hobie.

Presley's lips pressed together and she tried to not let her disappointment show. Her mother gave her a questioning look.

"Hi, Megan, you look lovely," Hobie greeted his employee warmly. Presley grimaced.

"Hello," Megan greeted them all, especially Presley, with a brightness that she could not return. All she could do was smile at Hobie's beautiful date and know the smile looked tight and unappealing, like the smile of a repressed librarian.

Despite her obvious misgivings, social pressure meant Presley was forced to introduce her to her mother and Agnus as well. As she did this Presley avoided eye contact with both her mother and Hobie. In fact, she avoided eye contact with everyone, using the age old tactic of looking at someone, yet looking right through them instead of focusing in on their eyes. It was the only way she could manage to appear at all normal. All of the elation and attraction she had felt earlier dropped into the pit of her stomach and boiled into a thick, bubbling tar that seethed with jealousy and wounded pride.

When Presley finally escaped with her mother and Agnus to join Ronnie and Pete who were standing with Mack near the fireplace, she only managed to give Hobie and Megan a cursory goodbye. She couldn't stand to look at them. If she did she was afraid she might lash out or possibly even cry, which would be ridiculous and immensely more humiliating.

As the evening progressed she steered clear of the couple and grew more and more miserable. Moping around the outskirts of the party, her mood was not lost on her siblings.

"What's wrong with you?" Pete asked after finding her lurking along a wall partially hidden by the live band.

"Nothing, I'm just not in the mood for this tonight," Presley gestured toward the party.

"Here," Ronnie handed her a fresh drink. "Is Mom driving you nuts?"

Presley shrugged and took a sip, intimating that her mother was driving her nuts, even though that wasn't the problem. At least not this time.

"I thought she was in a pretty good mood tonight," Pete looked across the crowded room where their parents were standing together, chatting and laughing with a cable TV mogul.

Presley sighed, "It's fine. Mom's fine. I just don't feel like being here."

Ronnie grinned over the rim of her glass and spoke right before she took a sip, "Is it Hobie?"

"Ugh," Presley waved her sister's words away like she might a pesky fly. "I'm not worried about him at all."

Ronnie and Pete shared a look, which Presley promptly ignored.

"So it doesn't bug you that Hobie's got that hot number on his arm?" Pete asked, grinning.

"I hadn't noticed," Presley said, taking a big swallow of her drink.

Ronnie peered into the crowd growing around the auction that was about to begin. "I bet she's going to bid on his charity," she said.

"Why do you say that?" Presley's curiosity got the better of her.

"Well, if I wanted to impress someone like Hobie, someone who runs this big charity, I would bid on his auction to win."

Presley thought about it for a moment, then asked as nonchalantly as she could, "What's the prize?"

Ronnie grinned at Pete before giving Presley a conspiratorial smile and answering, "A date in New York with the man himself, Mr. Hobie Brent."

CHAPTER 21

To say that Presley out bid Megan at the auction to win that New York date with Hobie would be an understatement. Presley squashed Megan's attempt. Completely annihilated any possibility that the younger woman might win along with the hopes of anyone else at the fundraiser who might be interested.

Money, after all, was not an issue for Presley Monroe, first born daughter of Mr. Money Bags. She had, quite literally, billions of dollars at her command. When something caught her eye, anything at all, Presley could absolutely afford it. No questions asked. Poor little Megan never stood a chance and by the end of the event Presley almost felt sorry for her. Almost.

At first, Presley just upped Megan's bids by a thousand dollars each time, certain that eventually Megan would run out of money. As the bidding went up and up, however, Presley's competitive nature took over and she finally ended the whole pointless scenario by bidding what, to some, might seem an extreme amount of money—$250,000.00.

"Madame?" The auctioneer's voice echoed through the room, which had fallen dead silent when she called the number out. He did not stutter, yet had to force his composure as he clarified, "Did you say *two hundred and fifty thousand?*" He annunciated each syllable carefully and Presley realized that perhaps upping the bid by more than $200,000.00 might have appeared rash. All eyes were on her and she nodded curtly at the auctioneer, reassuring him with her confidence while simultaneously avoiding eye contact with Hobie, her sister, her mother and father, her friends, virtually everyone.

There was some applause after the auctioneer hit his gavel on the podium. Presley smiled graciously and nodded, realizing that nobody need know her true motivation for the act. For all they knew she was simply donating a large sum of money to Suzie's House. Doing a good deed. Doing her part.

Faye reached her side among the hubbub, leaning in to say, "I hope you get your money's worth, darling."

Presley refused to acknowledge the innuendo and was about to grace Faye with a witty comeback when someone touched the back of her arm. She turned to find Hobie standing just behind her.

"It looks like you and me in New York, then?" he asked. His head was bent down, angled towards her as if he were about to kiss her cheek.

Her response caught in her throat and she had to swallow before answering. "Yes."

That was all she could say. All clever repartee escaped her mind as she stood captivated by Hobie's gaze. He was looking at her so strangely. There was a friendly, flirtatious air to his expression, true. But there was also something else, something she could see deep in his eyes. She tried, yet couldn't name the emotion. It was guarded. Protective. Whatever it was, the fierceness of it was a little intimidating.

~

THE NEXT MORNING Presley walked through a shabby parking lot belonging to the Pitkin Pet Shelter. Her Vivier high top boots crunched across shallow puddles that had frozen into thin sheets of ice overnight. She had chosen what she considered to be a casual outfit for her adventure with the homeless animals that Ruby was always trying to save. Charcoal grey flannel leggings were cozy and cute paired with the grey and white pattern on her boots. She had topped it off with a pale pink and grey geo sweater that fell just below her hips and was soft as an angora bunny.

"You look cuddly," Jaxson had told her after once again helping her pick out her clothes. The life of a personal assistant was eclectic to say the least.

"Do I?" She double checked the view of her backside in the mirror.

"Cute and cuddly, just like those adorable little puppies you're going to help save," he added.

"Is that a good thing?"

He shrugged, not committing 100 percent to the idea, but not dismissing the possibility either. "If you're someone who likes animals."

Presley sighed as she approached the smoky grey glass doors of the drab building. The Pitkin Pet Shelter was housed in an inexpensive to rent and unwanted area on the outskirts of town. It had a brown, municipal feeling to it that she found depressing. Maybe people would come looking for these stray cats and dogs if they were presented in a more appealing and lively atmosphere. Oh well, she was only here until noon, or when her presence was no longer useful, or when she couldn't stand it anymore, whichever came first. She perked up a little knowing that Hobie was also here and they were doing a photo shoot, which should make the whole experience more palatable.

As she stepped through the door, Presley's nose wrinkled involuntarily at the smell. It was awful. Wet dog, damp cement, some kind of rancid salami that must be dog food. Yuck, she was positive she would not be able to make it all the way to noon.

"May I help you?" A tubby middle aged woman with bleached blonde hair, dark black roots, and features that were pinched inside the roundness of her face, smiled brightly from behind a huge circular reception desk.

The woman's body was wrapped in logic defying skinny jeans, a tight purple t-shirt, and a tie on work vest that was the ugliest piece of clothing Presley had ever seen. It was a garish bright blue–a terrible, horrible blue–lined with bright yellow piping and Pitkin Pet Shelter embroidered across the front along with a smiling cartoon dog and cat. Presley was glad for the woman's sake that most of the living creatures she saw all day at the shelter probably didn't have any fashion sense. Although she wondered if even dogs and cats might be put off by that vest.

Presley glanced quickly at the name tag pinned to the woman's ample bosom. It read 'Patty'.

"Yes, Patty," Presley began. "I'm here for–" Chaotic noises interrupted her request.

Barking, shouting, and laughter came from a heavy door that was propped open behind Patty at the reception desk.

"Oh my goodness," Patty exclaimed, hopping up from her chair and hurrying to see what was causing the commotion.

More shouting came from the other room. It wasn't angry or fearful, which was good. But when Patty opened the door all the way it grew even louder. Patty gasped and looked at the ground in surprise. The clip, clip, clip of tiny nails on the tile flooring told Presley something was rounding the corner and she turned just in time to see a small dog-like creature racing around the edge of the receptionist's desk towards her feet.

"Sugar Pop!" Patty called out.

The tiny creature stopped at Presley's feet and placed two dainty paws on her shoes, looking up at her with urgency and wagging what was supposed to be a tail, but was merely a small nub on her skinny little rump. Presley gazed down in surprise at what must have been the ugliest animal ever created panting at her feet. The little thing landed somewhere between a Chihuahua and a bat on the cuteness scale—which wasn't saying much.

"Sugar Pop, come here," Patty said with good natured firmness. She waddled around the outside of the receptionist desk to retrieve the tiny animal.

"You're Sugar Pop, aren't you?" Presley said to the dog. The dog emitted a whine, which sounded a lot like a squeaky toy for a dog rather than a dog itself. Sugar Pop pranced her little paws on Presley's toes. Or at least Presley assumed she was a 'she'. What else could she be with a name like Sugar Pop?

Ruby appeared at the opened door and saw Presley. "Hi, Pres," she said brightly. "We have an escapee running around."

"Yes, she's standing on my foot."

"Don't pick her up, she bites," Ruby warned, but it was too late. Presley had already bent down and scooped the homely mixed breed runt up in her arms.

Sugar Pop was light as air and wriggled with glee, so much so that Presley was afraid she might drop her. She had short black fur, where she had fur, for much of her legs and paws, belly and neck appeared to be void of any fur at all. She had bug eyes and only one floppy ear, which stood cockeyed, making her look confused. The other ear was completely missing, whether she was born that way or had suffered an accident and lost her ear Presley couldn't tell. The dog's small tongue shot out of its mouth and stabbed at Presley, licking her hands and face wherever she could reach.

"She's not biting me, but she's going to lick me to death," Presley passed Sugar Pop to Patty's waiting arms.

"She likes you!" Patty said happily, even Sugar Pop yipped her disappointment at being handed over and made like she was about to nip Patty's nose.

Maybe some dogs did have fashion sense, Presley thought as she watched Patty wrestle a squirming Sugar Pop back into the other room.

"Come join us, we're in here," Ruby waved to Presley to follow them.

In there turned out to be a plain, windowless room that normally stored bagged dog and cat food, but had been turned into a photographer's studio of sorts. There was a backdrop of a meadow full of sunshine, a green shag rug on the floor in front of it, a sturdy table with the same shag rug laid over it, and several photographer lights on stands aiming towards the spot in front of the back drop.

And Hobie. Hobie was there.

As soon as Presley's eyes fell on him her mouth went dry. Wearing a pair of faded jeans and a long sleeve navy blue Henley shirt with the sleeves pushed up to his elbows, his dark curls falling into his eyes as he looked down into the camera on a tripod in front of him making some adjustment, he was casual as always. Casual and irresistible.

He looked up when she stepped into the room and caught her eye. All of the chatter going on between Ruby and Patty and the other assistants in the room faded into the background and all Presley could hear was the pounding of her own heart. She tried to swallow so she could speak, but her dry mouth made that impossible. She tried to smile coyly, to look away and make conversation with Ruby, to do anything but stare like a school girl with a major crush. She failed.

He straightened, holding her captive with his riveting eyes. A smile played at the edges of his lips and he opened his mouth to say something.

"Sugar Pop!" Patty's exclamation broke through their silent connection.

Patty and Ruby had repositioned Sugar Pop on the small table, presumably to have her picture taken, but the little dog was having none of their nonsense. She flew off the table in a feat of wild optimism and landed in a tumble on the floor. Unfazed, she raced directly to Presley again, stamping her minuscule front paws on her shoes as if demanding to be picked up.

Hobie laughed and the sound warmed Presley's whole body. "Well, somebody's found a friend."

Presley picked up Sugar Pop and was greeted with her tiny pink tongue. She tried to hold her at arms length to keep the dog from licking her cheeks, but Sugar Pop writhed around so frantically she was forced to hold her close or risk losing her grip.

"You really make quite an impression on dogs, don't you?" Hobie asked, bemused.

"I guess so," she answered, biting her tongue before she finished the sentence with 'not men, apparently'.

She placed Sugar Pop gingerly back on the table. When Presley took her hand away from the dog, she acted as if she was going to jump off again. So she put her hand back on Sugar Pop's black fur and looked to the others for help.

"Stay there," Hobie directed as he looked into the camera to frame the shot. "Keep your hand on her and I'll tell you when to take it off."

And so, once again, Presley stood uncomfortably in front of Hobie as he focused the giant, bulging lens of his camera in her direction. Every time she moved, Sugar Pop moved. If she tried to speak, Sugar Pop whined. Ruby and the others had already excused themselves to prep the next shelter animal for its photo shoot, so Presley simply stood mute and still while Sugar Pop licked her hand incessantly.

The camera clicked.

"Are you taking the picture?" Presley lifted her hand off of Sugar Pop who hopped up and down and let out a disappointed squeak.

"Not yet, you can leave your hand there," he answered. "I'm taking a few test shots."

She relaxed a little and realized that she liked the way he took over when he was taking pictures. She was off the hook for a while. No decisions to make. Nobody waiting for her next move.

Sugar Pop pressed her small cold nose against the inside of Presley's palm, making her smile. What an ugly little animal, yet she certainly was full of personality.

"Okay, I'm gonna make a sound that gets her attention and you pull your hand away when I do," Hobie instructed.

Presley nodded. "Got it."

Hobie kept his eye on the tiny screen on the camera and lifted a small rubber doggie toy shaped like a doughnut with pink frosting above his head. He squeezed it three times in quick succession and Sugar Pop sat up straight, her single ear at attention, her bug eyes full of life, riveted on the sound. Presley lifted her hand up and away and the camera clicked several times.

"Perfect," Hobie smiled at the screen, then at her. "Let's do it one more time." They did it one more time. Then another. After the third time Hobie waved her over. "You have to see these."

With Sugar Pop happily nestled in her arms, Presley stood next to Hobie and looked at the pictures as he clicked through them on the camera screen. They were hilarious and charming and she couldn't help but giggle at how he had captured Sugar Pop's wild and curious personality.

"These are adorable!" Presley announced. Sugar Pop licked her chin as if to say thank you.

Hobie's eyes twinkled, "You're really good with animals, you know. Nobody else could even touch that little dog without her trying to bite them."

Sugar Pop snuggled into Presley's neck and the softness of her sweater. "I think she finds me cuddly," Presley said, remembering Jaxson's comments about her outfit.

Hobie grinned. They were standing so close together to look at the camera that their shoulders touched. The intimacy was difficult to ignore.

Hobie dropped his gaze and let it wander over Sugar Pop in her arms then down the shape of her waist and hips, along the length of her charcoal grey leggings, then back up to her eyes.

"Cuddly," he said with a nod, agreeing with Jaxson's assessment.

"Are you going to take her home?" Ruby had returned and spoke as she joined them at the camera.

Hobie lifted his eyebrows in surprise at the suggestion, then realizing she was talking to Presley about Sugar Pop, his cheeks reddened ever so slightly. Presley giggled. Sugar Pop squeaked.

"I don't need a dog," Presley told Ruby.

"But she loves you," Ruby said. "Maybe you need a dog more than you think you do."

Presley shook her head and tried to hand Sugar Pop to Ruby, but the little stinker kicked and whined so much she had to pull her back into the softness of her sweater to calm down again.

"Dogs are great," Hobie agreed. "You can't buy that kind of devotion," he nodded towards Sugar Pop snuggling into Presley's neck.

Presley cocked her head at his choice of words. She wrinkled her nose and looked back and forth between Hobie and Ruby, who seemed awkward. Presley blinked and asked, "What are you saying?"

Before he had time to respond, a large unruly dog, burst through the open door and ran joyfully towards Hobie.

"Rocky!" Hobie called out.

Presley's body tightened. She knew what the presence of Hobie's big, slobbering dog meant.

Megan. That's what it meant.

And, true to form, the dark haired beauty followed Rocky into the room, raising Presley's stress level and, apparently, Sugar Pop's as well. For as Hobie greeted Megan with a big stupid smile and Rocky jumped around all of them, Sugar Pop cowered in Presley's arms.

At first Presley appreciated the company of the little dog who had latched onto her. It was like a child having a comforting stuffed animal to squeeze when they were feeling insecure. Sugar Pop's little heart beat wildly, probably at the antics of the out of control Rocky, and her body was warm against Presley's chest.

"You remember Presley," Hobie said to Megan.

Megan gave Presley a polite smile, "How could I forget the woman who out bid me."

Presley pinched her lips into a smile, her mind whirling with a variety of witty retorts, but she never got a chance to use one. The warmth of Sugar Pop against her chest suddenly became very warm and spread over her bosom and down to her stomach. Then something splattered on the toes of her Vivier boots.

Instead of saying something smart and cutting, Presley's mouth dropped open. First with horror then disgust. The others watched in surprise as she held Sugar Pop out in front of her at arm's length, revealing a wide wet spot on her cuddly sweater.

Sugar Pop had peed on her.

Ruby leaped into action and took Sugar Pop from Presley's outstretched arms. "Your sweater! I'll take her outside," she said apologetically as she whisked the dog out the door.

Sugar Pop's little bug eyes were full of remorse and fear and Presley felt sorry for her. She knew that Rocky's antics had scared the timid little dog and she hadn't meant to pee on her sweater. But Presley also felt sorry for herself, embarrassed and wretched in front of Hobie and the perfect Megan.

She wished she had handed Sugar Pop over to someone else to hold. She wished she hadn't given Jaxson the morning off so he could swoop in and assist her out of this mess. She wished she was anywhere but here, standing with a massive stain of rapidly cooling dog pee all over the front of her sweater while Hobie and Megan stared at her in shocked amusement.

"Here," Hobie stepped towards her holding some kind of red handkerchief he had pulled out of nowhere like a hillbilly.

"Don't touch me," Presley said sharply. He stopped in his tracks. She closed her eyes and took a deep breath to regain control. When she opened her eyes she kept them trained on the ground in front of her, not wanting to meet Hobie's or anyone else's looks. "I'm leaving," she said and turned firmly on her heel to walk out the door.

Nobody argued and nobody tried to stop her, which was

good, because she would have blown her top if anyone made one little peep about how she could change into one of the horrible blue Pitkin Pet Shelter t-shirts and finish helping with the photo shoot.

The only person that had the gall to speak to her as she left was Hobie. Just as she stepped out the door and left him and his little girlfriend alone, most likely to crack up laughing, he called after her, "See you in New York!"

CHAPTER 22

*R*uby called Hobie a few days later gushing with the news of their successful shelter dog photo shoot.

"Eighteen of them have already been adopted!" The excitement in her voice was contagious.

"That's good, right?" he asked.

"That's great! Over half of the dogs you photographed have found families in just a few days. I can't thank you enough for taking the time."

"It was my pleasure," he said, meaning every word of it. He had a soft spot in his heart for animals, dogs especially. Combine that with photography and he was happy to be involved.

Of course, throwing Presley into the mix had made it all the more interesting. Every time she entered the equation he kind of lost his equilibrium and didn't know quite what to focus on. After seeing her at the fundraiser and her outrageous bidding on his charity he hadn't been sure how to react. Not that $250,000 was a big deal to her bank account. Still, her presence at the photo shoot was definitely felt.

He had been hard pressed not to turn his lens completely on her instead of the dogs. The way her face changed from moment to moment fascinated him. He never knew what expression was coming next. Through the camera he could watch those changes without looking away and when he caught a tiny shift of her emotions, a mere glimmer of what she was thinking or feeling, it felt like he was capturing a piece of a dream.

"I hope...everyone had a good time." He had to catch himself to keep from singling out Presley in his comment.

"We all had a great time," Ruby reassured him. There was a slight pause before she added, "Well, I'm not sure Presley was too thrilled at the end."

Hobie had to chuckle. The peeing incident had really thrown her into a fit, a supremely controlled micro-fit that barely showed on her cool exterior, but a fit nonetheless. He smiled at the memory, wondering what exactly had been going through her mind when she stalked out of the room. Personally he liked seeing her human side, but it went in the face of what Danny had said about her. Ruthless business-woman she was not when she was being peed on by an ugly little dog.

He was struck by a thought, "How about Sugar Pop? Is she one of the lucky ones who got adopted?"

Ruby sighed sadly, "No, not yet. Sugar Pop is what you might call a tough case. She's high strung and a little strange to look at, it's going to take a special person to adopt her."

"She sure took to Presley, didn't she?"

"Yes, she did." This time Ruby chuckled, "But I'm not sure Presley was interested."

Hobie stretched his legs out in front of him, glancing down at Rocky sleeping at his feet. The private plane was roomy and luxurious, a far cry from where he'd first found Rocky. Or, more accurately, when Rocky had first found him. Undernourished, filthy, full of fleas, Rocky began his days as a street dog in Kolkata where Hobie had visited on one of his photography voyages.

He had set out early one morning to get some pictures of the sun coming up on a dilapidated building, dilapidated street actually, and Rocky had approached him like they were old friends, refusing to leave his side. Not that he had tried too hard to run him off. Surrounded by the extreme poverty of the poorest people in the city Hobie had found comfort in the dog's puppy-like excitement. Rocky's immediate devotion to him had been impossible to ignore and Hobie hadn't had the heart to leave the dog behind. After a few months to get the proper paperwork in order, he left India with Rocky at his side. Though that time it had been in a crate on a commercial flight.

"Sometimes they choose us," he said.

"True."

He didn't say his next thought out loud, but his opinion of Presley had skyrocketed when Sugar Pop so obviously took to her. Rocky liked her, too. Dogs knew a good person when they saw one, didn't they?

He had another idea. "Would you mind if I showed the pictures of the not-yet-adopted around?"

"Mind? I love the idea," Ruby answered, her natural enthusiasm bubbling through the phone. "Thank you for all of your help on this."

"No, thank you for involving me. And for putting Suzie's House in the auction."

"Yes," Ruby stretched the word out as if thinking of how to respond. "I'm glad the bidding went so well."

Hobie smiled. Ruby was a diplomat at heart. She focused on the positive and was keeping whatever her thoughts were on Presley's unexpectedly large bid to herself. A loyal friend.

"I'm not sure if our date in New York can live up to her sizable donation," he admitted.

"Oh, well, I'm sure she was only thinking about your charity," Ruby added quickly. "Although…"

"Although what?"

There was a pause and Hobie sensed Ruby was about to impart something important.

"Can I tell you something off the record?" she asked.

He sat up straighter in his chair and nodded, even though she couldn't see him, answering, "Off the record? Sure."

"If you want to win over Presley, don't listen to her."

"Don't listen to her?"

"I mean don't let her call the shots. Take control. Do something that takes her out of her comfort zone."

"Out of her comfort zone," he repeated.

"Yes, that girl keeps her world too tightly controlled. She needs to loosen up a little."

"Okay," he said, though he really wasn't sure how to go about taking control of Presley Monroe. There was one thing he was certain about, now that she was involved this New York charity date had to be over the top.

CHAPTER 23

Almost one week later Presley was feeling better about the whole Sugar Pop incident. Back in New York she was strengthened, the city was exactly what she needed. The weather was perfect, not too cool, not too hot, but sunny. The energy of the city always filled her with passion. The people were the perfect blend of competence, intelligence, and brusqueness. New York suited her and it was Presley's opinion that New York was the only place to be in the spring. Besides maybe Paris, of course.

With the Sugar Pop incident a fading memory, she was looking forward to her date with Hobie.

"You're still going?" Ronnie asked her over dinner a few nights after they both returned to the city.

Presley blinked, mildly confused at the question. "Of course I'm going. Why wouldn't I go?"

"Oh, I don't know, it seems like every time you're with him you get humiliated somehow," Ronnie said.

"I wouldn't say that. Not every time." Presley was annoyed at the suggestion. "Besides, I donated $250,000."

"True," Ronnie nodded. "Do you know what you're doing

for the date?"

She didn't. It was to be a surprise.

On the day of the date Presley sipped her spritzer and enjoyed the view of Rockefeller Center from her seat on the patio of Del Frisco's. She was meeting Hobie here. He had given her strict instructions on the time and place to meet when he called her to confirm.

"3:30 outside at Del Frisco's. They'll show you what table exactly," he had said.

"That sounds fine," she agreed, as coolly as possible.

She hadn't spoken to him in person since the disastrous photo shoot and the sound of his voice, deep and a little gravelly, gave her a tiny thrill despite her every effort to remain composed. When they hung up Presley reminded herself that this was not an actual date. She had been forced to pay for his attentions–donate to be exact. Regardless, she couldn't let her emotions get the better of her. She would allow him to follow through and she would try to enjoy herself and it would all go down in the books as a business transaction with flair.

Waiting at Del Frisco's, Presley felt perfectly composed. Settled into the table the maitre'd had offered per Hobie's arrangement she took in the scenery. She would have preferred to be further from the street, not bumping right up against the sidewalk and a line of orange cones that had been set out to obstruct traffic, but she didn't object. She was glad that she had made it on time and before Hobie. Plus she had dressed with confidence.

Since this was to be an afternoon date Presley had chosen a new black with white polka dot Dolce & Gabbana stretch silk dress she had been waiting to wear. Off the shoulder, scrunching and bunching in all the right places, clinging in the other right places, with a flirty skirt that kicked out just below her knees.

"You're all glamour today," Jaxson complimented her as she put on her strap back stilettos.

Paired with a simple pearl necklace, bracelet, and earring set from Tiffany's, a birthday gift from her mother a few years ago, she felt fresh and fun. So fun, in fact, that she had opted to wear a large brimmed black hat with white trim to top off the look.

"What do you think?" Presley asked Jaxson as she modeled the hat for him in her penthouse.

"Very Audrey Hepburn," Jaxson said with approval.

Sitting at Del Frisco's the tune of Moon River popped into her head. Smiling quietly, she hummed the song to herself, pleasantly distracted from her normally busy life.

Presley nonchalantly scanned the pedestrians strolling through the center, wondering when Hobie would arrive. While it was empowering to arrive on time and be poised to perfection when her date arrived, the empowered feeling lessened as the minutes ticked away. She took another sip of the fizzing pink spritzer and tried to avoid the stares from a small group of young tourists who were passing with their cell phones raised, talking and laughing loudly, probably live streaming their experience to Twitter or whatever.

She tilted her chin toward her chest slightly which caused her wide black hat to artfully cover most of her face. Even if the tourists did share her image with the world, nobody would know who she was, which was preferable. She silently congratulated herself on choosing to wear the hat and listened for the noise of their little group to disappear into the other sounds of New York; the buzz of businessmen talking over early drinks, cars making their way along West 51st, the occasional honking of a cab, the clip clopping of horse hooves on pavement.

Was that right? Did she hear horse hooves?

Presley turned and looked over her shoulder toward the

sound and was greeted with the sight of a horse drawn carriage coming down the street. Though a little cliché, Presley had always kind of liked these carriages. She, of course, wouldn't be caught dead in one, but she could see how tourists might enjoy them and they added to the general ambience.

This carriage was particularly classy, shining black with yellow spokes on its wheels. The horse pulling it was beautiful as well, huge and muscled with a pure black coat that matched in color and shine to the painted carriage it pulled. The black leather bridle and harness on the horse had silver plates embedded throughout and at the top of its head was a yellow plume of feathers, the exact color of the yellow spokes on the wheels. With a toss of its head, the black mane swung fluidly, the feathers rippled, and the bridle and reins jingled.

Presley was so caught up in the grace and majesty of the horse that she didn't notice the driver sitting atop the grand carriage right away. Not until the whole festive rig drew up on the street directly across from her and slowed to a stop did Presley look up at the man on the seat high above.

Donning a black shirt and jacket atop his signature jeans, along with a black top hat on top of his dark curling hair, Hobie sat atop the narrow driver's seat smiling down at her.

He tipped his hat, "Good afternoon, Miss."

Surprise and disbelief rushed across her face as she watched him climb swiftly off of the carriage. Another man in a formal black suit and his own top hat came from the back of the carriage and took Hobie's place at the reins. Presley stood up, a flutter of childlike excitement in her chest, but still without words.

Hobie's approach slowed as she turned to him. His cocky smile gave way to something more heartfelt as he took in her silk dress and Audrey Hepburn hat. Stopping a few feet on the other side of the low decorative hedge of plants that separated diners from pedestrians at Del Frisco's, he touched his hand to his heart. The gesture charmed her and she blushed, dipping her head, which made her large hat cover her face again. When she looked up at him from under the brim, he caught her gaze in his and held it there. Undeniable attraction. So strong it tugged at her heart.

Everything fell away from them. The buildings, the people, the city, even the horse and carriage disappeared. All Presley could see was Hobie and he did not look away. He would not release her, and it was as if they were bewitched with each other, sheer electricity sizzled between them. She felt powerless, gripped by something larger than both of them. Then it was as if she were falling, falling through a bright blue sky towards a warm, inviting ocean that was ready to envelop her completely. If the group of tourists were still taking pictures, Presley wouldn't have known. She didn't care anymore. Later, she could not have guessed at how long they stood there, connected by this invisible force, but it was Hobie who moved first.

He threw back his shoulders like someone about to salute, and with mock seriousness gave her a formal half bow. He straightened, his eyes twinkling, and said, "Nice hat."

Presley grinned, suppressing a giggle. She glanced at his ebony top hat then back at him, "You, too."

He laughed out loud at this, his smile lighting up his whole face as he reached out his hand to her, "Shall we?"

She placed her hand in his and the warmth of his touch made her fingers tingle. The falling feeling stopped, but not in a sudden, frightening way, as one might expect a long fall to end. No, it was something better, more exciting. Presley's sensation of dropping uncontrollably through the air had turned into the sensation of flying. As if she was soaring hand-in-hand with Hobie through a bright blue sky to a destination yet to be discovered.

CHAPTER 24

If anyone had ever told Presley Monroe that she would be riding through the streets of New York in a horse drawn carriage dressed like Audrey Hepburn and sitting next to Hobie Brent from high school wearing a top hat, she would have thought they were crazy. But they wouldn't have been. It turned out that she was the crazy one. Crazy to have ever thought that carriage rides were cliché and touristy, and crazy to have ever dismissed Hobie as unattractive, unappealing or uninteresting.

He was none of these. He was the exact opposite.

Nestled next to each other on the bench seat of the carriage, though not too close as the rims of their hats kept bumping, she couldn't stop laughing at his jokes or being taken in by his handsome, engaging smile. The smile that took over every part of her body and mind as they clip clopped towards West 59th Street.

"Never?" Hobie asked, astonished at her disclosure that she had never taken a carriage ride through Central Park.

"Never."

With a serious look on his face Hobie considered the

gravity of the situation then said, "We better make this ride perfect."

With that he stood and leaned forward to speak to the driver. Hobie had introduced him to her as Joseph, the proud owner of a carriage ride business, who had been born and raised in Brazil. Presley vividly noticed the loss of Hobie's presence when he stood up. The void he left in the seat next to her seemed exceptionally empty and she hoped he would settle in next to her again soon. She was so distracted by this desire that it took a few moments for her to realize Hobie was speaking in a different language to Joseph. Didn't they speak Portuguese in Brazil? Was he speaking Portuguese?

Hobie sat back down next to her, the weight of his body comforting. She opened her mouth to ask him how many languages he spoke, but Hobie lifted his finger to her lips and touched them lightly to shush her. For the first time in her life, Presley didn't mind being shushed.

Hobie cocked his head as if he was listening for something, so Presley listened. Nothing different that she could hear, but then...the music began. The sweet instrumental melody of Moon River floated through the air. She completely lost her train of thought.

"Joseph's got surround sound in here," he explained. "Do you like the music? I could have him put on something else."

He made a move to stand again, but Presley stopped him with a hand on his knee.

"No, don't change it. I love this song."

Pleased with this reaction, he remained seated next to her as they entered Central Park South. Trees rose up on either side of them as their carriage moved into the park and down the wide path that led carriages and bicyclists through the greenery. The park was already beautiful at this time of year and plenty of people were out enjoying the sunshine on the

Great Lawn. A teenager on a unicycle pedaled past them and they shared an amused look.

"It feels funny to be moving this slowly," Presley commented.

Hobie leaned comfortably into the seat and tilted his head back with his face toward the sky. "Central Park was built to be seen by horse drawn carriage. It was the most stylish transportation at the time."

She pondered that as they rode past a statue where two little girls were making huge bubbles out of wide ring bubble makers. The little girls stopped their bubble making and stared when they saw her, their eyes round as saucers. Presley smiled politely at them.

Hobie leaned closer to her, pointed his chin at the little girls and said, "You have fans."

"Fans?" Presley didn't understand. "I'm sure they have no idea who I am."

"It's who they imagine you are," he said.

"And who is that, exactly?"

"A princess," he offered. Presley laughed at the suggestion, but Hobie continued, "Look at you." His eyes went immediately to her hat, then wandered down her cheek and neck, then further. When he lifted them again to meet her gaze they weren't exactly smoldering, but they were close. "You look like a beautiful princess."

Heat moved up her neck and cheeks and Presley knew she was blushing yet again. Today had to be a record for her turning pink.

He nudged her gently, "Wave at them."

Now she was truly embarrassed. "I'm not going to wave at them."

"C'mon," he nudged her again, his eyes twinkling merrily. "Do the Queen of England wave."

"What's that?"

"You hold your hand stiff, bent at the fingers just a little, then you twist your wrist." Hobie demonstrated for her by waving at the little girls who, due to the slow movement of the carriage, were still in view. The littlest one waved back and Hobie nudged Presley again. With less confidence than she was used to having, she obliged and imitated Hobie giving a stiff hand, twisting wrist wave to the girls. They smiled and giggled and waved back enthusiastically.

Presley fell back into the seat and chuckled, "Where did you learn how to wave like the Queen of England?"

He wiggled his eyebrows and said, "I've been around, you know."

Over the next hour they passed many of the landmarks in Central Park; the Boat House, Cleopatra's Needle, the Alice in Wonderland statue, and ended up at Lasker ice rink, or pool, depending on the season. It being springtime, Lasker's was in between seasons, which was why Presley got confused when the carriage stopped there.

Hobie said something in Portuguese to Joseph, who responded in Portuguese, and Presley was nothing but puzzled when Hobie climbed deftly out and turned to offer her his hand.

"What are we doing here?"

Hobie offered his hand to help her down. "We have a little detour."

The detour turned out to be a pathway that led behind the ice rink/swimming pool where all of the industrial machinery and air conditioning units hummed. Presley thought she spied a garbage dumpster.

"And what are we doing *here*?" she asked again.

"Don't tell me you've never been to the North Woods?" Hobie asked.

She had not. She distinctly remembered her mother warning her to stay out of the North Woods and The Ramble in Central Park. Both were wilderness areas fraught with dangers like muggers and rapists, according to her mother.

Not wanting to look like a prissy girl who had let her mother scare her with embellished stories, Presley shrugged off his question and went for a more obvious excuse to not take his detour. She pointed at her feet, which were wrapped in sexy black and white stilettos.

"Do these look like North Woods shoes?" she asked.

Hobie gave her a good natured scoff, "Not a problem." He offered her his arm. "We're not going far. I'll take care of you."

With one parting look of longing towards Joseph and their carriage, Presley took his arm and let him lead her under the decidedly rustic arch that took them into the North Woods. She found that with Hobie's support her shoes weren't too bad on the pathway, at least it was paved. The woods were wilder than she would have imagined possible in the middle of Manhattan. No wonder her mother hadn't wanted her and her siblings wandering around in them. Tall trees, thick brush, great stones, bubbling brooks and a water-fall were all pleasant for sure—as long as you had some form of protection.

Walking arm-in-arm with Hobie she did feel protected. Protected and just a little bit off kilter, as if her command center was blinking out of control. She decided to ignore it. Maybe this was good for her. It was only for the afternoon anyway.

"Here we are," Hobie stopped and swept his arm in a wide gesture towards what looked to her like a wall of bushes.

She smiled, then gave him a confused look. "And where is here?"

"We're going in there." He pointed straight into the wall of bushes.

"I'm not going in there," Presley said, indicating her

stilettos again with a nod of her chin. It wasn't just her shoes that were worrying her, however. Did he really expect her to hike around in the wilderness in her Audrey Hepburn silk dress?

For a long moment neither of them said anything. They just stared at each other. Hobie with a plan and Presley nixing his plan. This felt familiar.

Suddenly, Hobie stepped to her side and said, "Allow me."

Without explanation he scooped her up in his arms like a fireman saving a damsel in distress, stepped off the path, and plunged into the wall of bushes.

CHAPTER 25

*P*resley had no time to coherently protest being manhandled into the deep woods. All she managed was a squeal as she clapped one hand on her hat to keep it from falling off and grabbed hold of Hobie's neck to make sure he didn't drop her.

Surrounded by rustling branches, leaves slapped at her face as he carried her through what she swore was a swarm of gnats. Presley closed her eyes and instinctually curled into Hobie's chest for protection. Part of her was absolutely incensed, but part of her, that new little piece of her heart that apparently enjoyed not being in control, kept her from kicking and screaming and demanding to be put down.

She didn't have time to be conflicted about this turn of events for too long. As soon as they emerged from the thick wall of brush, Hobie took a few more strides and placed her gently back on her feet.

Presley opened her eyes, her hand still on top of her hat, leaves and tiny pieces of broken twigs stuck all over her polka dot silk dress. Indignant, she made unintelligible stammering noises as Hobie watched with a bemused expression.

He reached out to brush a twig off of her shoulder and she smacked his hand away.

"Wh-what do y-you think you're do..." Presley's voice stopped abruptly as her eyes fell on the scene behind him.

A dining table draped with a white tablecloth, set with gleaming china and crystal goblets, and adorned with mounds and mounds of yellow, pink, and lavender flowers sat dead center in what must be a thicket. The wall of green bushes Hobie had carried her through was just one side of a full oval of green bushes. Presley had never been inside of a thicket, but she felt certain that's what this was. It didn't look man made. The only word she could think of as she took in the little romantic scene was...magical.

Black iron posts dripping with the same flowers that graced the table were set all along the inside edge of the oval. Two small fruit trees, both in bloom with puffy white flowers, spread their branches over the table. Someone had hung a crystal chandelier from one of the branches. Even though there was no electricity going to it, the sunlight filtering through the leaves of the fruit trees bounced off of the crystals and sent sparkling rainbow reflections over everything. The grass under their feet was almost as thick as a carpet and the bright green of spring.

There were two other people in the thicket with them, both of them wearing white tuxedos. The first, a man introduced to her later as Frederick, stood ready at the side of the table holding a bottle of wine. The second was a woman, Lian, seated with a cello next to one of the posts with flowers. As if on cue, she ran her bow across the strings and began playing.

Hobie, obviously pleased with Presley's reaction of stunned silence, touched the brim of his top hat and dipped his head in a polite nod.

"I thought you might get hungry," he said, sweeping his

arm gallantly toward the table and offering her his arm to lead the way.

She took it and was surprised to notice that her fingers trembled as she reached out to him. He noticed too and flicked his eyes to hers to check that she was fine. She was. More than fine. Presley had never felt so fine as she did in this moment.

They dined on radicchio and romaine salad with truffle-lemon vinaigrette, seared black sea bass with fingerling potatoes, a tray of selected French cheeses served with grapes and raspberries, and coconut sorbet. The cellist was talented, the waiter refined, the ambience reached fairy tale levels. More than anything, however, Presley found herself lost in conversation with Hobie, learning things she had never known about him and revealing herself in new ways.

"It's short for Hobart?" she giggled.

"Yes, my grandfather's name. Hobie was as good a nickname as any I guess. I don't think I'm much of a Hobart."

"Do you know what my actual first name is?" She wondered if he had ever heard it when they were in school together.

Hobie pretended to think hard, then guessed, "Elvis?" Presley hit him lightly on the shoulder in protest. "You've probably heard that joke a thousand times," he said apologetically.

"A million. Try again." She took a sip of wine, it was the sweeter Pinot Grigio she liked far better than Chardonnay, while she waited for him to guess.

He gave up and shrugged, "I have no idea. What is your real first name, Ms. Monroe?"

"Lorna."

"Lorna?"

"I know, it's awful isn't it?"

"No worse than Hobart."

"It was my grandmother's name," she explained.

Hobie raised his wine glass to hers and clinked them together, "Here's to passing on horrible names to your kids." They both took a drink and Hobie looked at her thoughtfully.

"What?" she asked, wondering if she had radicchio stuck in her teeth.

"Are you the kind of woman who wants to have kids? If you don't mind me asking."

The question came out of nowhere and her initial reaction was to say something sarcastic, but she sensed sincerity in his voice. And, surprisingly, she didn't mind him asking.

"I used to want kids, actually," she answered.

"Used to?"

A twinge of sadness poked at her heart and she blinked a few times before redirecting, "What about you?"

Hobie took her hint and didn't push for an answer. His response came out almost as a sigh, "I'm too much of a wanderer to have a family I think. After my Mom passed away I couldn't settle down long enough in any one place to find a wife." This comment hung in the air between them, a statement of depressing reality. He smiled at her, trying to deflect the sadness, one of his dark locks had fallen forward into his eyes. "And I figured I needed a wife before I had the kids."

Presley had to tell her hand to stay put and not raise up to push the lock of hair back into place. She had to find something to distract herself. "I was married once," the words sort of fell out of her mouth before she could put a halt to them.

Hobie looked genuinely surprised, "You were?"

"Well, for about two minutes. It didn't work out," she waved her hand weakly in the air, erasing an imaginary chalkboard. Hobie remained quiet, and something about his undivided attention made her ramble on, "It was right after college. Big mistake. He cheated. It was over before it even started…" Presley would have kept going. For some inexplicable reason she wanted to tell Hobie about all of the times she had waited up all night for her then husband to come home, the way her father had had to bring in the family's law firm to manage her divorce, and the humiliating pain of it all, but a knot tied up the back of her throat and she couldn't keep speaking. She put her hands in her lap and looked down at them, blocking her face from Hobie with her hat.

"I'm sorry that happened," his voice was soft and kind… and close. He had moved his chair nearer to hers and she watched as his hand reached into her lap and covered both of her hands easily, gently.

Hot tears welled up in her eyes and she blinked hard to control them. One escaped and dropped directly onto the back of Hobie's hand. Presley panicked. She had to think of something to say or do to pull back from this… this…intimacy.

"I'm sorry, too…about your Mom," she managed to get that out at least, with a minimum of sniffling. And the sentiment was sincerely felt, she was sorry that he had lost his Mom. She wasn't just saying it to distract from her own mini-break down.

He didn't answer, but he didn't move his hand either. They sat together with Presley's eyes cast down into her lap and his hand generating so much warmth that it seemed to be moving through her clasped hands into her legs beneath. She gathered her courage and looked up at him, but he had leaned in so close that the brim of her hat smacked into the brim of his hat, knocking it askew.

"Oh!" they both said in surprise.

Hobie grabbed at his hat with both hands and she felt the loss of his hand on hers as keenly as she had felt the emptiness on the bench seat of the carriage when he had stood up.

"Whoops," Hobie said, catching his hat just as it slid off his head. His hand turned quickly, like a magician, and flipped the hat high up in the air. Presley watched it tumble over once then land back on top of his head. He wiggled his eyebrows and smiled, looking for a reaction.

She laughed out loud at this showmanship and he beamed. He was trying to lighten the mood, which was sweet.

A light hearted melody filled the air, cutting through their shared amusement and the beautiful playing of the cellist. A cell phone.

The happy smile slipped off Hobie's face as he fished his phone out of the inside pocket of his jacket. What replaced it was a mixture of annoyance and a darker heavier look of concern.

"Excuse me," he said as he stood and turned his back to her. "Hello?" he spoke curtly to the caller.

Presley sat in that uncomfortable place reserved for people who are in earshot of a phone call they know they aren't supposed to hear. She fiddled with the napkin next to her empty sorbet dish and thought about Megan. The young woman's name and face hadn't even crossed her mind since the carriage had arrived and she felt guilt creep into the polite, calm expression she held steady on her face. Apparently, Hobie had forgotten about Megan as well.

"I thought–you said–" The cello music was cutting through the sound of his voice and Presley could hear only pieces of what he was saying.

She willed the woman to stop playing. She dared not ask, because then it would be obvious that she was listening to Hobie's phone call. It turned out that she didn't have to ask. Hobie waved his arm impatiently at the cellist and she stopped. The last note reverberated through the late-afternoon air inside the thicket, weighing it down.

"I can't...right, yes, of course..." Hobie was pacing as he spoke. When Presley glanced at him sideways, trying to act like she was engrossed in her wine glass, she could see that all of the color had drained out of his face. "I will," he said with finality and disconnected the call.

A few beats went by and Hobie stood very still, staring into the space on the ground in front of him as if she had disappeared both from this thicket and his mind. Presley realized she was holding her breath, waiting for him to break the dark mood that had descended on their little picnic with that one phone call.

When he did speak, it was with the last words she expected to hear.

"I have to go. Frederick and Joseph will take you home."

obie ran through Central Park. Unfazed by the looks he received, whether they were because of his top hat or the frantic way he was racing past every other person in the park he didn't know. He didn't care.

His own heartbeat pounded in his ears. The hurt and shock on Presley's face burned in his mind. She was all right, he told himself. Frederick and Joseph would take care of her. But her face. A sharp pain stabbed at his heart and it wasn't from being out of breath or running full speed. It was her. Her confusion at him leaving. The emotional wall that had slipped away during their date slamming back up around her as he told her he had to go.

He wanted to stop and turn around, go right back, tell her he was sorry. But he couldn't go back. Not now. He shook off the urge and pushed faster, harder, along the paths of the Ramble, darting around small crowds, making his way to the street where he could hail a cab. East 79th was closest, Miner's Gate.

"Hey, buddy, you lost your hat," a man's voice called after

him, but he ignored it. Hobie didn't care about the top hat. He needed to get out of the park and get a cab.

When he emerged at East 79th he had to stop and catch his breath. He bent over and leaned on his knees, the stabbing pain was still there whenever he let an image of Presley in her beautiful hat and dress enter his mind. So he fought them. All of them. Pacing back and forth like a caged lion he closed his eyes and pressed the heels of his hands against them, growling in frustration. When he opened his eyes the pedestrians on the sidewalk were making a wide berth around him. Good. That would make it easier to get a cab.

Or so he thought.

The first one slowed for a few moments then sped up and passed him by when the cabbie saw his sweaty, unkempt appearance.

"Thanks," Hobie shouted at the bumper of the cab as it drove away.

He turned and scanned the oncoming traffic for another one. Several drove by. None even slowed. As he waited for a cabbie that was willing to take a risk he wondered at the timing of that phone call.

What did it mean that it came just when he and Presley were were connecting, just when he thought maybe, possibly, he might have found someone in this big wide world who was even lonelier than he was? Someone he could relate to?

A cab came to a screeching halt in front of him, bringing him back to the moment at hand. With relief he reached out to grab the handle when another hand beat him to it. Before Hobie could stop him, a bald guy in a black suit jumped into the back seat and shut the door, stealing his ride.

"Hey!" Hobie hit the top of the cab with his fist, but neither the cabbie or the bald guy even looked at him.

A slurry of emotions boiled in his stomach and threatened to explode in one form or another right there on East 79th.

He couldn't let that happen. He couldn't lose control. And, apparently, he couldn't get a cab.

Instead of waiting one more moment on that sidewalk, Hobie took off running again. Away from Presley and all of the emotions she brought up in him and towards where he was needed most.

CHAPTER 27

Mack Monroe was no fool. He knew what it took to be successful in life, how to make money, to win arguments, to control his destiny. He had never failed at anything he had set out to do in his life. Not once. Not ever.

That's why he was utterly perplexed.

How had he come so far, galaxies beyond where he had begun, only to realize that he may have been going about everything all wrong?

"Another drink, sir?" The waiter appeared at his side with another gin and tonic ready and waiting on a silver tray.

Mack waved the drink away, remembering to say 'no, thank you' a little too late. The waiter had already disappeared.

Mack sighed. Ronnie would have been disappointed at his treatment of the wait staff. Presley may not have noticed. And what about Pete? Pete would have rolled his eyes at the tardy politeness, knowing it for what it was, an attempt to make up for years, decades, of his father's general disinterest in his fellow man.

His son was the most ruthlessly honest of his children. Mack understood this the older he got. It was why Pete couldn't stand to be around him for any great length of time, at least not without arguing.

They had argued just minutes ago with Pete storming out of the restaurant like he had so many times. A repeat of bad behavior brought on by a lifetime of poor parenting.

Pete's blue eyes, the mirror image of his own, had burned hotly at Mack's suggestion that he take a job at one of Mack Industries' companies.

"Why, so you can keep closer tabs on me?"

"No, son," Mack had tried to keep his own temper from flying off the handle. "I think if you took part in the day-to-day of running a company you would..." Mack searched for the right words.

"I would *what*?"

Grow up. That's what Mack wanted to say, but he held back, afraid of Pete's emotional instability and acutely aware that they were in a very public place having a highly personal conversation.

"You might find some direction," Mack said, happy with his word choice.

Pete was less happy.

"So I can slave away like Presley? Fill the overflowing coffers with more and more gold and never have any kind of life?" Pete scoffed and looked away from his father towards the exit. "No, thank you."

Surprised at Pete's intimation that Presley had no life, Mack decided to move past that comment and press the issue in a different way. "Maybe you don't want as much responsibility as Presley has taken on, but Ronnie has a great business going for herself. You could build something of your own." He made this suggestion with real hope. Mack's intentions with business had changed since his heart trouble. He had begun to entertain the idea that running a business could mean more than merely making money.

Pete looked at him for such a long time Mack's infamous hard shell almost cracked. Before it did, however, Pete spoke up.

"Are you cutting me off, Pops?" His eyes were hard and filled with cold amusement.

Taken aback, Mack shook his head in disbelief, "That's not what–"

Not waiting for Mack to finish his thought, Pete leaned forward, his face reddening with emotion. "Because if you think I'm gonna beg, I'm not."

"Beg?"

Pete stood abruptly and continued, not worried about the spectacle he was making, "Do what you want, Dad, but I'm not gonna take some handout job title that everyone knows I didn't earn. And I'm not gonna beg." With that parting shot his only son had left him alone at the table.

Mack sighed, letting his gaze drift across the room. Several people sitting at nearby tables averted their eyes quickly away when he looked in their direction. Whether they knew who he was or had overheard Pete's outburst he didn't know. It didn't matter. He had bigger concerns than the opinions of strangers.

Were all three of his children as miserable as Pete seemed to think? It was no secret that Pete struggled. There was the drug use and the continual attitude he'd had ever since he was a little boy. Mack had thought it was because he was a boy, that being a boy made him more rebellious and he needed to butt heads to prove he was tough. But were Presley and Ronnie also unhappy? His little girls?

The possibility filled his heart with deep sadness, which was not something he was used to feeling.

Mack put his elbows on the table, folded his fingers

together and leaned his forehead on his linked hands almost as if he was praying. It was at times like this he missed Judith's presence. She knew more about their children's personal lives than he did. It would be nice to at least talk to her about them…or have her tell him that he was a good father and everything would be all right.

But she was on an extended trip in Europe. Again.

He let his hands drop to the table and used the white cloth napkin to wipe his eyes, which had teared up unexpectedly.

"Old fool," he muttered under his breath. He didn't bother to look around to see if anyone had overheard him.

CHAPTER 28

"I will never forgive him," Faye declared with a swishing motion of her manicured red nails.

Ronnie screwed her face into a frown. She wasn't one to make grandiose negative declarations. Instead she squinted sympathetically at Presley and said, "That was a pretty awful thing to do."

Presley lifted one shoulder and let it drop nonchalantly, as if she could brush off the hurt and humiliation of being abandoned at Central Park without another thought.

"It wasn't like it was a real date," she said dismissively.

The memory of making her way in her stilettos out of the thicket on the arm of the waiter with no Hobie there to carry her through the wall of bushes flashed through her mind. The embarrassment of riding alone in that ridiculous carriage back to the edge of the park rose up in her chest again, making her cheeks flush red. Presley took a deep drink from her wine glass, trying to blot the whole incident from her mind. Thank goodness for Jaxson, who had arrived with her limo driver, Penny, to rescue her after she texted him from the thicket.

"Never!" Faye said louder than before and lifted her wine glass into the air with defiance.

"Calm down, Faye, it didn't happen to you." Ronnie glanced around at the diners at nearby tables and gave them all an apologetic smile.

Faye covered Presley's hand with hers and squeezed, saying, "It happened to one of my best girls so it may as well have happened to me."

Presley gave Faye's hand a return squeeze of thanks before pulling hers away and trying to change the subject, "So Grace isn't going to make it after all?"

Ronnie shook her head, "No, she's in the Bahamas or something? Research for a new movie, I guess. Ruby's not going to be back in the city until next month."

"Hmm, I haven't heard about this new Bahamas adventure," Presley said.

"Well," Ronnie gave her a sly smile. "You've been preoccupied."

Presley flushed at the insinuation. Preoccupied with business matters, maybe, but that wasn't what Ronnie was saying. As she stewed over whether she should point out to her younger sister that she most certainly was not preoccupied with the likes of Hobie Brent and his tendency to abandon her without rhyme or reason, Faye motioned to the waiter for more wine.

"You'll come with us today, darling," Faye stated matter-of-factly.

"Shopping?" Presley didn't feel up to that.

"No, not just shopping. We're shopping for fine art," Faye swiped the air with an open palm as if showing off a prize on a game show.

"We're going to Frieze's, it'll be fun," Ronnie coerced.

"Good art always lifts the spirits," Faye informed them both knowingly.

Presley wanted to insist that she didn't need her spirits lifted and that they both needed to stop trying to cheer her up, but that might sound too gloomy and defensive, which would prove their point. She sighed and took a sip of her wine. Maybe an afternoon away from the office would do her good.

"I have to be back for a dinner meeting," she said.

Faye arched her eyebrow and asked, "Will the beast be there?"

Presley chuckled, "Yes, but not just him. We're meeting the Count and Countess, finalizing some plans."

"We should be back in plenty of time," Ronnie said, delighted that her sister may take an afternoon off to spend time enjoying the arts. "I'll send for the car."

"Penny is already on standby, she can take us," Presley offered. "I need Jaxson to come, though. Make sure I get something done during the ride."

Ronnie all but rolled her eyes. Presley chose to ignore her. The responsibility of the entire Mack Industries fortune did not ride on Ronnie's shoulders, so she had never understood Presley's dedication to work.

"As soon as we're there you will forget all about work and all of the ugliness with that horrible man," Faye announced.

And she was right. Almost.

Presley did enjoy Frieze's. She took in all of the avant guard installations along with the more traditional paintings and sculptures, all of it was thought provoking or beautiful or both. She even came across a small ceramic sculpture of a nude woman, heavy in the hips and arms, who had a hole that went through the center of her stomach all the way through to the back. The only piece of clothing on the sculpture was a flat basket she wore as a hat. The basket was full of different sized buttons and the sculpture woman's head was bent forward as she neatly sewed a button on one side of the hole in her belly. She was sewing herself up. Presley was drawn to that idea. She liked the little sculpture so much that she bought it.

The afternoon did do a lot for her spirits, but it didn't erase all thoughts of Hobie as Faye had promised it would. Much of the artwork brought up thoughts and feelings that Presley wished she could talk to him about, the way they had talked in the carriage and at lunch…before the phone call from Megan. Free and easy.

Plus she knew she was going to see him later in the evening and she couldn't wipe that thought out of her mind. By the time she returned home to change for the dinner meeting, Presley's stomach was tightly wound again.

"She's beautiful," Jaxson praised the button woman sculpture as he set it up on a corner table in her home office. He leaned back and studied the piece with admiration. "What is it called?"

"Buttons, her name is Buttons," she smiled.

"Perfect!" Jaxson was delighted with the piece. Once again she was reminded of her number one assistant's good taste. He turned to her crisply. "Now, what else do you need from me to prepare for this big meeting with the Count?" She glanced down at the slacks and blouse she had worn all day, then met his gaze. "To the closet!" Jaxson declared.

PRESLEY WAS sure Jaxson had helped her nail down the perfect look for her dinner meeting. Poised and confident in a sleeveless black wool crepe dress by Givenchy, cut short to show off her legs and including a short cape that wrapped stiffly around her shoulders, she captured the eye of every man in the room as she swept through the restaurant to their reserved table. With her blonde tresses swept into a chignon and her favorite brooch, a Chanel diamond feather, pinned to the cape, the final addition of simple diamond stud earrings and a single diamond encrusted cuff bracelet added just enough glitter to the look.

"Bellisima," the Count boomed as he stood to greet her.

She smiled graciously and allowed him to take her hand and kiss it before kissing her on each cheek.

"Count," she said kindly, "Countess."

Presley nodded at the Countess who shimmered in a pure white dress of abundant ruffles. Hobie and Megan were also there, which she had expected, but the sight of them sitting by each other sent a stab of jealousy through her that she hadn't expected.

Megan wore a strapless blue cocktail dress of some unknown origin. In fact, it was slightly gaudy and obviously off the rack. For one moment Presley almost felt sorry for her. Hobie's girlfriend may be younger and would probably be considered more beautiful than Presley, but she lagged behind on class and power. There was another glitch, however, the only empty spot remaining at the table was the seat between Hobie and the Count.

Hobie, too, had stood when she arrived. He had been the first of their group to notice her as the maitre'd escorted her through the room, past the other diners. As she approached his dark eyes had not left her and Presley's stomach flipped over several times before she managed to get a grip on herself. She was not going to falter under his charm again. Presley Monroe rarely made mistakes, and she never made them twice.

The maitre'd pulled her chair out and just before she sat down Hobie leaned towards her, his mouth coming very close to her ear where her diamond stud sparkled in the candlelight. "You look beautiful, Presley," he said in a low gruff tone that might almost be considered a whisper.

Chills tickled across her skin, wrapped behind her neck and shot down her spine. What was he playing at, exactly? How could he be so blatantly flirtatious with her after what he'd done at the park, at a business meeting, and in front of his girlfriend? She pressed her lips together in a tight smile, aware that the whole table was watching her and refusing to give Hobie even the slightest amount of satisfaction.

"Good evening," she said evenly, immediately turning her attention away from him and to the Count and Countess. They were why she was here after all.

His abhorrent behavior didn't stop there. During the appetizers and soup Hobie continued to say funny, interesting things to her. He asked her opinion and listened attentively to her when she spoke. She noticed that his attentions to her were causing him to neglect Megan sitting on his other side. This made her feel triumphant on one hand and incensed at how he was treating his girlfriend on the other.

He pressed on, leaning in so close to her that their shoulders brushed and the enticing scent of his cologne tickled her nose. He kept saying things like, "What are your thoughts, Presley?" or "I am confident Presley has considered every angle." Every time he said her name the sound of his voice was like silk in her ears and she had to allow herself a moment to recover before she could focus again.

As they enjoyed each delicious course and drank more wine, the flattery continued non-stop, but Presley was not swayed by Hobie's steady, thoughtful considerations. She met every pleasant overture he made towards her with a cool calm that she knew could stop any man or beast from toying with her. She wasn't about to let her emotions get the better of her again. Not in front of the Count and Countess, and certainly not in front of little lovely Megan.

Right after a special dish of braised brussell sprouts the chef had sent specifically to their table was set in front of them, Hobie took advantage of the moment of distraction from conversation to lean even closer into her ear and speak softly, "I'm sorry I had to leave suddenly." Presley shot him a look, though he didn't seem to realize right away how much sharpness the look held. "Sometime I'd like to explain..." he searched her eyes for a chink in her armor. Finding none, he continued, "I wish we had taken some pictures."

He said it with such a sweet sadness, Presley's chilly reception almost warmed. Almost, but not quite. Hobie sat back in his chair and pushed his brussell sprouts around with his fork.

Triumphant, Presley turned her attention to the business at hand. By the time her entree of sautéed Sepia ribbons and squid ink risotto was placed in front of her, she had successfully squelched any and all intimate moments with Hobie. She sensed a shift in the way he looked at her, from curious to confused, from flirtatious to quiet, almost sullen. Her indifference to his feelings was palpable and she continued to expertly guide the dinner conversation of the entire table towards business and business alone, ignoring his cheerless sulking. Was it her job to make him feel better after he ditched her on their date? She didn't think so.

"Ah, it has been a while since we enjoyed such a decadent meal," the Count said, waving his hand at the waiter, gesturing for the check. He glanced at the Countess, whose expression had suddenly tensed, a flash of embarrassment unmistakable in her eyes. Drawn away from her obsession with being cold and unapproachable towards Hobie, Presley noted a curious look between the Count and his wife. Secretive and strained, as if they were having a silent argument.

Hobie noticed it, too. Presley could read it in his eyes, with which she unwittingly shared a look. Those damned dark eyes that pulled her in every time, as if they, too, were involved in a long term relationship. Tension filled the air as the waiter did as he was bidden and placed a black leather binder containing the check for their dinner next to the Count. Hobie gave her a meaningful stare and indicated the check by pointing his chin at it. Presley didn't understand.

The Countess looked away from the Count and into the middle distance of the busy restaurant as he reached to pick up the check, his Italian accent booming, "This has been a wonderful night with wonderful friends."

Presley watched him curiously. There was something wrong, but she couldn't put her finger on what it could possibly be.

Suddenly, Hobie leaned forward and around Presley, forcing her to press into the back of her chair to keep from being elbowed in the face. He lifted the black leather binder swiftly out from under the Count's lingering hand and sat quickly back in his chair.

"Please, this is Barcom's treat," he said, tucking the binder safely between he and Megan. The Count's cheeks reddened as he protested, but Hobie only shook his head and responded, "I insist."

Despite boisterous declarations that he must pay for their dinner because it was him who invited them out, a look of relief had washed over the Count's face. And the Countess'. She even gave Hobie a shy, grateful smile, which he returned with a gracious nod. Presley recalled what Agnus had told her at Ruby's fundraiser gala. The Count was experiencing some kind of financial difficulty, or something of that nature. Presley had forgotten all about that until now. Obviously, Hobie hadn't.

Before anyone could say anything to move them all past this uncomfortable social faux pas, a vibration buzzed out of Hobie's jacket. Presley watched with irritation as he pulled his phone out and lifted it to his ear.

"Yes?" Hobie answered.

Honestly, the instant he started to improve in her estimation there was one of these interruptive phone calls. Presley stewed as she eavesdropped, flicking her gaze occasionally to Megan to see if she, too, was annoyed. She couldn't tell.

"Right away," Hobie said, clicking off the call and lowering his phone. He looked around at everyone, his gaze landing on Presley. "I've–"

"You have to leave, I know," she said crisply. And then, with more than just a little sarcasm in her voice, "How did I ever guess?"

CHAPTER 29

Once again in a span of only a few days Hobie found himself trying to hail a cab on a busy New York City street. Once again Presley was top in his mind, putting his emotions on edge. This time, however, he wasn't torn about returning to the dining room of the restaurant and apologizing to her for leaving early.

This time he was furious.

He tugged at the tie around his neck to loosen its grip. He hated ties, but he had dutifully put one on for this meeting. It was more professional, plus the restaurant required it, something Hobie had always found annoying about high end restaurants.

But he'd worn the stupid thing without complaint, arrived on time, kept up with his end of the conversation with the Count and Countess, and been a complete gentleman to everyone at that table, especially Presley Monroe. What did he get in return? The cold shoulder. More like the glacier shoulder. Icy, mean, unmoving, stilted, any and all of these words could describe Presley's treatment of him throughout dinner. And what was that snarky comment about him having to leave after it was over?

"I have someplace to be," Hobie muttered. What business was it of hers if he had other commitments? He wasn't slacking on the Count's project and she obviously didn't want him around to have a civil conversation.

Thoughts of the Count brought back the painfully awkward moments before Hobie was able to take hold of the check for dinner. Presley had seemed oblivious to the whole interaction. Didn't she remember what her friend, Aunt Annie or whatever her name was, told her about the Count's finances? He remembered. Could Presley really be that obtuse to the money problems of other people in the world?

Hobie scoffed at this question. "Of course she could," he mumbled as he scanned the street for a cab. "She's a spoiled brat."

He took a deep breath and tried not to look as angry as he felt. He had learned the hard way at Central Park how cabbies don't like to pick up an already angry rider. He had sent his driver and car to take Megan home since he needed to go in the opposite direction. He wasn't one hundred percent sure he could get a cab, but he didn't have far to go and could run again if he had to.

As far as Presley went, Hobie was glad to be outside and on his way somewhere where she wasn't. After showing up drop dead gorgeous in that shapely black dress she had shown her true colors. He had learned more about her personality tonight than he ever had before, even when they were kids. And the feelings he'd thought he had for her during their carriage ride date were souring. Despite his physical attraction to her Hobie was pretty sure Presley Monroe was not the woman for him.

As if on cue, a cabbie with a number of tiny brightly colored statues glued across his dashboard and fringe dangling along the tops of his windows caught Hobie's eye, giving him a barely perceptible nod. Hobie relaxed as he waited for the cab to make it across two lanes of traffic to get close enough to pick him up.

The symbolism was hard for Hobie to ignore. It seemed that when he pushed aside any romantic interest or physical attraction he felt for Presley, his life got easier almost instantly.

CHAPTER 30

"Home, Ms. Monroe?" Penny asked from behind the wheel of the limo.

Presley sat fuming in the back, her body resting snugly in the plush leather seat, her gaze set out the window. She stared fiercely at the traffic passing them on the street, offended by the people in all of the cars who knew where they wanted to go. They must. They were heading toward their chosen destinations with such singular dedication, while she couldn't put two thoughts together, let alone instruct her chauffeur where to drive.

The audacity of that man.

She was overcome with anger, reliving the way he had given her a nasty glare before storming away from the table, his ridiculous girlfriend on his heels, leaving her to make nice with the Count and Countess and leave the dinner meeting with at least a modicum of grace and civility.

What did he have to be angry about? She was the one being interrupted all of the time. She was the one who had to put up with his inability to finish a meeting. To finish a date. How many times had he done this now? So many she had lost count. This whole mess with him sent her reeling from seething anger all the way to pulsating insecurity.

Penny peered over her shoulder through the open glass partition, waiting for Presley's answer. Presley gave her a nod. Home it was. She had nowhere else to go this evening and even if she had her mood was shattered.

Penny turned her attention to pulling the sleek, black limo into traffic. Presley's gaze shifted back out the window just in time to see a man wave down a taxi on the other side of the street. A man that looked a lot like Hobie.

She squinted, trying to see through the tinted window as well as the streams of cars and pedestrians moving past. Yes, there he was again. It was definitely Hobie and he was ducking into a yellow taxi that had been decorated by its cabbie with pink and red fringe on the inside of the back window.

The glass partition behind Penny's head slid up as the limo pulled smoothly away from the curb. Presley was unable to contain her curiosity, she strained to find Hobie's taxi in the stream of cars. There it was again. The unmistakable fringe. Her heart beat quickly, as if she was in the middle of a game and about to score the winning point. Suddenly Presley knew what she wanted to do.

"Wait!" she called out just as Penny's chauffeur hat disappeared behind the gliding glass. Its upward motion stopped and started down again.

"Yes?" Penny asked.

Presley pointed a manicured finger into the traffic and gave the instruction, "Follow that cab. The one with the fringe."

As thrilling as it was to give the command, Presley was not expecting Penny to take it to heart so completely. Before Presley could brace herself in the back seat, her eager chauffeur stepped on the gas and turned sharply, cutting in front of several cars. Presley toppled to the side, nearly bonking her head on the tinted glass window.

"Discreetly, Penny," she said.

"Yes, Ms. Monroe."

The limo smoothed out and besides a melee of angry honks from drivers they had just cut off following them, they blended into the throng of traffic as well as any other black stretch limousine could, which was to say quite well. There was no shortage of black stretch limos in Manhattan. Just as there was no shortage of cabs. Penny left the glass partition down pending further instructions from her employer, but mostly focused on keeping up with the smaller, spryer vehicle.

Presley's initial excitement at pursuing Hobie to whatever secret location he was scurrying off too, was slowly replaced by a sickening feeling that maybe she didn't want to know. Maybe he had yet another woman waiting in the sidelines who Megan was oblivious to as well. He hadn't struck Presley as the philandering type, but then again, he had taken her on a wildly romantic date even though he was seeing Megan.

Why wouldn't someone like that keep multiple women on strings around the city, or even around the world. He was a world traveling photographer after all. Never been married. Maybe his line about not meeting the right woman all these years was just a cover up for being a player. Was this really something she wanted or needed to know about Hobie?

About 15 minutes later the limo slowed to a stop and Penny's eyes found hers in the reflection of the rear view mirror. "They've stopped," she said, waiting for further instruction.

Presley didn't want to appear too eager, plus she couldn't see the cab in front of them from her position in the back of the limo.

"Is anyone getting out?" she asked.

Penny nodded. "Yes, it looks like Mr. Brent. He's going into the building."

Presley peeked cautiously around Penny's head to see what she could see through the windshield. She couldn't see much. Her heartbeat had quickened when Penny said Hobie's name. A surge of nervous energy filled her stomach.

"Do you want me to follow him?" Penny asked. Her tone surprised Presley, eager to step up and do something covert.

"No," she responded automatically, though her voice sounded more sure than she felt. What did she want to do? She hadn't really thought any of this through. Of course he wasn't going to do whatever sneaky thing he was doing right out on the street in full sight. Someone would have to follow him inside.

Penny looked at her expectantly in the rear view mirror and for an instant Presley considered sending her chauffeur in after Hobie, but realized Penny wouldn't know what to look for since she didn't know why they were following him to begin with.

"I'll be right back," Presley said, popping open the limo door and slipping out as discreetly as possible before Penny had time to react and open it for her. Heart pounding, she hurried across the sidewalk and ducked into the door Hobie had entered just moments before.

The lobby lights were bright, not mood lighting at all. Presley quickly realized that if Hobie was just ahead of her and turned around for any reason he would see her immediately. Spying a sitting area immediately to her left, she took the chair furthest from the door because it was out of the direct line of sight of people moving through the lobby and it had a large ficus plant in a planter next to it, which would mask some of her at least.

Presley wondered for the first time what the name on the

sign outside of this building had said. She had been so focused on following Hobie, she hadn't stopped to read it. Peeking through the thin green leaves of the ficus, she scanned the lobby for more intel.

It was clean, but not plush. Comfortable seating areas like the one she was hiding in were positioned in each corner of the lobby. Each contained single chairs and loveseats in muted, calming colors that faced each other with standard coffee tables holding short stacks of magazines in the center. Artwork on the walls was beautiful, but also neutral. Not too flashy. It matched the light fixtures. Tasteful, but definitely not a high end apartment building or even a luxury office building.

Stumped, Presley squinted through the ficus at the sign hanging behind a front desk being manned by two competent looking receptionists. Before she could read it, Hobie stepped in her line of sight and she shrank back behind the plant. His back was to her as he leaned casually on the front desk talking to the receptionists. One of them, a slim young woman with pale blonde hair, laughed out loud at whatever he said.

Could the blonde be who he was here to see? Was he visiting one of his girlfriends at work? As if in answer to her question, Hobie knocked his knuckles on the counter signaling the end of his lively interaction with the receptionists and walked past the front desk into the well lit hallway that Presley assumed led to the elevators. The pale blonde watched him go with a kind smile and Presley was even more confused. The look wasn't necessarily a romantic look, though it was tender.

The blonde's eyes left Hobie's retreating back and moved across the room, falling on Presley. Her blonde brow wrinkled in question, as if she was about to ask Presley if she needed any assistance. Presley whirled around in her chair and pretended she hadn't just been peeking through the frail limbs of a potted ficus.

She smoothed her skirt with her palms and wondered if there was any way she could sneak by the front desk without being noticed now that she had been spotted. With each passing moment she expected to hear the soft voice of the pale blonde asking her why she was here and if she was expected. How was she going to come up with a viable story without knowing what business was housed in this building?

Presley picked up a gossip magazine from the table and flipped through its wrinkled pages. Perhaps she could buy a few minutes to figure out what to do by acting like she was simply waiting for someone.

Just then the front doors opened and a large group of people entered. Even though it was a big crowd, they all appeared to be related. They kept streaming through the door, grandparents leading grandchildren, parents leading children, older siblings, aunts and uncles, all of them talking loudly and some of them carrying brightly wrapped gifts, flowers, and balloons.

"We've brought the birthday party here," the boisterous voice of what must be the patriarch of this group announced to the receptionists. Presley couldn't hear how the pale blonde or the other receptionist responded over the noise of the rest of the traveling birthday party.

A small girl, about five years old, caught Presley's eye and came to stand next to her. She had dark hair, deep blue eyes, and was holding tightly to the string of a purple balloon.

After a few awkward moments where the little girl stared at her silently, Presley smiled and said, "Hello."

The little girl did not smile back, just stared and blinked a few times in that way children did because they hadn't learned how inappropriate it was to gawk. Finally she spoke,

"My name's Nita. We're going to see Aunt Karla for her birthday."

"That's nice," Presley said politely. She scanned Nita's family who now almost completely filled the lobby, wondering if her parents were nearby or if anyone in the group was paying attention to this odd little girl who was making conversation with a total stranger.

"You're pretty," Nita said.

"Thank you…so are you."

Nita smiled, revealing a big gap where her two front teeth used to be.

"I'm bringing Aunt Karla a balloon," Nita said, lifting her gaze to the balloon floating over their heads then dropping it back to Presley. "Do you want to come to the party?"

Presley started to politely decline, then stopped. She scanned the room again, taking in Nita's large, loud family with renewed interest. A thought formed in her mind. A way to get into the building without having to explain herself to anyone.

She turned her attention back to Nita, smiling with more warmth, as if they had been acquainted for far longer than two minutes.

"I would love to come to your Aunt Karla's party," Presley said kindly.

Then she stood and followed Nita and her family past the pale blonde receptionist onto an elevator and up into the mystery building to look for Hobie.

$\mathcal{P}$resley decided if anyone asked, she would be the distant, rarely seen, well dressed cousin to Aunt Karla. But to her relief, nobody asked. She rode to the 7th floor with the rest of Nita's family, standing at the back of the elevator trying to blend. When they filed out of the elevator she went with them, hanging back just a bit, and finally slipping into a nearby hallway as Nita and her bobbing purple balloon disappeared to wherever Aunt Karla was staying.

Hurrying down the wide, brightly lit corridor she knew immediately that this was a hospital or a clinic of some kind. If the sterile smell wasn't enough to tip her off, the men and women donning scrubs with stethoscopes hanging from their necks would have been a major clue. Presley became very aware of her chic black dress and glittering jewelry as she walked, the clicking of her high heels echoed through the clinical atmosphere.

What in the world was Hobie doing here at this time of night? It dawned on her that he may not have gotten off on the 7th floor. Perhaps there were other floors in this building that were not full of physicians and nurses and families visiting their Aunt Karlas.

She sighed, the click-click-click of her heels slowed as she pondered what to do next. A pair of handsome young doctors walked by and smiled at her appreciatively. She glanced down at her clothes, certain now that she was sticking out like a sore thumb and could soon be exposed as an imposter with no reason to be here.

To avoid too much eye contact, she turned to a long bulletin board that ran the length of the hall. Squinting hard at the items stuck there with thumbtacks, as if the flyers for ice cream socials and hand signed cards thanking the staff for all of their hard work were of the utmost importance to her, she tried to act like she belonged. Her eyes swept past a series of pictures of patients and their caregivers smiling and laughing. This certainly was a happy place for being full of what she presumed must be sick people.

The images on the bulletin board blurred together as her mind wandered back to her predicament. Finding Hobie in this building. He could be anywhere by now. Her musings on Hobie stopped when her gaze came to a picture of a dog, all by itself, seemingly grinning at the camera but not accompanied by a human. There was another picture of a dog next to that one. And another. A whole series of dog pictures stared back at her as she tried to make sense of why they were hanging on a bulletin board in a clinic.

Presley's eyes fell on one image in particular and she stepped closer. This wasn't any old dog. The single ear, the bug eyes, the frantically joyful expression.

"Sugar Pop?" she said under her breath.

"Presley? Is that you?"

A voice sounded behind her, deep and familiar, and Presley whirled around with a start like a little kid who'd been caught with their hand in the cookie jar. Hobie had found her.

But it wasn't Hobie. It wasn't Hobie at all.

Standing behind her wearing a plush navy blue housecoat was a tall, thin man. His pale legs stuck awkwardly out of the bottom of his robe and his feet were clad in blue velvet Versace bedroom slippers. His hair was extremely short, almost not there, and he was quite thin, but his eyes were the same beautiful brown eyes she had adored as a teenager.

Danny. Danny Brent.

Yet not quite the Danny she remembered. Pale and bony, bluish purple rings under his eyes, his head shorn of its thick, dark locks, he looked like a ghost appearing out of nowhere. It was as if her memory of Danny had blown into the corridor, but hadn't fully formed in front of her yet. He was a shadow of his former, athletic, high school self.

He spoke again, "Presley Monroe, it is you."

His voice was exactly the same as when they were young, deep and resonating. And, she noted, almost identical to his little brother's now that they were both grown men.

"Hi Danny," she tried not to gape at his state of undress… and his state of illness.

"Fancy meeting you here in these strangest of circumstances." He indicated his bathrobe with a sweep of his hand.

Presley relaxed a little. It helped knowing that he knew it was awkward.

"You look good," she lied.

He tilted his head and gave her a shrewd look. "I look like death warmed over." He smiled and some of that old Danny Brent charm shone through. "But you…you look amazing."

It was her turn to smile and she blushed at his comment, and at his state of undress, and at having been caught snooping after his brother.

"I see you found Hobie's pictures," Danny helped her out by creating a safe topic of conversation.

"Oh, these are his?" She feigned ignorance as she turned back to the wall.

Danny moved next to her so they both faced the dog photos. Sugar Pop's picture was smack dab in front of them. She fixed her gaze on the tiny dog's quirky expression and tried to look amused and interested.

"Yeah, he's quite the photographer these days," Danny said, a hint of pride in his voice.

She cleared her throat before answering, "Yes, I've heard a little about that."

"He should be here any minute," he offered. Presley's heart jumped into her throat as Danny continued, "I'm assuming you're here to see him…aren't you? About the charity donation?"

Presley's face froze and she kept her eyes trained on Sugar Pop. If she looked at Danny he might guess she had ulterior motives for following Hobie into this most intimate of spaces. The place she knew now was Suzie's House where Danny was undergoing treatments. He had given her the best possible excuse by guessing it was because of her $250,000 donation. It was a weak excuse, but she was going to embrace it.

"Yes, yes, I wanted to talk to him about that…and, you know, other things."

"You're welcome to wait with me, he'll be by to see me soon I'm sure."

Presley didn't have any good reason to refuse Danny's suggestion so she had to follow him to his room. Or, more precisely, his rooms.

What must have been four or five hospital size patient rooms had been joined together and redecorated into more of a high end hotel than a cancer research patient room.

Although glimpses of the medical treatment were visible throughout the space.

An IV stand with a full bag of clear solution stood waiting next to a large red leather reading chair. It almost looked like a gaudy standing lamp, but not quite. Along the walls various types of plugs for electricity or compressed air were grouped together with disposable medical equipment hanging next to them in sterile plastic bags. Everything anyone might need for a medical emergency.

"Please excuse the decor," Danny said as he noticed her eyes roaming over the room. "We've done what we can to make things more comfortable here in 722B, since I'm here all the time these days. I was commuting, you see, staying at our penthouse and coming in daily," his eyes were fixed on the IV stand as he spoke. "Then the travel just became too tiring I'm afraid."

A lump rose in Presley's throat and she tried to swallow it back. Danny looked at her and smiled again, gesturing for her to take a seat on a nearby couch. She did while he settled into the reading chair.

"I have managed to bring some of the finer pieces I enjoy most," Danny looked to the wall where a Felin Putole painting hung over a cherry wood dresser. "Do you know Putole?"

"I do, I just saw some of his newer pieces at Frieze's," she answered. The modern artist's clean lines and bright color swathes were easily recognizable. "I like him, too."

"Do you? I've found most people either like his work or despise it." He looked at Presley for a long moment then asked, "Are you thirsty?" He reached for a tan remote with three large buttons. One blue, one green, and one red. Playing host came naturally to him due to his upbringing, she was sure, but it didn't exactly feel comfortable in their current surroundings. She felt like she should be bringing him a get well gift rather than being treated like a guest.

"No, thank you," she said. She wasn't thirsty at all. In fact, she didn't know what she was—sad, confused, embarrassed, wishing she had never told Penny to follow Hobie's cab.

"Thank you, by the way, for the donation," Danny interrupted her inner melt down, another bright smile shining at her from under his faded exterior.

Red creeped up her cheeks, she was ashamed in the glaring light of his gratitude. "Oh, no, it was nothing." This was true. It was nothing. She knew it and he did, too. In her kind of vast fortune $250,000 was easily thrown away and forgotten. She urgently didn't want him to think she thought of him and his condition, of this research center named after he and Hobie's deceased mother, as a throw away charity. "I– I was happy to help," Presley cleared her throat. "I hope I can help more."

Danny relaxed into his chair and smiled, "You've helped more than you know."

"Oh, surely not," she brushed his comment aside.

Danny's eyebrows lifted as he nodded knowingly, "You've certainly brightened Hobie's mood, which helps this whole place. He's been under a lot of pressure since I got sick and he had to take over everything."

Presley's heart skipped and she felt the red in her cheeks deepen, she shook her head in dismissal, "I doubt I have much impact on Hobie's mood."

With an amused chuckle, Danny looked away from her, his eyes landing on the closed door. "Did you see all of the pictures out there?"

"Of the dogs?"

Danny nodded and looked back at her. "Not just dogs."

Presley furrowed her brow, trying to remember the other images on the bulletin board. "The patients and staff?"

He nodded again. "Those, too, but there are also some of you."

"Of me?" She was truly surprised and looked towards the door herself as if she might see through it into the hallway.

"With the funny little dog."

"Sugar Pop?" She looked back to him, trying to put the pieces together.

"Is that her name?" Danny chuckled again, then leaned forward to explain. "Hobie brings in pictures all the time. Pictures of things he thinks might interest or amuse those of us who are stuck in here all day and night." He paused, giving her a chance to respond. She didn't, so he continued, "He started taking pictures of our mother when she became ill. I've always thought that's where his love of photography really took off." He leaned back, his eyes warm yet sad as he spoke, "It's how he communicates, really. I think he takes pictures of things that he cherishes…and things he's scared he won't see again. It's like he's afraid he's going to forget them."

"Oh," she said, her throat tightened at Danny's distant tone. A rush of grief overwhelmed her at the memory of Hobie as a quiet, gawky boy. At the end of their time in school together he had been suffering through the death of his mother and she, a popular and self-centered teenager, hadn't given it one thought. Another emotion rushed through her–shame.

"I guess maybe I should be worried that he's been taking a lot of pictures of me lately, shouldn't I?" Danny coughed out a laugh.

Presley could not help but laugh, but it came out more as a choked guffaw instead of her normal, more practiced, light and airy laugh. She covered her mouth with her hand, shocked at the donkey like sound she had just emitted.

Danny looked at her with surprise and they both froze,

their expressions locked in comical horror. A smirk lifted one side of Danny's mouth and moments later he cracked up laughing. So did she. The strangeness of their meeting here mixed with their familiarity from childhood, bubbling up and out of them in fits of the giggles. Soon they were both doubled over, struggling to catch their breath between peals of laughter, tears streaming down their faces.

"Well, now, something's struck a funny bone in here, hasn't it?"

The voice came from the door and startled Presley more than Danny. An elderly man, finely dressed in crisply ironed black slacks and a grey cashmere sweater entered the room. Thin and stooped, he moved with a kind of calm grace reminiscent of fine gentlemen in old movies.

"Dad," Danny wiped tears of laughter from his eyes with the back of one hand as he motioned toward Presley with the other. "You remember Presley Monroe, don't you?"

The old man's eyes, warm and brown like his sons, brightened as he looked at her. Presley moved as if to stand, but he reached out and patted the air in between them to stop her.

"No, no, miss, don't get up. You look quite comfortable where you are." For a long moment he gazed at her with obvious delight, then he clucked his tongue and shook his head in disbelief. "All grown up and so beautiful, too. Though I shouldn't wonder, your parents were always a handsome couple."

Mr. Brent, Daniel Brent Senior, founder of Barcom Incorporated, father to Danny and Hobie, and one of her own father's oldest friends, was a stranger to Presley. As she smiled and accepted his complement she wondered at that fact. How had they not met in business or at least in a social setting over the years? She was certain they ran in the same circles, yet somehow she couldn't recall a single time she and the elder Brent had ever spoken.

"She's come to see Hobie," Danny explained as his father settled onto the love seat next to Presley. She focused on holding the friendly, calm expression that had settled onto her earlier, but felt stiff and strange at the mention of Hobie's name.

Mr. Brent's eyes twinkled, "Oh, he'll be glad of that I'm sure." Danny shot his father a look of mild reproof, which made the older man chuckle before he turned his attention back to her and smiled warmly, "How are your parents, Presley? Are they well?"

It took her a few moments to think of an answer. How were her parents, really? Normally her answer might be tinged with complaints of her mother's incessant social climbing or her father's partial retirement that had left her in the predicament of being left in charge yet always under his watchful eye. But with his own wife passed away so long ago and his eldest son sitting opposite them suffering from the same insidious disease that had taken her too young, Presley's family issues were petty and superficial.

She started to answer, but the sound of the door opening interrupted whatever benign response she was about to give. Both Brent men looked towards the door, but Presley didn't have to, she already knew who it was. Heart pounding, mouth dry, nervous sweat sweeping across her skin, there was nowhere for her to hide and no path to escape.

CHAPTER 32

*P*resley stood quickly. Even though she had been caught in the act of intruding and her stomach was a ball of twisting nerves, she turned to face Hobie head on. The smile Hobie expected to give his brother faded into puzzlement as he laid eyes on her. His forward motion through the door slowed to a graceless stop. Their eyes locked and she saw with dread the good humor in his look turn into a sharp question. *What in the hell are you doing here?*

She felt his words just as clearly as if he had spoken them out loud. And even though she longed to explain, give a believable reason that would erase the shadow of distrust on his face, she remained quiet, willing her response instead – *I'm sorry...I didn't mean to invade your private family space. I didn't even know Danny was here...and I didn't know he was this sick. I just wanted to know if you were meeting another woman.* Even unspoken, the words sounded hollow echoing inside of her head.

"Presley came by to see you," Danny offered. He pushed himself up from his chair as if to play host again, but his attempt was weak and he seemed off balance. With a stinging glance, Hobie dismissed her presence and went to his brother's side to assist him.

"Don't get up," Hobie said as he guided Danny back into the great red reading chair. The caring in his voice squeezed her heart. After settling Danny, Hobie straightened and turned to her again. He had found his composure and was all polite formality, as if she was a dried up, barely remembered, old family friend who had stopped by unexpectedly at a bad time.

Presley didn't know which hurt her more, his initial reaction of barely controlled displeasure upon seeing her or the cold aloofness that had taken over.

"Presley came to visit," his father said encouragingly as he patted the seat next to him that she had just vacated. "Sit down, dear, no need to run off now."

She blushed furiously as Hobie looked her up and down, his eyes shrewd and dark. What must he think of her? They had only just left their dinner meeting and here she was standing bold as brass in his brother's sick room.

"No, no," she stammered. "I don't think this is a good time after all. We can talk later. I'll have Jaxson make an appointment."

Ignoring the protests of both Daniel Senior and Junior as politely as she could, Presley managed an artless escape out the door and into the hallway without locking eyes with Hobie again. She almost stumbled over a cleaning cart and the surprised hospital custodian who steered it as she hurried away.

Face burning from embarrassment she pressed her lips together fiercely and tried not to cry. This was ridiculous. Why was she so upset? She was Presley Monroe, she did not cry over imagined social faux pax. Presley Monroe did not cry over anything.

Heels clicking hurriedly on the smooth, shining floor she

was almost to the elevator when a strong hand took hold of her elbow.

"What are you doing here?" Hobie whispered thick in her ear. The sensation of his breath on her neck made her shiver.

She didn't look at him, but tried to pull out of his grip. He did not let go.

"Excuse me," she said haughtily, glancing back and up at him with an angry scowl.

The muscles along his jaw clenched then released and she felt his fingers slip off of her arm. But his eyes, still storming and deep brown, almost black, continued to glare. He reached out and punched the down button on the elevator.

"I can find my car by–" she started.

"I'll walk you out," he said brusquely. She dared not argue.

They waited for the elevator doors to open in silence. Presley alternated between red hot humiliation at being caught in a petty and meddling act, and seething anger at Hobie's gruff treatment of her. The elevator bell dinged, the sound almost comical amidst their angry silence. A few moments went by as the elevator settled then the doors slipped open smoothly and he gestured for her to go first.

Presley huffed in. It was empty so she stepped all the way in and squared her back so she was facing the front, glaring up at the numbers above the door. Hobie entered after her, viciously punching the 1st floor button with a stab of his forefinger.

The elevator moved under their feet and she felt the familiar drop in her stomach as it started down.

"What are you doing here?" he asked again, still coldly irate.

She pressed her lips together and glared at the numbers glowing above the door as they descended – 7...6...

There was a loud smack and the sickening anti-gravity feeling of an elevator ride suddenly halted lurched in her stomach. An obnoxious alarm squealed through the small enclosed space. Presley looked at Hobie in shock. His hand still hovered near the bulbous red emergency button.

"You hit the emergency button?" she asked, incensed.

"We're not going anywhere until you tell me why I came to see my big brother and found you in his room chatting up him and my Dad."

"What?" For someone who moments before had been feeling guilty about doing exactly what he was accusing her of doing, Presley was surprised at the indignity she felt in being called out on it. The shrill pulsing of the alarm wrapped around them and penetrated her ears. She wanted to scream at him to turn it off and make the elevator move again. Instead, she narrowed her eyes, stepped right up into his chest and jabbed straight into it with her finger as she spoke, "If you do not stop this nonsense I will call the authorities. I will get the New York Fire Department here in minutes and you will have to answer to them and to the owner of this building."

He did not back down. If she didn't know better, Presley would have sworn he moved closer each time she poked him. His eyes narrowed and a smirk lifted one side of his mouth.

"I own the building," he said, his voice boldly quiet. She blinked at him in surprise and his lips twitched in an almost laugh. "And the firemen would be on my side."

"I hardly think this is funny."

Hobie smiled despite himself and the protective fury in his eyes receded. A calmness settled over him and his shoulders relaxed as he watched her with more curiosity than anger.

"Why are you here, Presley?"

The change in his demeanor quieted her own emotions and she sank back into the wall of the elevator. He waited for her answer until she was compelled to say something, anything, that might appease him.

"I wanted to see this place. See where my donation went to." It was a feeble answer, she knew. Hobie knew it, too.

"Bullshit."

Unscathed by his language, Presley continued, "$250,000 is a lot of money. I have every right to know whe–"

"That's pocket change for you," he interrupted. His eyes, fiery from her lack of truthfulness, searched hers for the answer he wanted. She matched his intensity with her own and they remained like that, locked together, both of them refusing to look away first, the blaring alarm dimming into the background.

Without taking his eyes from hers, Hobie reached out and hit the emergency button. The alarm ceased, leaving a ringing in her ears and a palpable emptiness in the stuffy elevator air. She wrinkled her brow. Why had he given in?

Before she could ask what he was playing at, the elevator jolted into its descent once again. Not ready for sudden movement, Presley flopped into his chest, which was quite the opposite of how she might hope to fall into a man's arms. He caught her and held her steady, but he did not push her off of him.

The warm strength of his chest pressed against her breasts. His hands held her arms firmly so she wouldn't topple over. With her face almost nuzzling into his neck, the heat of his breath tickled her ear sending goose bumps up and down her arms.

Presley lifted her eyes just as he turned his face to look at her. They were so close that his lips barely missed her mouth, brushing against her cheek instead. The sensation was so light against her skin she could not be certain he had actually touched her except for the tingling sensation left behind.

He peered into her eyes, searching, probing, seeking something she wasn't sure she wanted to give him. Her heart pounded like a drum, surely he could feel it. Mouth dry, breath shallow, she could only stand, flustered, in his arms, and wait for him to speak.

"You're so…so…," his voice was low and growling.

"So…what?" she whispered.

"Difficult."

She pulled back, her face screwing into a scowl. "Me? *I'm* difficult? What about you?"

"What have I ever done that's difficult?"

Pushing against his chest with the palms of her hands, barely able to ignore the way his muscles flexed under her fingers, she pulled away from him. Hobie kept hold of her arms even though the elevator was now moving smoothly down and there was no danger of her falling.

…5…

"You're always leaving," she said.

"Leaving?"

"Every business meeting, every phone call, even the… the…" she looked for the word to describe their Central Park picnic. Reluctant to call it a date, she chose something more suiting, "The charity lunch in Central Park. You left me stranded in the middle of nowhere. It's very unprofessional, you know. Leaving early, dropping everything, wasting time. Money is time, Mr. Brent, and my time is valuable."

A wave of power surged through her and she straightened her shoulders, taking a step back from him, forcing him to release his steadying hold on her arms. He dropped his arms to his sides and stared at her in silence. She smoothed the skirt of her dress and jutted her chin out sternly, turning her attention to the glowing numbers above the door.

…4…

They stood in stony silence as the elevator dropped.

Presley shot a look at him, expecting him to be sufficiently shamed for his behavior. But he didn't look ashamed at all.

...3...

Hobie shook his head once in disgust, lifting his eyes to the ceiling. With a frustrated sigh he directed them back at her like a laser finding its target.

"Have you ever lost anyone?" he asked, then looked away with a brief scoff before answering his own question. "Of course not. You've led the perfect rich girl existence your whole life, haven't you?" He zeroed in on her again. "Well, I can tell you it sits in your gut...and you never forget what it feels like to realize that the last time you saw someone was the last time you will ever see them again. They disappear and you can't even remember what they look like without seeing pictures." His voice cracked as he spoke and the power Presley had felt after scolding him drained swiftly away. "Nothing, no amount of money, no business deal, nothing can replace the chance to see someone you love once more before they're gone forever."

...1...

The elevator bell dinged. Heat burned the back of her throat and she was alarmed to find fat tears welling up in her eyes and blurring her vision. The doors began to slide open and Presley made a move to escape only to be blocked by Hobie's arm as he stopped her forward progress.

He leaned down so his mouth was almost touching her ear. Though his voice was even and deep, this time it did not make her tingle with excitement. "Don't cry, Ms. Monroe. Instead of crying, why don't you try doing something meaningful with all of that money and good luck you're so blessed with?"

He dropped the arm that blocked her and Presley made a quick exit, blinking back tears and avoiding the looks of total strangers as she practically ran out of the lobby.

$\mathcal{D}$anny settled back into his red leather chair and pondered what he had just witnessed.

His father had sighed heavily after Hobie stormed out of the room, presumably to chase down Presley, and said, "To be young again." Then he'd picked up the book he had left there earlier and turned his attention to reading, leaving Danny to mull over the situation between his younger brother and Ms. Monroe.

Hobie's feelings for Presley had always been clear as glass, even when they were kids. Any possibility that Hobie had grown out of his boyhood crush was erased when Danny saw them together. He couldn't remember the last time he had seen Hobie so agitated.

"Hmm," his father turned the page on his book. He had taken to making quiet mumblings to himself as he went about his day. Little old man sounds, which in another time and place Danny might have found annoying, but he had come to appreciate.

His father spent more time with him during treatments than anyone else. It was a strain for his wife and kids to spend all their days with him, especially when he felt really sick. He didn't like them to see him so unwell. He wanted them to go to school and have a nice home life, not watch him deteriorate. Hobie came to see him whenever he could. When Danny went downhill after a treatment or just needed to talk, Hobie dropped everything and came to be with him. But Hobie was also handling the daily business of Barcom and Danny felt bad intruding on his time.

His father, on the other hand, had all the time in the world at his disposal. And, perhaps even more importantly, he had experience sitting bedside. Danny had grown to appreciate all the little ways his father tried to make him comfortable as well as the funny sounds he made under his breath.

A wave of nausea came over Danny and he closed his eyes, letting his head drop back against the chair.

"You all right?" his father asked. Nothing escaped him, even when Danny thought he wasn't paying attention.

Danny lifted a hand and waved his concern away weakly. "It'll pass."

The nausea did pass, usually. As did the fatigue and the dizziness. Still, Danny was growing weary of their continual return and was glad this run of medical intervention was nearing its end. Suzie's House was providing him with the best possible cancer treatment available. Sometimes, however, he wondered if it was all worth it. What if it didn't work? Would he be glad that he spent his last months of life fighting through the sickness that the treatment caused? Fleeting though they were, these thoughts still popped into his head occasionally.

The door clicked open. Danny's eyelids were so heavy he didn't want to open them. He didn't need to. He knew it was Hobie.

"What was that about?" he asked, trying to sound stronger

than he felt. It didn't work. His voice came out dry and scratchy.

"What?" Hobie responded.

"All that...*tension* between you two."

"Tension?" Hobie was pretending to not care. Again. One of his first and strongest defensive reactions.

"Oh, come on, Hobie," Danny continued, still with his eyes closed and head resting back.

"It's not the business deal," their father stated, as if he had read the situation and knew instinctually that the issue was personal.

"The business deal is fine," Hobie countered. Danny heard him slump onto the love seat with a sigh before continuing, "She's really headstrong and we don't have all of the details agreed upon yet..." his voice trailed off.

Danny opened one eye to take a look at his kid brother and was surprised at his troubled expression. Since their mother passed away Hobie had learned to hide behind his camera or run away to the far sides of the globe in order to avoid painful emotions. His current distress brought back memories of their childhood. Hobie a little out of place, a little uncertain, not knowing how to proceed. Haunted by feelings he didn't know how to express. Presley must really be getting to him.

"But it will all get worked out in the end. I will make sure of it," Hobie added.

"But it's personal," Danny said.

"What?"

"This thing between you and Presley Monroe," Danny insisted.

"Thing? There's not a thing," Hobie looked down at his hands in his lap.

Danny scoffed and closed the eye he'd had on his brother. He didn't have much patience for denial these days.

"Have you told her?" he asked.

Hobie's silence spoke volumes.

"You should tell her," Danny said, a little wistfully.

"I thought you said she was ruthless," Hobie said.

Danny shrugged. "A ruthless businesswoman maybe, but that's not an insurmountable problem…if you really like her."

Hobie scoffed, "*Like* her?" He laughed, a little wryly, before saying, "One minute she's charming and beautiful and the next minute she's throwing a fit. She's stubborn and spoiled and bossy, thinks the world revolves around her, and wears the most ridiculous, impractical shoes." Hobie paused for a breath then added, "She's impossible."

Danny grinned and peered at his brother through one eye again, trying to think of a suitable response. It was their father who came up with one.

With a grave shake of his head, Daniel Brent Senior said matter-of-factly, "The best ones always are."

CHAPTER 34

*P*resley and Jaxson sat reviewing her schedule for the upcoming day. Jaxson, positioned in the chair opposite her desk, had his tablet open and was busy touching and swiping the screen with his stylus. Presley gazed out her window at the Manhattan morning, distractedly tapping a pen on the armrest of her chair.

Still looking out the window, she blurted out, "I do good things, don't I?"

The question might have been unexpected, but it didn't surprise Jaxson. He was rarely surprised by anything.

"You do something good every day," he answered without looking up.

She turned her attention to him. "I do?"

Jaxson paused and returned her look, "Don't you?"

"What are you talking about?" She swiveled her chair away from the window and faced him.

He lifted his eyebrows at her request, "You want a list of specific good deeds?"

She nodded. Jaxson sighed tersely.

"Let's see," he made a show of thinking hard. Presley

scowled at him. "You employ me and you pay me well," he said brightly.

"That doesn't count."

"You employ a lot of people," he offered. She shook her head, dissatisfied, but Jaxson wouldn't let it go. "Employing people is important. People need jobs."

"That's not what I'm asking," she said, disappointed that there wasn't something more touching that he could point at to make her feel better, more than just throwing money at people.

The question stayed on her mind all morning.

"Would you say I do good things?" Presley asked Ronnie, Faye, and Grace over lunch later. Once again, she was disappointed at their blank faces.

"What do you mean, darling?" Faye asked, mildly bemused as she skillfully lifted a juicy pink piece of tuna sashimi with her chopsticks and popped it into her mouth.

"Like Ruby?" Ronnie asked.

Of course everyone's mind would leap to Ruby. She had been helping the poor, saving the animals, and cleaning up the earth since they were kids.

Flustered, Presley tried again, "I mean do I do anything to help people? Or animals? Or nature? Or anything, really?" Grace had a thought and opened her mouth to speak, but Presley was still struggling to explain, "And it can't be about money. Something truly good that doesn't involve me just transferring money somewhere." Grace closed her mouth, her thought squelched by this new direction.

Presley sighed heavily and pushed her California roll around with her chopsticks on its small, square plate.

"What is this about?" Ronnie asked.

Presley gave her sister a listless shrug. The topic was making her gloomy.

"Your existence is a gift to the world," Faye said with a flourish of her chopsticks.

This did not lift Presley's mood.

"What's the matter, Pres?" Ronnie eyed her carefully.

With another shrug Presley took a sip of her ice water. She hadn't told any of them about what Hobie had said to her two long days ago. She hadn't even told them about her ill fated visit to Suzie's House and running into Danny, or how terrible he had looked, or how horrible it had all ended with Hobie in the elevator.

The whole situation was tumbling around inside of her and there was something so personal, so awful, so shameful about it that she didn't want to tell her best friends. Not even her little sister.

"Are you having philanthropic urges now that you're getting older?" Grace teased.

She was referring to Presley's birthday, which was coming up. In a few short months she would mark another trip around the sun on this twirling ball of dirt and what, if anything, did she really have to show for it? She had a lot of material things, true. She had her family business, an honest to goodness dynasty, but one that she had inherited, not something she had built on her own. She had a decent family and a few good friends, this was also true. But Hobie's words still rang in her ears. Had she ever done anything meaning-ful–anything at all? Nothing came immediately to mind, which was an utterly depressing thought.

Her mother had given her a nickname when she was growing up, but only used it when Presley was being particu-larly morose, Miss Moody Blues. Presley smiled wryly at the memory. Staring at her partially eaten lunch she allowed her thoughts to wander into that childhood melancholic place. The sad part of her heart she suspected nobody else knew existed. When she looked up, Ronnie and the others were all staring at her.

"Aren't you?" Ronnie asked.

"Aren't I what?" Presley answered. Apparently she had stopped listening and missed a question.

"Meeting with Dad later?"

"Oh, right," Presley remembered. Jaxson had reminded her this morning. She had a 2 o'clock with Mr. Money Bags himself. Heaven knew she was not in the mood.

"Are you sure you're all right?" Ronnie's bright blue eyes were concerned.

Presley waved her off, but could sense Ronnie wasn't totally satisfied.

"I'm just preoccupied. This meeting with Dad and everything."

Presley wasn't completely lying. She wasn't looking forward to it. He had called her and asked for the meeting. More like demanded it. He hadn't wanted to give her any details over the phone, which made her uncomfortable, like a kid being called in to see the principal.

"Where is Ruby?" Faye had moved past Presley's search for meaning in her life and on to the one friend of theirs who was always doing good.

"She's delivering dogs," Grace said with a grin. "It seems all of that work that she did with Hobie taking pictures of the shelter dogs got a lot of attention. Now she's adopting dogs out to new owners all over the country."

"How marvelous," Faye responded, eyeing Presley for her reaction.

They were all looking at Presley…again. Every one of the women in her life knew something was going on between her and Hobie, but she had nothing positive to report. She averted her eyes back to her beleaguered California roll and refused to look up until they had moved on to another topic of conversation.

Nothing about her early morning workout, her in house mani-pedi taken before she left her penthouse for the office, her busy morning at work commanding everyone and everything that came before her, not even her lunch out with friends helped. Nothing could burst the bubble of depression that had encircled her since she left Hobie in the elevator.

Tortured by the memory of his tone when he had told her not to cry, she couldn't let go of how his voice had been laced with scorn, barely audible as he spoke, yet present in his hardened features and the glittering enmity in his eyes.

He hated her. Everything that she stood for disgusted him. All of the moments she thought they had shared and even believed to be evidence that he was attracted to her meant nothing. That much had been clear. And that knowledge was eating Presley up from the inside out as she moved through her day like a robot.

"And how's my Pumpkin today?" Mack Monroe entered her office like Poseidon riding a wave, except her father's wave was made of pure power and charm and went with him no matter if he was on land or water.

Presley smiled thinly and leaned forward when he approached to let him kiss her on the cheek. "Fine, Dad, how are you?"

She leaned back in her chair and assessed him. Though he was undoubtedly aging gracefully, he was still aging and she couldn't help but worry over his health.

"I'm fantastic," his blue eyes sparkled then clouded as they looked more deeply into hers. "But you're not. What's the matter?"

"Nothing's the matter."

He grunted. "I think I know when something is the matter with my daughter."

"Nothing important is the matter." She saw he didn't believe her, so she clarified, "Nothing for you to worry about."

He waited a few moments to see if she was going to elaborate. When she didn't, he gave her a warning look as if to say she had better not be keeping important secrets from him. But he didn't push the issue as he settled into one of the chairs placed next to the floor to ceiling windows that overlooked Manhattan. She joined him.

"I spoke to Drew Beeker yesterday," her father said, his eyes still focused out the windows.

Presley bristled. Why had he spoken with the president of their European hotels division? She nodded as if Drew and her father were old friends who spoke all of the time, which they weren't as far as she knew.

"How is Drew?" she asked.

He flicked his eyes to her, "You don't know?"

She shifted uncomfortably in her chair. Had something happened to Drew or their European hotels that she should know about? Having been distracted the past few days, she couldn't say with certainty that nothing had happened. She wished Jaxson was in the room and could tip her off, but she'd sent him for refreshments.

"Has something happened?" she asked.

"One of the most important projects Mack Industries has ever had and you don't know?" His tone was full of admonishment.

Presley's face burned with the reprimand, but she was still confused. The project at Villa Pallotta vineyards was big, but it most certainly wasn't the most important thing Mack Industries had ever taken on.

Her head was too full for this back and forth, she bit the bullet and asked, "What are you talking about?"

Her father leaned towards her chair and pressed his

pointing finger into the pure white silk upholstery next to where her hand rested. "This partnership with Barcom is important to me. I thought I stressed this to you."

Presley's brow pinched together as she tried to think of what might have gone wrong with the Count's project. She came up blank.

"Everything is going according to plan with Barcom, Dad." It pained her to even say the name of Hobie's company, but she successfully disguised her feelings. "We just met with the Count and Countess a few nights ago and everything is on track..." she paused as she could tell this was not addressing his concerns. "What is it that you're worried about, exactly?"

Her father leaned back into his chair, though he looked anything but comfortable. He turned his attention out the window, but didn't seem to be focusing on the view, rather he seemed to be looking for an answer. Presley watched him with growing concern. What did she not know about this project? What was going on?

Her father pressed his lips together and sighed, shifting his eyes away from the window to focus on the floor in front of his feet. She wanted to speak, to demand that he tell her what was on his mind, but she knew better than to press Mack Monroe for an answer. She watched and waited.

When he spoke his voice sounded worn, "I owe him."

She wasn't sure she had heard him correctly. "What?"

He lifted his eyes to hers, so blue, so sharp, even with age, and repeated himself, "I owe him."

"You owe who?"

"Daniel Brent."

Her stomach twisted at the mention of the Brents. She cocked her head, not understanding. "What do you owe him?"

"Everything."

"Everything?" Her voice rose a little in surprise.

He leaned back in his chair, the shadow of an apology in his eyes as he tried to explain, "When we were building our business in the very beginning, Daniel and I..." Something like a smile crossed his face at the memory, "Seems like two lifetimes ago now." Seeing she was impatient, he cleared his throat and continued, "You see, we worked together, all the time. Everything we did in that first store, and I mean all of it, was Daniel's idea. I worked hard, I'm not saying I didn't work hard. But Daniel...well, he worked better. Smarter. I've never admitted this to anyone, Presley, but without Daniel Brent I wouldn't have been an early success." He watched her face, waiting for a reaction, a comment. When there was none, he kept going, "And without that early success, I wouldn't have had anything to build on. There would have been no store chain, no company, no international invest-ments, no Mack Industries." He waved his arm around to encompass her penthouse Manhattan office. "None of this would exist."

Presley followed his gesture with her eyes, taking in the luxurious white on white office, the sleek furnishings, the pale blue Faberge egg that she kept on her desk. She looked back to her father and shook her head, "Dad, I don't think-"

"You don't know, Presley," he cut her off. "I know. I was there and I know."

She nodded respectfully.

He sighed and looked down into his lap for a long minute before continuing, "When Suzie got sick...I should have been there more for him. I was never any good at that kind of thing. Neither was your mother...but you know that." He caught her eye and again she saw an apology on his face. "I didn't do everything I could have. I was so intent on the busi-ness. On making money." He shook his head in disdain for the man he once was. "I could have been a better friend to him…to Suzie…to those boys. And now Danny's sick, really sick, did you know that?"

Presley's stomach clenched. She swallowed hard and said, "I do, yes."

He reached out and patted her hand, his own hands so large over hers, yet lighter somehow. Older.

"I don't know what I would do if anything ever happened to you or your sister or brother," he said, his eyes wet. "It's heartbreaking and I…well, I don't know what to do for Daniel now. I can't make up for what I haven't done in the past….I just want to do everything in my power to…to help."

A thought struck Presley, "Is Barcom in financial trouble?"

He thought for a moment and shook his head, "I doubt it."

"You didn't…cheat him out of money, did you Dad?"

"No, no, nothing like that. It's not about the money at all. I wasn't the best person I could be. I'm still not. That's why I need you to help me."

This request from her father, one of the richest and most powerful men in the world, was unsettling. Midday Manhattan sunshine streamed through the windows and bathed them in an ethereal glow. An other worldly light. Presley felt an unseen pressure pushing against her head and her chest.

She cleared her throat to clear the lump in her throat, "What is it you want me to do?"

He smiled sheepishly. "I don't know exactly. That's part of what you need to figure out, Pumpkin."

CHAPTER 35

Tasked with righting the wrongs of her father's past, Presley found the rest of her daily schedule nothing more than a distraction. She dismissed everything on her plate that wasn't a necessity, which she decided meant virtually everything.

"Shall I reschedule these for tomorrow?" Jaxson asked.

"No, I don't want to have to think about any of this for as long as possible. Two weeks at least."

"Okay," his expression remained even, but Presley detected a note of concern.

"I'm fine, Jaxson. I just need to focus on Villa Pallotta and the Count's project without any distraction."

"Is there anything I can do to help?"

She thought about it for a few moments, tapping her fingernails on the smooth surface of her desk. She had already come to terms with the Count as far as the finances, but she knew she hadn't really thrown her support behind the environmental aspect of the deal. Being that this was the one piece that was most important to Hobie and Barcom, that's where she would start.

"Get me a meeting with Hobie Brent…and Megan," she said, trying not to betray any emotion with the request.

"Right away," Jaxson stood and left the room, his cell phone already up to his ear.

Presley took a deep breath. Her heart was pounding in her chest, her palms sweaty, as if she expected Hobie to come running through the door of her office the instant Jaxson reached his secretary. Silly…but still, the thought of it made her stomach tremble with anticipation.

"Knock, knock," a man's voice called through her half open door.

Presley's heart leapt in her chest and she froze where she stood, staring at the door. When her brother appeared in the doorway instead of Hobie, it took her a few moments to gather her composure.

"What's up, sis?" he rambled into her office and flopped into the chair facing her desk. When she didn't say anything he gave her a crooked smile. "What's the matter?"

"Nothing," she sat down.

He chuckled and rubbed his chin with his hand. "Did I scare you? You look like you just got caught sneaking out of the house after you'd been grounded."

"I never snuck out of the house when I was grounded," she retorted.

He sighed and gave her a smirk, "I know." His eyes twinkled as he teased, "Did you ever get grounded?"

Her little brother, the youngest of the three of them, looked disheveled, like he'd been out partying all night and just gotten up. Probably because he'd been out partying all night and had just gotten up.

"What are you doing here?" she asked, wanting to shift the attention anywhere but her emotions.

"Can't a guy come visit his big sister?"

"Yes, of course," she smiled. "But usually that guy has a reason to come all the way in to the office."

He stuck out his bottom lip and shook his head, "Naw, just wanted to say hi, see how you're doing." Presley narrowed her eyes and Pete raised his palms up, deflecting her suspicions, "Seriously, no agenda. Just in the neighborhood."

"Okay, well, I'm kind of busy right now."

Pete glanced around the empty office. "Are you?"

"I just have a lot on my mind. I have a lot of things to think about and plan..." her voice trailed off. She didn't really want to get into the whole Barcom, Hobie, change the world conversation with Pete. He could be a little cynical and her emotions were already so raw.

He slapped his hands on his knees and stood up, "I understand. How about I come by another day. I'll take you to lunch?" He pointed at her with his finger like it was a gun.

She agreed they would have lunch soon as she bustled him out the door. She needed time alone right now, time to think.

Presley pulled open a drawer on her sleek desk and took out a brand new legal sized pad of paper and a fat, black writing pen. Some of her best ideas had been written out by hand while she was alone.

She pressed the end of the pen and it made a satisfying click. Then she swiveled her chair so she was facing the brilliant Manhattan view and started writing down every question and concern she had about the sustainability aspect of the Count's project. As she wrote, not only questions popped into her mind, but ideas too. Ideas on what she could do to make the project something that would make her father proud by pleasing Daniel Brent.

Writing furiously on the page, the emotions that had been tangled up in her core since her last interaction with Hobie, pulling her into a pit and making it hard for her to eat or think straight, all began to unravel and rise-up, up, up, into her chest. With their rise a sense of purpose and excitement rose, too. She felt lighter, brighter, and full of hope.

As the black ink flowed and her cursive filled the white paper from top to bottom and edge to edge, Presley dared think that maybe, just maybe, she could prove to Hobie that she wasn't just your average, every day, spoiled rotten rich girl. And if she could prove it to him, maybe she could prove it to herself.

The next morning dawned magnificent. Her high spirits carried her through her routine like she was the lightest of feathers dancing on a happy summer breeze. Jaxson had wrangled an appointment with Hobie and Megan that would begin at 10:00 am and Presley was there well before 9:00 am to ensure she had all of her thoughts put together.

Dressed to the nines she wore a stylish Herrera sheath dress in vibrant coral and a pair of bright white heels. Today she wore her hair down to match her free flowing mood and for the final touch she had chosen her favorite Tiffany pearls as a kind of good luck charm.

"You're glowing," Jaxson said as he placed a tray with coffee and croissants on her desk, nodding with approval at her ensemble.

She smiled. She had asked him to meet her at the office instead of at her penthouse, feeling the need to center herself around her feelings instead of her schedule. This meant she had dressed herself without any advice from him, giving more weight to his compliment.

"I'm in creative mode," she told him, taking a scrumptious bite out of one of the croissants.

"You don't have anything until your 10 o'clock."

"Good," she munched as she spoke and pulled her notepad out from her desk drawer, reviewing her handwritten notes with interest. "I need to brainstorm more ideas before that meeting."

"Shall I step outside?"

She nodded, taking another bite of the flaky, buttery goodness, "Please."

Jaxson moved efficiently to the door and paused, looking back at her. "Do you want music?"

She grinned at him. Jaxson was amazing. He always knew exactly what to do. Her mouth too full to speak, she gave him a happy nod. He turned to a discreet console set up on a shelf on the far wall of her office and touched a few glowing buttons.

"What are you in the mood for?" he asked. Still chewing, she gave him a mischievous grin. After barely a moment's hesitation he responded, "Prince it is." With a flourish he pressed a few more buttons and her office filled with the famous artist's funky music.

The first song, "U Got The Look", had her feet tapping as she finished her croissant and sipped her coffee while reading through her notes.

Her biggest question about sustainability was how to make sure it was implemented in a way that was...well... sustainable. Meaning she didn't want to set something up just for show. She wanted to make sure it was set up to last and not leave the project floundering after five years. And she had decided that she would bite the bullet and spend the extra money if necessary to make sure that happened.

By the time "When Doves Cry" came on Presley had completed her review of the business side of things and moved on to some of the other general do-good ideas she had come up with. Among them was a much larger donation to Suzie's House and a plan for a shopping trip to pick up more Felin Putole artwork and have it delivered to Danny's wing. This idea was one of the most exciting. For a few moments she entertained the idea of delivering the paintings herself. In her mind's eye she could see the pleasure in Danny's eyes as she unveiled the artwork. It felt good to know that Hobie would know about the event, perhaps even witness it, and have to look at her in a new light.

She stood up to stretch her legs. One of Prince's classics, "Kiss", ended and she moved to stand next to the window and take in the full view as the next song began. The unmistakable organ chord of her all time favorite Prince song filled the room and she spoke out loud, matching the singer in his intro, "Dearly Beloved…"

Chords changed and the music swelled. Presley spoke along with Prince, performing the introduction towards the window like she was in front of an audience. "Let's Go Crazy" always made her want to move.

The beat dropped and she swayed her hips to match the rhythm. Lost in the sound and in her soaring mood, she shook her shoulders, flipped her hair and grimaced like a rock star. When Prince declared that she should go crazy she was fully engrossed, dancing and singing along as if she was standing next to him on stage. Eyes closed, derriere wiggling, strutting back and forth to the rhythm, Presley let loose and channeled one of the greatest artists of all time.

A loud, cartoon-like sound of someone clearing their throat cut through the music. Followed closely by a woman's voice exclaiming, "Oh!"

Presley whirled around to see Jaxson frozen in an awkward pause at her office door and none other than Megan standing just behind him.

Red faced, Presley tried to catch her breath and compose herself. The song continued to pump through the room adding to the strangeness of the moment. Jaxson didn't seem to know what to do, which was unlike him. Presley glanced meaningfully at the console and he hopped to it, turning the music off with the press of a button.

Silence was even more oppressively bizarre than Prince's lyrics.

"Good morning," Presley said calmly as she smoothed her hair back from her face and ushered Megan into her office.

Megan gracefully took the chair Presley offered and accepted Jaxson's offer to bring in some coffee. As he left, he looked over his shoulder and gave Presley a cheeky grin.

"I didn't mean to be early," Megan said as she took in the luxury decor.

Presley waved her hand in the air as if shooing away a fly, "That's not a problem. I wasn't..." she was about to say 'busy' then realized how obvious that statement was and decided to leave the sentence unfinished.

Megan smiled and Presley had to admit it was a beautiful sight. Full of sweetness and good humor, her smile added to her already stunning beauty. Presley sighed inwardly. She could see why Hobie was attracted to the young woman.

Megan leaned forward and spoke in a conspiratorial whisper, "Prince is the best."

Presley laughed, "Yes, yes he is." She relaxed into her chair. Maybe it was the dancing or maybe it was her decision to put all of her energy and support behind the Count's project, but she felt all warm and fuzzy inside, like everything was going to be okay. Better than okay. "I'm looking forward to this meeting, Megan," she said. "As soon as your boss gets here we can really dig into the meat of it."

Megan's smile slipped. "Oh, I thought you knew. He's not coming."

Warm and fuzzy dropped to instant chill. Presley managed to keep her face relaxed as Jaxson entered the room with a coffee tray. She looked to him for the answer to her question, "Mr. Brent won't be joining us?"

"No, I found out just before Miss Adams arrived. I was going to let you know when we came in..." here Jaxson stopped talking. They all knew what had happened when they came in.

Disappointment sank in and for a brief moment Presley considered cancelling the whole thing. The meeting. The push for more of what her father wanted in this project. Everything.

"Don't be ridiculous," she muttered, angry at her lack of fortitude to proceed without Hobie present.

Megan leaned closer as if to hear what she had said, "I'm sorry?"

"Nothing," Presley answered with determination. Giving the younger woman a reassuring nod she continued, "We will have to forge ahead without him, I suppose. I have a few questions and then," she took the coffee Jaxson offered and raised it as if to salute Megan, "I would like you to explain everything you know about the Villa Pallotta project and how we can set it up as the most forward thinking, sustainable, eco-friendly collaboration of our time."

Megan's eyes sparkled with this encouragement and she proceeded to answer all of Presley's questions with whole hearted explanations. The young woman took such care to give her all the details and address all of her concerns, that Presley couldn't help but be impressed. No wonder Hobie had been so keen to bring her in on this project.

Suddenly, understanding jolted through the pit of Presley's stomach. Hobie hadn't brought Megan in because they were dating. He had brought her in because she was brilliant and exactly what they needed to achieve success. Blinded by jealousy and insecurity she had discounted Megan's abilities and dismissed her ideas. She had been such a fool. So what if they were dating? Presley had lost sight of the bigger picture because of it and that was her own fault.

"Do you have any other questions?" Megan inquired.

Presley leaned back in her chair and considered Megan from her new perspective. Not only as a sustainability expert, but as a woman who she had misjudged and labeled. She would not make that mistake again.

"I want you to tell me what you think I should know about running a sustainable company. I'm here to learn from you," Presley said.

Megan paused then her face lit up. "Thank you, Ms. Monroe. I hope you know how much I appreciate this opportunity."

"I'm grateful to you for helping me understand."

Pleased with the praise, the young woman began, "Well, one of the first things I think is important to know, especially for someone in your position, someone who has financial interests in any sustainability project, is that, by and large, most companies who undertake the changes necessary to 'go green'," she made air quotation marks with her fingers, "find that not only do they see a full return of their initial investment sooner rather than later, but within three to five years their costs are significantly lower and they are making a higher profit overall. And that profit is, well, it's sustainable."

Presley considered this information for a moment, then asked, "So, you're saying that we can, in essence, have our cake and eat it, too?"

Megan nodded enthusiastically, "That's what I'm saying."

Before Presley could relay the pleasure this gave her, there was a knock on the office door and it pushed open. Her mind flew to Hobie. Her stomach did a flip-flop and she stood nervously. He had come after all.

"Knock, knock," Pete said as he stepped into the room.

Not Hobie. Presley was flustered, somewhere between disappointment and relief.

"Pete–" she started, but Pete had seen Megan and his attention was zeroed in on the extremely attractive young woman who was not his sister.

"Well, hello," Pete practically loped over and extended his hand to Megan, all smiles. "I'm Pete." He laid his second hand over hers to avoid letting go and cocked his head, "We've met, I think…Aspen?"

Megan smiled back, "Yes, I think we did. At the fundraising party."

"Right, you were there with Hobie." He made a face of mock despair, "Don't tell me he's your boyfriend. It will break my heart."

Megan giggled. Pete had a natural charm that made him popular with the opposite sex, sometimes too popular. Presley was about to inform him that they were in the middle of a business meeting and he was interrupting, when Megan answered his question and shocked her back into silence.

"No, no, no, nothing like that," Megan said. "We are strictly professional. He's just my boss."

CHAPTER 36

The moment Faye saw Presley she knew something was wrong.

"What is it? You look horrible!" she exclaimed as she rushed past the maid who had let Presley into the foyer to get to her friend.

Presley shook her head, unable to speak, her face screwed into a grimace. Faye had seen that look before when they were girls and Presley got hurt on the soccer field. Not wanting to cry, but fighting the tears back was an especially unattractive expression. After childhood Faye had only seen that look once on her friend's face, when she found out her ex-husband was cheating on her.

Faye put her arm around Presley's shoulders and guided her into the parlor, waving frantically at the maid behind Presley's back and stage whispering, "Brandy, get us some brandy."

Presley sort of crumpled onto the gold silk damask sofa and took the crystal glass of brandy offered by the hurried maid. Faye took one, too, gesturing that the girl should leave the bottle on the glass coffee table.

The brandy burned the back of her tongue and took her breath away for a few seconds. She made sure to give Presley a moment after sipping hers, then Faye asked, "What in heaven's name is the matter?" When Presley still couldn't answer, Faye narrowed her eyes. She knew what was the matter, or rather who. "It's that beast, isn't it?"

Presley looked up, her eyes wet with tears she would not allow to fall, and shook her head vehemently.

"I don't believe you," Faye exclaimed. "He's done something, hasn't he?"

Presley covered her mouth with her hand and shook her head again, her eyes pleading.

This was ridiculous. Exasperated, Faye went off, "What in the world are you doing worrying about that horrible man? He's not worth your time, darling." She scowled at Presley's mute reaction. Picking up her phone, Faye declared, "I'm calling Ronnie. Maybe she knows what happened."

"No," Presley's hand flew towards Faye's cell phone and fluttered madly to stop her. "Ronnie's in the middle of a fashion show. Besides, nothing happened."

Faye put her cell down on the coffee table with a sigh. Patience was not one of her virtues. "Then tell me what's the matter."

"I was wrong," Presley blurted out. When the declaration wasn't followed by a stream of uncontrollable blubbering she seemed to gain confidence and the story flowed out of her. "Hobie isn't dating Megan. She told me herself. And the reason he's been leaving unexpectedly is…is…" here her eyes welled up with tears again. Faye put her hand on Presley's and patted it. Presley took a deep breath to retain control and said, "It's Danny."

"Danny?" Faye had to think for a moment to catch up. "Danny Brent?"

Presley nodded. "He's undergoing treatment for his cancer and…and…oh, he looks awful, Faye."

"You've seen him?"

Pursing her lips gravely, Presley nodded and took another sip of her brandy.

Faye's heart sank. Danny Brent's illness was a sad subject, but she never expected to come this close to knowing the details. A part of her recoiled at the idea of Danny on his deathbed. Another part of her leaned in for more information.

"Where did you see him?"

"At their cancer research place, Suzie's House."

Faye nodded soberly before being overcome with curiosity, "And why did you see him?"

Presley pursed her lips together again. It was a tense look, but a hundred times better than the 'trying not to cry' ugliness of a few minutes before.

"I had a…meeting with Hobie," she began, hesitated, then waved her hand around like she was erasing her thought out of the air, "It doesn't matter. What does matter is I want to do something nice for him."

Faye blinked at her friend, not certain what she meant. "For whom?"

"Danny…and Hobie…and all of them. The whole research center. Something really, really nice, Faye. Something wonderful that will…I don't know…something that's thoughtful. A gesture. Not just giving a little money."

Faye peered at her friend. There was more going on here than Presley wanted to reveal, obviously. However, there were two rather unusual points that stood out to her as most important.

First, Presley Monroe had an honest to goodness love interest in Hobie Brent, something Faye had not witnessed in years. She was delighted for her friend and happy to be in on the secret, even if Presley hadn't yet realized it herself yet.

Second, and this was perhaps the most remarkable, Presley had come to her for help.

Faye smiled, genuinely thrilled to do just that. She patted Presley's hand again and said, "What can I do for you, darling? Name it."

CHAPTER 37

It would take three full days to purchase all of the artwork for Suzie's House, plus have it suitably prepared, packed and sent for delivery. Presley was grateful she had enlisted Faye's help to complete this task. There was nobody, absolutely nobody, who knew how to drop cash on high ticket items in a rush like Faye.

"That one, and that one…and that one, you definitely want that one," she told Presley as she pointed at Felin Putole's paintings.

They were in the painter's studio where his newest work was placed on the floor leaning against the walls as if to dry. Huge canvases, each one brilliant and unique, were still larger than life even if not quite ready for display. Unframed, rough around the edges, they were not yet available to the public. However, Faye knew the artist personally and had convinced him to let them have first pick.

"It's for a wonderful cause, darling," she had crooned into her cell phone in the back of the limo as they made their way to the studio. Felin had eventually agreed, as everyone did when Faye insisted.

"They know my work already?" Felin asked from the corner of the room where he was smoking a cigarette and watching the two women shop.

"Yes," Presley said. "There is already one piece of yours in one of the rooms. But I think it would lift everyone's spirits to have more displayed throughout the center."

Felin seemed pleased with this, which meant he wasn't completely put out about them invading his studio and demanding to go on a shopping spree. He continued to take slow, thoughtful drags from his cigarette as she and Faye 'oohed' and 'aahed' over each glorious canvas.

Presley had already put Jaxson to work on her second phase of assisting Suzie's House. This one was purely financial, a 50 million dollar donation. Nobody could say that was just pocket change. And even with the money she had available at her fingertips, it still took some doing to transfer 50 million dollars in cash. Jaxson had been delighted at the challenge.

"When do you want this completed?" he had asked her as he tapped the information busily into his tablet.

"As soon as possible. Tomorrow?"

His eyebrows lifted in a an almost childlike surprise. As if she'd just told him Santa Claus would be coming to visit tomorrow.

"Is that going to be a problem?" she asked.

He paused for a millisecond then shook his head, "No, I don't think it will be a problem. But I need to get started on it right now."

"Go," she waved him out of her office.

At the door, he turned and asked, "Do you want this to be in Mack Industrie's name or yours?"

"No name," she said quickly.

"Anonymous?"

She nodded, a smile that she could not control spreading rapidly across her face. "Anonymous."

"Anonymous it is."

A warm fuzzy feeling was growing exponentially inside of her and had been ever since she fought back a small bout of overwhelm and regret in Faye's penthouse. The minute Pete had taken Megan out to lunch after interrupting their meeting, Presley had felt a barrage of emotions. Now that her good deeds were underway she felt a lot better. She wanted to attribute it to the fact that she was running around like Daddy Warbucks and throwing money at good causes with no thought to profit margins or shareholder meetings, but she knew there was a little more to it than that.

Hobie and Megan were not an item. And from the way Megan reacted to Pete's invitation to lunch, Presley could tell that Megan and Hobie were never going to be an item. Hobie Brent was single. Not only that, he had been single when he took pictures of her in the snow, and when he took her on their picnic in Central Park. A little rush of butterflies flew through her stomach every time she thought about that fact.

They were fluttering in her stomach still as they rode back from Felin's studio. Faye had dropped back into the comfortable leather of the limo seat and she was softly snoring, wiped out from shopping. Presley watched the traffic and buildings go by outside the window, thinking about how fun it was going to be to show up with the shipment of paintings and surprise Danny and the staff at Suzie's House. She liked this, being the good guy. It was uplifting.

A buzz from her purse interrupted her thoughts. Remembering that she had put her cell on private while in Felin's studio, she dug it out of her purse and saw instantly that she had missed a call from Hobie. The butterflies in her stomach roared into action and she almost cried out in excitement, but caught herself just in time.

Glancing at Faye to see if she was still sleeping, Presley touched the screen to listen to her messages. Sure enough, the first one was his incredible voice.

"Hi, Presley..." Just the sound of him saying her name sent a tiny shiver along her shoulders and she had the crazy thought that she would never delete this message. "I just talked to Megan about your meeting. Sorry I couldn't make it, by the way, something came up..." Presley uttered a sympathetic sigh. Danny was probably not doing well. "Anyway, Megan told me how open and enthusiastic you were about...well, everything," he paused and when he continued, Presley's heart melted at the sweetness in his tone. "And I just wanted to say thanks. Thank you for committing to making the Villa Pallotta project something we can all be really proud of....I appreciate it...I should say, we all appreciate it. And, um, well, I guess I'll see you soon."

With another swift glance at Faye snoring, she played the message again, luxuriating in his voice.

A warm tingle moved through her legs and arms, it had been quite a workout going through all of Felin's work at his huge art studio, but Presley knew the feeling was more than just physical. It was a sense of satisfaction, the pleasant knowledge that she was in the middle of a success story of her own making. There was not a thought in her mind to return Hobie's call. She would arrange to meet with him after her good deeds were in place and she could look him in the eye without flinching.

She placed her cell phone back in her purse. No need to continue listening to Hobie's message over and over again, because his words were running on a loop in her head. She sank into the sweetness of her success and smiled quietly out the window.

Two days later Presley met the delivery team at the door to the lobby of Suzie's House. Flawless in a pair of white

Palazzo pants and a wide striped blue and white Ralph Lauren shirt, she relished the moment. There had been rain the night before and the bright summer morning was fresh and full of possibility.

With the flourish of a skilled realtor she pushed the double doors open and stepped confidently into the lobby. The same lobby where she had so recently tried to blend in and been discovered by little Nita and her purple balloon.

Today she had no desire to blend.

Presley walked with purpose to the front desk where the same pale blonde receptionist and a different coworker watched with big eyes. Followed by a dozen burly moving men who were carrying six huge canvases between them, each carefully wrapped and boxed in specially built boxes, Presley knew she was quite a sight.

When she reached the desk she pulled her white framed Chanel sunglasses off for dramatic effect and said, "We have a delivery for Daniel Brent, 7th floor."

As the young women hurried to look up the details, Presley scanned the lobby. Tapping her bottom lip with the earpiece of her sunglasses, she mused about the last time she was here. What a fiasco. Today would be different.

"Um," the pale blonde was looking confusedly at some hidden computer screen. "Did you say Daniel Brent?"

"Yes," Presley's brow puckered.

"Junior?"

Presley waved away the question with a flick of her sunglasses, "Junior, Senior, or Hobie Brent," saying his name made her feel even more confident. "It doesn't matter, darling." Now she was channeling Faye, "I'm sure my assistant scheduled it."

Flustered, the pale blonde's cheeks reddened, "Yes, it's just–"

"Come, come," Presley interrupted. "We don't have all

day. I'm paying these men by the hour." She turned and gave the foreman of the movers a wink to reassure him that she had the situation under control.

"Of course, I see there is a delivery scheduled. But I think you might–"

"No thinking required," Presley interrupted again, hardening her smile so the pale blonde knew she meant business. "If there are any problems, please send someone to the 7th floor. Otherwise, we'll be on our way."

With that she ushered the movers to the elevators so they could begin their ascent.

The ride up was magnificent. Her stomach twirling with happy anticipation, her heart bursting. As the floors ticked away under them Presley, and the two movers carrying one of the biggest paintings, rose silently. Presley stood at the front, staring at the closed doors and trying not to giggle at her own excitement. It was difficult. She was flushed with the thrill of her big, generous, splashy gift.

When the elevator doors swished open they weren't met by a group of applauding patients, which was, frankly, a little disappointing. There were two nurses who gave her a sideways glance as she held the door open for the movers, but they moved quickly on their way.

Presley had envisioned a little more grandiose of an entry, but tried to brush it off. Jaxson had arranged this delivery, but he had kept the details and her name out of it per her instructions. Of course nobody was expecting her or the expensive artwork she was gifting.

She smiled sheepishly at the foreman as he emerged from his elevator ride with two more paintings and their carriers. "That's why it's called a surprise," she said. He looked confused. Realizing he had no idea what she was talking about, she tried to say something more sensible, "It's room 722B. Just around the corner."

Her eyes switched impatiently between the two elevators. The glowing numbers above them indicated that they were stopping at several floors between here and the lobby. Ill at ease, she wondered how long it would take for them to go all the way back to the lobby and all the way back up with the remaining movers and their paintings.

"Maybe I'll just go check on the room, make sure it's open," she said. The foreman shrugged his indifference. "As soon as the others get up here, go down this hallway," she walked swiftly in the direction she was describing as she continued to explain over her shoulder. "Then to the right. 722B." She didn't know if the foreman nodded his understanding or not, she was on her way.

With every step, elation rose in her heart. She was near giddy with anticipation as she passed the familiar photos on the bulletin board, noting Sugar Pop's silly little face as she saw it out of the corner of her eye. Her mind raced with scenarios. Would Danny be in his room? Would Hobie be there with him? No matter what she encountered she was so convinced of the positive response she would receive that what she did see when she strolled through the open door of 722B didn't register at first.

The room was empty.

No people…no furniture…no red reading chair. No IV stand where there should be a lamp, no Felin Putole on the wall. Nothing.

Completely and utterly empty. Void of any sign of life. No Hobie. No Danny. What could have happened?

The sight of the abandoned room had stopped her in her tracks. But the terrible possibilities that flooded her mind sent Presley's soaring heart plummeting into the pit of her stomach.

CHAPTER 38

The wrong room. She must have walked into the wrong room. Presley stepped back to find the brushed gold plate attached to the outside of the door. It read '722B'.

A gasp of dismay escaped her as she lifted her hand to her chest. Eyes flying around the room she searched for an answer. The pale blonde receptionist's reluctance to let her and her movers go to the 7th floor flashed into her mind. And there was the fact that Hobie had cancelled last minute and not come with Megan to their last meeting. The sweet tone of his voice in his voicemail. Had he sounded sweet…or sad?

"Oh no," she said to the empty room, clutching her Ralph Lauren shirt at her heart. "What happened to Danny?" Hot tears sprung into her eyes, the room seemed to spin around her body. What could she do? This was horrible.

"Excuse me," a man's voice came from behind.

Presley turned to find Hobie and Danny's father looking small and rumpled and bewildered at her presence.

"Oh! Mr. Brent, I'm so sorry," she stammered her apologies at intruding.

"Hello Presley. I didn't know it was you," he gave her a weak smile as he wiped his eyes with a pocket handkerchief, like the kind her grandfather used to carry.

She was at a loss for words, so deeply saddened that her own tears swelled and dropped from her eyes.

Mr. Brent noticed and concern filled his eyes, "Whatever is the matter? Are you all right?"

Still choked up, she swept her hand behind her at the empty room.

Mr. Brent followed her gesture and took in the space. "Well, take heart. He has moved to a better place."

It was too much. Presley dropped her face into her hands and let out a small sob. This was awful. Here she'd been so wrapped up in buying things and donating money she hadn't even been in touch with Hobie or his family enough to know that Danny had passed away. No amount of money in the world could make up for that.

"Presley?"

She dropped her hands to see Hobie walking up behind his father. His eyes caught hers and filled with concern at the state she was in, just like his father's had. It was so kind of him to be worried about her at a time like this.

"Oh, Hobie," she managed to say even as her bottom lip trembled terribly.

"What's the matter?" he stepped forward and reached out, taking her by the elbow and looking at his father for an explanation.

"I don't know, son," Mr. Brent said.

Presley blinked at them both and sniffed, then said, as if it was obvious, "Danny."

"What about me?" Danny appeared from behind Hobie.

Presley's mouth dropped open at the sight of him–alive.

Not only alive, but looking much better than he had looked the other day. She stared at him in shock as all of the Brent men shared puzzled looks with each other.

Presley shook her head, trying to grasp the new reality where Danny Brent was, indeed, alive and she was just some crazy lady crying in an empty room. She pointed at the empty room as some kind of proof and stammered, "I–I–um…you weren't here and…I…"

"Yeah, Mr. Brilliant here thought it would be a great day to go out and take some pictures with the dogs," Danny slapped Hobie on the shoulder.

"The dogs?" she asked, befuddled by everything that was happening.

"It's Rehab Dog Day," Hobie explained to her. Then to his brother, "And it is a beautiful day, just a little muddy from the rain."

"My allergies," Mr. Brent complained as he wiped his handkerchief across his watering eyes.

"Oh…" she said with sudden understanding. Everything was starting to fall into place. But still, the empty room. "Your room…?"

All of the Brent men looked into the yawning maw of 722B then back at her.

Danny was the first to understand her confusion. "Yes! Everything's gone. I'm going home!" he replied brightly. His charming smile, the one she remembered, filled his face and she couldn't help but smile back. Though she decided not to tell him she had just thought he was dead.

"That's great!" she said, truly delighted at this news.

"So, is there something wrong? You seemed upset," Hobie moved slightly closer to her. The protectiveness in his body language was so kind…so masculine.

She opened her mouth to explain, but Hobie's attention, as well as his brother's and father's, shifted suddenly to something over her shoulder. She turned to see what they were looking at just as the last movers carrying the last boxed painting between them turned the corner. Led by the foreman, her delivery team was taking up most of the wide hallway.

"Where do you want these, Ms. Monroe?" the foreman called out to her in a thick New York accent.

She turned back to the Brents whose perplexed gazes were now back on her.

"Well, see, I was trying to surprise you," she said, feeling suddenly insecure about her idea.

"What are these?" Danny stepped over to the first box where the movers were placing it carefully on the floor so it leaned against the wall.

"They're Felin Putole's," she answered.

Danny's eyes flew open in surprise. "What? All of them?" He looked down the hallway at the five other boxes.

Hobie was watching her, waiting for an answer, as Danny and Mr. Brent's attention shifted to the paintings.

"I thought...I knew you liked his work and I thought I would bring some more. You know, to brighten the place up," she glanced up and down the hallway where a small audience of nurses, doctors, and patients had gathered on either side to see what the commotion was about.

Danny let out a great guffaw of laughter, "That's amazing, Presley!"

Mr. Brent gave her a polite nod of approval and added, "That's kind of you, my dear. Very kind."

Pleased, Presley smiled and dared to look up at Hobie. His eyes were still fixed on her and despite everything going on around them, she couldn't look away. The happy sounds of Danny asking the movers questions about the artwork they carried, for which they had no answers, drifted into the background and were replaced by the sound of her rapidly beating heart.

Hobie was so close she could sense the warmth of his body. Losing control momentarily, she breathed in deep to smell his cologne.

A smile crinkled the corners of his eyes and he leaned his head down towards her, like he had in the elevator, but sexier this time. His lips parted as if he was about to say something. The anticipation of his voice whispering something low into her ear sent a shiver across her shoulders. But before that could happen the sound of raucous shouts and jingling dog tags interrupted them.

"Rocky, no!" Danny's voice came to her just before the large, wriggling, muddy body of Rocky leapt between her and Hobie. The force of Rocky's greeting knocked them away from each other, scrambling to catch their feet.

Hobie fell against the wall and was able to stay standing, but Presley could not. She felt her feet sliding on the wet mud Rocky had brought in and promptly plopped onto her bottom. Ignoring the shouted commands of Hobie and Danny, Rocky came to her aid by placing his large, muddy paws on her lap and licking her face.

Hobie grabbed Rocky to pull him off while Danny and Mr. Brent took one arm each and heaved Presley back onto her feet. Hobie called out instructions to the movers so they could get the very expensive paintings somewhere safe. Mr. Brent called out to a nurse to come check Presley out to make sure she hadn't been injured and also sent for a custodian to clean up the mess.

After the commotion was over, Mr. Brent insisted she come to lunch.

Looking down at her intensely soiled white Palazzo pants, Presley shook her head 'no' and said, "I'm afraid I need to change first."

Mr. Brent halted her refusal with a raised palm, "I insist. It's the least we can do after Rocky practically mauled you." He looked at Hobie sternly. "Honestly, son, you need to teach that dog some manners."

Hobie tried to explain, "He's not normally like that." Looking sideways at Presley he continued, "He just kind of loses it when Presley's around."

Presley blushed. As flustering as it was to have the unfiltered attentions of Hobie's dog, it was also flattering. So much so that she agreed to join them for lunch in her mud splotched clothes.

It turned out she needn't have worried about the impression she was going to make at a restaurant, because they didn't go to a restaurant. They went to the cafeteria for Suzie's House, which resided on the top floor of the building.

Presley contained her surprise at this choice. She could not remember the last time she had eaten anywhere called a 'cafeteria'. To be fair, it wasn't bad. Casually decorated and lacking any pretense, the cafeteria took up most of the top floor. It was light and airy, too, with sweeping views of the city along the outside walls, which were floor to ceiling glass.

And it smelled delicious.

"You've got to try the hamburgers," Hobie said.

He stood close behind her holding a tray, still doing that protective masculine thing, even moresoe after Rocky knocked her over. Danny and Mr. Brent had moved forward in the line and were selecting salads from a variety of choices in a refrigerated glass display. Though the salads were prepackaged, they looked decent.

"I was thinking about getting a salad," she said.

"Naw, I'm telling you, they make a mean fried pickle burger here."

She looked back at him over her shoulder. He wiggled his

eyebrows at her in encouragement. She caught a whiff of the delicious smell of grilled beef.

"Fried pickle burger?" she asked incredulously.

He nodded, "You will not be sorry."

"It sounds…"

He waited.

"Fattening."

Grinning, Hobie let his eyes wander down her backside. No doubt taking in the wide mud spots on her white pants where she had landed on her bottom. Or maybe not. His look was so risqué she was a little worried his father might see it and scold him.

Hobie raised his eyes back to meet hers and gave her a flirtatious wink. "I think you can risk it."

She had to press her lips together to contain her smile.

"What would you like, Mr. Brent, the usual?" the woman behind the counter asked him.

"Yes, thank you Sandra," he answered.

Presley scanned the woman for a name tag, there was none.

Sandra smiled warmly and switched her gaze to Presley. "And for your friend?"

Hobie lifted his eyebrows at Presley with the silent question. She caved. With a wide grin he told Sandra, "She'll have a fried pickle burger, too."

The burger was good. Really good. So were the fries. When Hobie placed it in front of her after carrying it to the table Danny had procured in the far corner of the eating area, the burger looked gigantic. She didn't think she could even come close to finishing it.

Danny laughed as she stared at the thing with wide eyes, "We can get you a doggie bag if you need one."

"You won't need one," Hobie said with confidence before taking a big, juicy bite of his burger.

Surprisingly, Hobie turned out to be right. After a tentative first taste, Presley dug into her lunch, relishing every deep fried, greasy bite.

As they ate she forgot about her nervous elation at delivering the paintings, the horrible misunderstanding when she'd thought Danny had died, and even being knocked down and muddied up by the ever excitable Rocky. The Brent men were so interesting and funny, so kind and attentive, so laid back, so…normal. Presley relaxed into their lunch with ease and enjoyed every minute of it. Especially Hobie.

Seated next to each other, it was impossible for Presley to take his presence casually. Their knees occasionally brushed against each other under the table, as well as their shoulders and arms above the table. With every touch Presley felt an electric excitement at being so close to him. So much so that she couldn't bring herself to scoot her chair over just a few inches in order to avoid this constant contact. But, she noted with pleasure, neither did he.

In between bites of the delicious burger they all made pleasant conversation and it didn't take long for her to feel like one of the guys. Something she'd rarely, if ever, felt before in her life.

"What shall I do with the paintings? Since you're going home?" she asked Danny. "Do you want me to deliver them there?"

"No, no, let's have them here. They belong here with the patients and the staff," Danny answered. His generosity warmed her heart. He would be missed in this place. That was obvious from all of the people who kept approaching their table to say their farewells and give him best wishes on his recovery at home.

During one such side conversation when Danny and Mr. Brent were chatting with two nurses who had stopped by to wish them well, Presley reached for her water glass. At the very same time, Hobie reached for his and their hands brushed against each other. Again she felt the electric thrill shoot through her arm, but she didn't pull her hand away. Instead she looked at him and found his gaze on hers, a strange new look in his eyes.

Conscious of the fact that anyone might look over and catch them in this intimate moment, Presley tried to make conversation. "Wh–" her voice failed her and she had to clear her throat. His expression was so distracting she almost forgot what she was going to say. "Where will you hang the paintings?"

It was a meaningless question, but at least she had managed to say something.

He grinned, eyes sparkling, and Presley thought she might melt into a puddle right there. "I don't know for certain. But everyone will be glad to have something besides my pictures to look at."

"I'm sure that's not true," she responded. "Those are great pictures. And don't they help dogs get adopted?"

He nodded, finally moving his hand from hers and lifting his water to his lips, "That they do."

"Do you take them down when the dogs get adopted?" He nodded and took a sip. She thought for a moment then said, "I saw Sugar Pop was still on the wall."

He nodded again, his grin widening and his eyes filling with amusement. The memory of Sugar Pop peeing on her sweater flashed through her mind and Presley was almost sorry she had brought it up, even as she felt a pang of sadness for the odd little dog.

"So she hasn't been adopted yet?"

He shook his head 'no' and placed his water back down. Leaning back in his chair, he took a long look at her before looking out across the cafeteria and answering, "No she hasn't. Not everybody's taste, I think. She's a hard one to place."

His words went straight to Presley's heart. Sugar Pop's sweet buggy eyes flashed through her mind. The way her tiny little paws had scratched at her feet. Sadness weighed in her chest at the thought of the homeless little thing shivering in her cage at the shelter.

And there was something more. Something deeper in his meaning. Everything in his tone and expression, the way he was holding his body and not looking directly at her when he spoke, gave Presley the distinct impression that Hobie was not talking about Sugar Pop at all.

CHAPTER 39

"Uncle Hobie, Uncle Hobie," his youngest niece, Liza, pulled on his shirt. "Are you staying the night with us?"

Barely four years old, Liza was always excited at the prospect of a sleepover.

"I'm staying with Grandpa, remember?" Hobie lifted the little girl up and placed her gently on the chair next to his. They were enjoying some sunshine on Danny's extensive rooftop patio. "Besides, I think your Dad probably wants to be alone with you guys for his first night home."

"Want a beer?" Danny asked as he motioned towards his butler, Franklin, who was lurking nearby awaiting instructions.

"I think Liza's a little young for beer, don't you?" Hobie feigned shock at Danny's question. Liza giggled and he tickled her waist, increasing the giggles.

"Two, please, Franklin. And a pitcher of lemonade for the little ones," Danny instructed his man while idly dismissing Hobie's joke. He relaxed into the pillows on his wicker chair and Hobie thought he could already see some color returning to his big brother's face, which made his heart glad.

Hobie didn't have to help Danny move home and settle back in with his family. There were plenty of movers and paid staff to do whatever was needed to make a smooth transition. He didn't have to be there, but he wanted to be there. For his brother. For his sister-in-law and his nieces. For his Dad. But especially for his Mom. He'd felt her tugging at him to do more for Danny and his Dad ever since Danny got sick, and Hobie was not going to let his Mom down…not again.

"It is good to be home," Danny said. Little Liza scurried down from her chair and climbed into her father's lap. Danny wrapped his arms around his youngest daughter and kissed her on the top of her head.

"You look better already," Hobie said.

"That's not saying much, is it?" Danny laughed.

It was good to see him laugh. Hobie was glad their father hadn't joined them on the patio, though. Seeing Danny laugh would probably make him cry. His emotions had gotten the better of him over the past week. The relief of seeing Danny recover from the same disease that had taken his wife so many years ago was taking a toll on him. Hobie felt it, too, an intense bittersweet.

"It won't be long and I'll be back to work," Danny said, a gleam of hope in his eyes.

Hobie liked his enthusiasm, but he didn't want him to overdo anything. "How about we give you a few days to recuperate completely before we send you back in the boardroom with the sharks."

He meant it. No way was Danny going back to work before he was good and ready and they were sure he was healthy and strong. Still, Danny's comment made him pause. Hobie hadn't even entertained the idea that he might possibly return to his photography any time soon. If ever.

His only focus had been to take care of the family business, and take care of his father and his brother the way he should have done when his mother was ill, instead of retreating from them emotionally and running away across the globe at the first opportunity.

Everything was different now that Danny's treatment had gone so well and he was home. Hobie suddenly realized there would be a time, possibly soon, that he could have his old life back. As soon as the thought solidified, the memory of Presley eating a fried pickle burger flashed through his mind. Looking gorgeous in her mud smudged clothes, relaxed and flirting, the thought of her made his heart skip a beat.

"Do you like doing Daddy's job?" Liza asked. She sure was full of questions today.

Surprised, Hobie found that he didn't have an answer. Did he like running Barcom? Would he be sorry to have to hand the reins back to Danny when the time came?

Danny's eyes sharpened on his little brother, noticing how he fumbled for an answer. "Don't tell me you're making plans to stay in charge forever?" he teased.

Hobie tried to pass his hesitation off with a laugh and a quick shake of his head. "No, no...I was just trying to remember where I put all of your stuff that I cleaned out of your office."

Danny chuckled, "Right." He took a thoughtful swig of beer and leveled a curious gaze at Hobie. "Is there a more personal reason you want to stay on?"

Hobie glanced down and away from his brother, feigning nonchalance. "Like what?"

"Like who, you mean?"

Hobie understood the question, but he didn't know how to answer. There were still a lot of unknowns regarding Presley.

Danny figured he wasn't getting an answer, so he pressed on, "You do like her, don't you?"

Oh, he liked her all right, there was no denying that any longer. Everything about Presley Monroe made his heart spin, and his head. The way she took control of business, the way she moved with such confidence and grace, and the way all of that strong beautiful shell fell apart at times. It was enchanting. She was enchanting.

Hobie had to admit this was true, just as he had to admit that he could allow himself to fall in love under the right circumstances. No doubt about that fact. For whatever reason, however, he couldn't bring himself to admit it to Danny.

He took a swig of his beer and shrugged noncommittally, "I guess I do, but I don't think this is the right time for anything serious."

Danny grunted his response. Hobie couldn't tell if it was a positive or a negative grunt, so he left it alone.

"Who do you like, Uncle Hobie?" Liza piped up from her position on her father's lap.

"I like you, little Liza," Hobie gave his niece a wink and she giggled.

Danny grunted again and when Hobie ignored him, Danny warned, "You can't wait your whole life for the right time. Trust me, you never know what's going to happen."

The words struck Hobie right in the chest and for an instant he was compelled to call Presley right away and ask her out on a real date. He shook the feeling off. The timing still felt wrong.

What he couldn't do was let his personal feelings get in the way of his family. He had done that once and lost something in the process. A connection to home. A reason to hold still and raise a family of his own.

Danny was home and recovering. The Count's project

was well on its way. Soon Danny could return to his Barcom duties and Hobie would go back to the world he loved, traveling to distant lands and seeing them through the lens of his camera. Everything would go back to the way it was before…right?

A twinge of uncertainty sat in the center of his stomach. Hobie drank his beer and sat in silent company with Danny, looking out across the city skyline shining under the bright yellow sun. The twinge did not go away. Slowly, Hobie understood what the twinge meant.

A piece of him was changed. Changed forever. He knew this because for the first time since he began roaming the world as a teenager he found himself wondering what it would be like to take someone with him.

CHAPTER 40

The sun hung lower and lower on the horizon, a great orange globe overlooking the rolling green hills that surrounded Villa Pallotta. It was magnificent.

Soon it would be dusk and the land would bathe in the pink glow of the globe sun as it dipped below low purple hills and night fell. Fat lightbulbs that criss crossed over the patio would turn on and the much anticipated opening night party of Count Bolsena's Villa Pollata's vineyard hotel would commence.

But sunset wasn't for another hour or so, and for the time being Presley was free to stand alone on the patio and look out over the beautiful Umbrian countryside.

Construction on the addition to the winery that was now a cafe selling locally grown food and employing locals from the nearby villages had not taken long once the plans were in place. Walking and biking paths through this gorgeous area had been carefully laid out with appropriate signage and protection for the natural countryside, the vineyards, and the traditional village they would be showing off to tourists.

Renovations were well under way on the ancient and

long unused flour mill on the edge of the Count's land, which would create dozens of beautifully simple, and affordable, rooms to let to those tourists. This would be run by the local villagers and underwritten and overseen by the Count himself. More luxurious get togethers, such as weddings and large parties would all be held at the Count's grand estate home in the ball room where he and the Countess could provide the special zing of royal charm.

This project had come together with so much positivity and cohesiveness. Presley couldn't remember another time when everything in the planning and construction of a project had flowed so well and been such a delight.

Megan had been key in all of the planning. She had thought of everything, even seeing to it that other local businesses in the area had a word in what was happening. It was her idea to include smaller nearby vineyards on the team to provide their wines and special outings for guests. It was a win-win for everyone involved.

Villa Pallotta was set to be a beautiful, inclusive escape for everyone instead of an elite play place for only the wealthy few who could afford it. And all of the well thought out tourism would only enhance the prosperity of the local community and preserve the beauty of the surrounding nature, instead of destroy it or cause strife between the people who were visiting and those who had lived there for generations.

Daniel Brent Senior Was thrilled with how their company's had worked together and Presley was satisfied that she had done exactly what her father requested her to do. That was a good feeling.

She smiled and took a sip of the semi-sweet style wine known as Orvieto Abboccato, a blend that was only made in this region of Italy, which the Count had finally pinpointed as her favorite.

"We just opened this new blend, Ms. Monroe, and I think it is perfect for you!" he had declared at one of the several trips she had made to the Villa over the past few weeks.

With hints of pear and melon complimented by a light lemon and honey, it was juicy, a little sweet and smooth. She really did like it. So much so that Count Bolsena had decided to name it after her. "Presley's Dolci Amici" was on the wine list at the cafe and she was truly flattered by his gesture.

Everything about the Villa Pallotta project had given her a kind of sweet contentment, and Hobie...well, Hobie had been the absolute best part.

He had been a dream to work with over the past several weeks, giving his all and never– not once–rushing away to something more important. Ever since Danny returned home Hobie had gone all in and been the hardest working person on the project. Helpful, charming, and full of fun, he not only made every day productive, but he also had great ideas, was practically a business genius, and he made her laugh. Knowing Hobie and his family better than she had before the day she delivered the paintings, all of her previous misunderstandings about his behavior made perfect sense and she had no more complaints.

Well, maybe one.

Even though they had spent countless hours, days, and weeks together, meeting with their respective finance people, Italian policy makers, chefs, and construction crews, sharing private airplanes back and forth to Europe, planning together, eating together, even staying at the Villa as the Count's guests, they were still operating just as business associates. Maybe friends. She would feel comfortable calling him a friend, but besides a few daily flirtatious interactions, and a growing sense of warmth between them, he had not made a move to ask her out or steal a kiss or anything like that. Not once.

This vexed Presley.

She inhaled the rich, warm smell of the summer evening and let the air out in a sigh.

"Wow, that sounded heavy," Ronnie said. She was topping the steps that led to the patio from the grounds below. The same steps Presley had nearly toppled off of so many months ago when Hobie had caught her in his arms. "Is everything all right? Do you need any help with the party?"

Lost in thought, Presley hadn't heard her sister approaching the patio. She shook her head 'no' to the offer of help and motioned for Ronnie to join her and enjoy the view. Ronnie was here for the big opening party, as were Ruby, Grace, and Faye. Faye wouldn't miss a party if she could help it. Presley was glad to have all of them here. The feeling that something wonderful was ending hung in the air and Presley was afraid she would get morose without her sister and her friends around.

"Everything's done," Presley said. "I'm just relaxing out here for a few minutes."

Ronnie nodded and glanced around at the cocktail tables draped with deep purple linens, each topped with a heavy glass jar containing a fat white candle. "It all looks wonderful, Pres, everything. The party, the cafe is gorgeous, and the reno on the flour mill is stunning. You've done a great job."

Presley smiled. "It's been a new experience, all of this eco-friendly business planning is kind of amazing."

Ronnie gave her a mischievous look. "And maybe not just the business has been amazing?"

Presley feigned confusion even though she was fairly certain where this conversation was headed. "What do you mean?"

"Anyone with eyes can tell that you and Hobie have something going on." Presley's stomach did a flip flop at the suggestion, but she stayed silent. Ronnie continued, "I'm just saying that maybe he's the reason this whole thing..." she waved her hand encompassing the patio, the vineyards and the orange globe sun, "...has made you so happy."

Presley's eyebrows puckered, "Is that what I am? Happy?"

Ronnie laughed, the silvery sound floating out over the picturesque vineyard below. Several musicians from the small band Presley had hand picked to play live music on the patio during the party appeared at the top of the stairs and began setting up. The two sisters watched them for a few moments.

Her eyes still on the musicians, Ronnie said, "You're allowed, you know."

"Allowed what, Ron?" she lifted her glass to take another sip of her namesake wine.

Ronnie switched her gaze back to Presley and waited for her big sister to meet her eyes before saying, "You're allowed to be happy."

Presley's wine glass froze in place directly in front of her mouth. A knot sprung up at the back of her throat and she dared not take a drink or she might choke. She tried to swallow the knot away, it didn't work.

Lowering her glass, she asked, "You don't think I'm happy?"

Ronnie thought for a few seconds before responding, "I don't think you allow yourself to be happy. You always take on so much responsibility..." She turned her gaze back to the musicians, "I don't know, it's just you've been so happy working with Hobie for the past weeks. It would be nice if you could relax a little bit and let someone like Hobie make you happy."

A thrill rushed through Presley's chest and stomach and she smiled, the blushing smile of a teenager that couldn't be controlled no matter how much she tried. She looked down into her wine glass and considered how to respond, but before she had a chance, a voice came from behind them.

"Ladies," Hobie greeted them.

Both sisters whirled around in surprise then looked at each other. How long had he been standing there?

Presley's face turned beet red. She looked to Ronnie for assistance, but Ronnie was just as flustered at the possibility they had been overheard that she giggled. Ronnie's giggle tapped into a sisterly connection that made Presley giggle in response. She tried to stop the giggle short, which made her snort. The sisters stared wide eyed at each other for a beat.

Hobie chuckled, his deep brown eyes alight, "Have I interrupted something?"

"No," Presley managed to answer. "A little too much wine," she lifted her half empty glass up as proof.

He eyed her glass and smiled in such a soft, sweet way, Presley thought her knees might buckle.

Hobie had ditched his brown corduroy sport coat for a more sophisticated look this evening. In black slacks and a bluish grey button up shirt that fit him perfectly from his wide shoulders down to his narrow waist, he would stand up to any fashion police. His hair had grown longer and was a well controlled, curly mane of black that almost reached his collarbone. Still no tie, but that hardly mattered. Striking to look at and charming to boot, she had decided a while ago that Hobie wasn't the kind of man who needed a tie.

Eyes glittering with fun he leaned into Presley a little, "I was wondering if you would like to take a walk with me." He tilted his head toward the vineyard below.

A thrill rippled down her neck. She looked at Ronnie who was watching their interaction with more than a little amused delight.

"I've just been, it's a lovely walk, you should go," Ronnie

backed away, excusing herself from the possibility of being a third wheel.

"Sure," Presley tried to sound light and nonchalant, but the word came out in more of a croak. She turned as if to start for the stairs leading down to the vineyard, when she noticed the half empty glass of wine in her hand. She turned back awkwardly, holding the glass away from her body like a banana peel she needed to throw away.

Hobie wrapped his hand gently around hers and the wine glass and used his other hand to remove it from her grip. "We can leave that here," he said as he set the glass down on a nearby table.

Presley got the distinct feeling she was being maneuvered. She didn't mind. Not exactly.

A bundle of nerves in her stomach flickered and danced when Hobie placed his hand on the small of her back and guided her down the path. The air was warm and heavy with the scent of grapevines and the freshly turned earth from the vineyard. The ground felt buoyant beneath their feet, as if it had a life and a heart of its own that invited them to walk further and further into the evening.

Presley had chosen a flowing geranium print chiffon Dolce & Gabbana dress with a pair of the designer's green high heeled sandals for the party. The shoes were comfortable in normal circumstances, but once again she found herself on uncertain terrain as Hobie led her down the gravel path into the setting sun.

"Here," he offered his elbow for support and the sensation of his muscled arm underneath the smooth grey fabric of his shirt tingled through her fingertips. He placed his hand over hers for more stability. Presley's heart flip-flopped inside her chest.

Silently they meandered in the light of the glowing sunset. Reds, oranges, pinks, and purples stretched across the sky as if painted by a wild haired eccentric Italian artist. Though she had been in countless beautiful places during her life, there was something about this place, this moment, that seemed a level above the rest.

Presley didn't mind the silence. It wasn't uncomfortable. She was so comfortable she didn't feel the need to break the silence and was content to listen to the crunching of the gravel under their feet and the occasional bird song bidding the sun good night.

"Would you like to stop here?" Hobie motioned toward a small stopping point that had been built along the path specifically for its gorgeous view of the rolling countryside. There were a few small shade trees, a wooden bench, and a decorative iron fence set up for extra charm.

She said yes and they stood side-by-side against the fence looking at the view. Golden light from the sunset washed over them as the sound of musicians warming up floated softly across the vineyards. Presley sighed and Hobie glanced sideways at her.

"It's beautiful, isn't it?" he asked.

"It really is." Presley's gaze remained on the amazing vista before them, but all of her other senses were captured with Hobie's presence. The feeling of his arm brushing against hers, the sound of his breath, the slight shift of his body as he cleared his throat.

"I know about the money," he said.

She turned her head to look up at him. "What money?"

He wrinkled his brow as if she was asking a silly question. "I think you know what money."

The 50 million. She was sure that's what he was talking about. She returned her gaze to the view, not wanting to give away that she was the anonymous donor, uncertain of how he would respond.

"I'm not sure what money you're referring to, Hobie," she

said calmly. This could be true. There had been a lot of money moving between their two companies for several months now. His deep, soft chuckle reached her ear sending delicious warmth down her neck and into her shoulders.

"Someone donated 50 million dollars to Suzie's House anonymously," he said.

Feigning surprise, she said, "My, what a generous gift."

"Yes, it was generous. It's not every day we get a donation of that size."

"I suppose not," she focused on the rich colors in the sunset to avoid eye contact, but could feel his eyes on her watching for a reaction.

"I wish I knew who they were. I would like to thank them," he said.

She nodded and put her hands on the fence in front of them, leaning forward a little and searching through the scenery for something more specific to stare at to keep from looking at him. If she looked at him she might blurt out the truth, which would seem pathetic and needy. Not something she wanted to portray. In the near distance she saw an old well with stone sides and a teetering wooden roof. Locking her gaze on the well, she managed a carefully worded response.

"I'm sure someone who gave anonymously doesn't need to be thanked. That's the whole point of being anonymous, isn't it?"

"Yeah, I guess so," he said quietly.

Silence enveloped them, but it wasn't exactly a comfortable silence. This silence buzzed.

Hobie placed his right hand on the fence next to her left. Their pinky fingers touched and the same warmth from a few moments ago tingled up her arm.

Braving a sideways look, she saw he was definitely not looking at the sunset. His undaunted gaze tugged at her and, unable to turn her attention back to the old well, she shifted slightly so she was looking up into his beautiful brown eyes.

It felt so natural, their bodies close together and facing each other. He took her hand from the fence and held it tenderly. If she had been about to say something, she couldn't remember what it was.

"Presley...I..." his voice faltered and he looked down at her hand in his. A few curling locks of his hair fell forward and before she knew what she was doing, Presley reached up with her free hand and pushed them tenderly back. His eyes shot up to hers, but she couldn't pull her hand away. Her fingertips barely traced his temple.

Hobie searched her eyes, looking for an answer to a question. But she couldn't guess the question and she didn't have any answers. She didn't want to talk about the money anymore. Or about business. She wanted him to kiss her.

With that thought her gaze dropped to his mouth. She moved her fingers slowly...gently...down the side of his cheek and along his jawline. The whiskers of his signature close shaved beard were impossibly soft. Hobie squeezed her hand and pulled her into him, wrapping his free hand around her waist, holding the small of her back firmly so she couldn't pull away. A needless move in her opinion, because pulling away was the last thing on her mind.

He was hot. Heat traveled from his hard, muscled abdomen to her belly as he squeezed her closer. Presley's chest rose and fell quickly, her breath shallow with the thrill of it all.

Her fingers reached his mouth and she lightly traced his bottom lip. Firm and warm, all she could think about was how it might feel for him to press his lips against hers. Hobie closed his eyes for a moment and tilted towards her hand so his jaw pressed against her palm. He opened his eyes, those deep brown eyes. They were full of longing, piercing into her with such passion that she sucked in her breath and could not move.

Ronnie's silvery laugh carried across the balmy air. Presley ignored it. She was used to hearing her sister laugh.

Hobie paused. His lips were only inches away from hers and all she wanted in the whole world was for him to bend his head forward and kiss her full on the mouth.

"What was that?" he asked in a hoarse whisper.

"Nothing," she whispered back, but her answer was lost in the sound of crunching footsteps coming down the path.

CHAPTER 41

"There they are," Faye's voice cut sharply through the sunset glow. Ronnie's unmistakable giggle followed it, much closer than Presley had thought it was just a few moments before.

Instinctively, Hobie stepped back, putting some space between them. Though they were partially hidden by the shade trees, anyone who got very close would see their embrace. Presley understood he was trying to be chivalrous, not allowing anyone to see their intimate moment, yet she felt a stab of disappointment.

"Presley?" Ronnie called out, presumably to warn her that she and Faye, and who knew who else, were crashing their romantic moment.

"Yes?" Presley turned glumly to see Ronnie, Faye, and Jaxson round the shade trees.

"I told you they were back here," Faye said over her shoulder to her companions.

Ronnie caught Presley's eye and mouthed the words 'I'm sorry' while pointing at the back of Faye's head, blaming her for the intrusion. Jaxson gave Presley a quick nod of agreement, indicating he agreed with Ronnie. Hobie stepped further back and the energy between them fizzled.

"It's gorgeous," Faye exclaimed with approval. Her eyes danced and she threw her hands out as if she was going to hug the final few minutes of glowing light from the setting sun.

Sighing inwardly, Presley tried to smile.

"You two have done a marvelous job on Villa Pallotta," Faye was still gushing as she claimed the space on the other side of Presley next to the wooden fence. She leaned over the fence to catch Hobie's eye and give him an excited smile.

"Thank you," Hobie replied. "But really it was Presley and Megan. They were in charge of the aesthetics."

Faye sniffed her disapproval of him mentioning Megan. Presley had avoided speaking to her friend about anything to do with Hobie or Megan because of Faye's tendency to be, well, Faye. Maybe that had been a mistake. She wondered if Faye was going to say something unnecessarily nasty about the young woman and lead Hobie to believe that Presley had been talking badly behind their backs.

"Megan was great to work with," Presley said in a tone that meant she didn't want any snarky comments from anyone. Faye sniffed again. Presley looked at Hobie, "But I think you're understating your part in the planning."

Hobie ducked his head and smiled at her with a secretive twinkle in his eyes. His look awakened the tingling warmth on her skin where he had been touching her just moments before. It weakened her knees. So much so that she held more firmly to the fence to make sure she didn't wobble.

"Oh, who cares?" Faye waved her hand around at all of the surrounding beauty. "It turned out lovely no matter who gets credit for it."

"Right," Ronnie agreed. She rubbed her hands together, "Well, I guess we've seen all there is to see. We should head back up to the party." Jaxson, who had been discreetly checking out Hobie's non-corduroy jacket look, nodded in agreement and turned as if to leave.

"Nonsense," Faye dismissed the suggestion with another wave of her hand. "We only just got here." She leaned over the fence to look around Presley at Hobie. "So, tell me Hobie, did your brother enjoy the paintings?"

Hobie thought about the question for a moment, then asked, "The Putole's?" He looked at Presley for clarification even as Faye answered.

"Yes, the Putole's, what other paintings would I care about?"

"He liked them very much," Hobie said politely. "And so does everyone else at Suzie's House."

Faye raised her eyebrows, "Do they? I'm glad. His work doesn't always translate across..." Faye searched for a word and as the seconds ticked away, Presley grew more and more uncomfortable. She doubted any word Faye chose was going to sound right. Finally, Faye's eyes lit up and she finished her thought, "Tax brackets."

Hobie gave her a long look. "You don't think people in different tax brackets can appreciate fine art?"

Faye gave him a patronizing smile, "Of course I don't think that, anyone with taste can appreciate fine art. But not everyone can afford a Putole painting. Especially not several of them." She winked at Presley with the last comment, which only made Presley wish Faye had stayed on the patio even more vehemently.

Hobie got the hint, but when he responded Presley sensed a coolness in his tone, "It was very generous of Presley to donate those paintings."

Faye scoffed, "Not only the paintings."

Hobie raised his eyebrows in mock surprise and looked to Presley for an explanation.

She was fuming. She had confided her plans to donate the 50 million anonymously to Faye during their trip to Putole's studio. What about 'anonymous' did Faye not understand?

"Ms. Monroe," Jaxson's smooth voice interrupted them. All eyes turned to him, he was looking at his cell phone. "Your father wants you. The party is about to begin."

ON A SMALL STAGE in the ballroom, standing next to her father as they listened to the Count speak into a microphone to the crowded room, Presley couldn't have been less interested in the sea of smiling faces looking up at them. Her father had insisted she join him, the Count, the Countess, Hobie's father, and Hobie on stage to officially open Villa Pallotta, but all Presley could think about was Hobie's hands on her waist pulling her into him. How close their lips had been to touching. The sensation of his cheek under her fingertips.

"....and, of course, everything that went with it," the Count turned to look at her with a big smile. A murmur of laughter moved through the room and Presley realized he must have been saying something about her, but she had stopped listening. Hoping that he didn't expect a response, she beamed at him and nodded as if she got the joke. Satisfied, the Count turned back to his audience.

Keeping her beaming smile stuck to her face she searched the crowd for Jaxson and found him watching discreetly. Though he was positioned off to the side, he was still at the front of the crowd and could easily see her and everyone else on the stage including Hobie.

Presley tried to catch his eye. She needed him to keep her on her toes during this little introduction. What she didn't want was to flounder on stage just because the thought of kissing Hobie had overtaken her mind.

She blinked at him, tilted her head at him, and did everything that she could–which arguably wasn't much while she was on full display to the world– to get his attention. But try as she might, she couldn't get Jaxson to look at her. His gaze was fixed elsewhere on the stage and he had a strange, dreamy expression on his face, lost in thought. She bulged her eyes at him, hoping she didn't look like an insane, smiling frog. Nothing. What was he looking at? She leaned a little forward and tried to follow his stare.

If she wasn't mistaken, Jaxson was fixated on none other than Hobie. Seriously? Presley fought to keep a scowl off of her face and switched her hand back and forth at her side, a tiny semi-hidden wave at her personal assistant.

"…if she hadn't taken the reins the way she did, we would not have the amazing future we now have. A round of applause for Ms. Presley Monroe!" The Count turned to her again as did everyone other pair of eyes in the room, including Jaxson.

Applause and shouts of "Bravo" lifted from the crowd and she froze in place, forcing her smile even harder. At least the cheering had broken Jaxson's trance.

It was difficult for Presley to smile at the crowd and also glare at Jaxson for not paying attention. But she tried. Without skipping a beat Jaxson ignored her annoyance and gave her a meaningful look, then flicked his eyes to the other side of the stage and back to her, then back to the other side and back to her again. He was trying to get her to look at something.

Presley never thought she would be thankful to have the Count continue talking, but when he started in again on another tangent, she was grateful for his long winded tendencies. It gave her the chance to lean back a little and look behind the backs of everyone on stage to try to figure out what Jaxson wanted her to see.

All she saw were the back sides of her father standing next to her, the Count and Countess, Hobie's father, and Hobie on the far end. While he definitely had a nice back side, she wasn't sure what Jaxson had been insinuating with all of his eye movement and head twitching. Presley started to straighten when a movement caught her eye and she paused.

Hobie was tilting back to look behind everyone as well. When their eyes met he grinned mischievously and gave her a quick wink. She immediately turned pink and had to suppress a giggle. Hobie let his eyes wander down her dress and when Presley realized he was focusing on her derriere she almost lost her balance, teetering precariously on her designer heels.

Her eyes flew open spontaneously, the sensation of falling backward overriding her flirtatious instincts. The sexy gleam in Hobie's eyes switched to fear and he took a step back from the line they stood in to come to her rescue. Just then she felt her father's hand grab her elbow and pull her back to standing.

"Careful, Pumpkin," Mack said.

Still flushed, both from the near fall and Hobie's wink, she tried to regain her composure. Heart fluttering, she grasped her hands in front of her and concentrated on standing up straight. No more fooling around in front of the world. Her eyes wandered over the audience and she found Jaxson again. He was still watching her, but now with a suppressed smile. She sniffed and flicked her gaze elsewhere.

"And now," the Count's booming voice was wrapping up

his speech. Thank goodness. "Mr. Brent senior has foregone my invitation to say something to you all. But! Not to worry, my friends, no to worry, he has asked his son, Hobart, to say a few words in his stead."

Two things swirled through Presley's mind. First, was she expected to say something? Nobody had told her there were going to be speeches. How had she missed that detail? She shot a look at Jaxson who appeared to be just as confused. All he could muster was a weak shrug. She scowled at him. Honestly.

The second more pervasive thought pushing her heart rate up was that she wouldn't be able to remain calm and collected on stage while Hobie was speaking. Heat was already creeping up her neck and into her cheeks. The whole world was going to see how she felt about him, it would be written all over her face. Presley prayed his comments would be short.

"Let me begin by saying what an honor it has been to be involved in this project…" Hobie began and as much as Presley had been unable to listen to the Count drone on and on, she found herself riveted to every syllable that came out of Hobie's mouth. "Filling the shoes of my big brother has been quite an experience and I especially want to thank," he turned to give Presley and her father a big smile. "Mr. Mack Monroe and his…incredible daughter, Presley Monroe, for taking the lead with their intelligence, insight, and creativity."

Her father put one arm around her waist and beamed at Hobie. Hobie smiled back at him then caught her eye before he turned back to the crowd, pausing for a moment as if he wanted to say something else, but couldn't.

She was lost in his eyes. Completely lost. It was good that her father had hold of her waist because she felt weak and feathery and might float away if he let go, over the heads of the people in the crowd, twirling and laughing and calling out Hobie's name as she did.

And she could see it in Hobie's eyes, too. A feeling that matched her own. A desire to go back into the vineyard and finish what they had started earlier. He smiled, softer this time, before dragging his eyes and away and returning to his speech.

"You all know that Mack Monroe is the richest man in this room? Heck, he's probably one of the richest men in the world, isn't he?" Murmurs of agreement from the crowd, a few cheers. Presley stiffened, wondering where he was going with this line of thought. Hobie continued, his voice as smooth and pleasant as always, "And when people say that money can't buy happiness, I'm not sure they've met Mack Monroe." Some laughter and louder cheers. "Because when you look around at what Mack Industries has done here, I know in my heart that the investment they made, along with Barcom, is going to bring happiness to a lot of people for years to come. People in this community and nearby communities, and people who come here from all walks of life to experience the beauty and the joy that only Villa Pallotta can provide."

Presley relaxed as applause rose from the crowd and Hobie gave a head nod to the Count, his father, and hers, who was bursting with pride and accomplishment at his kind praise. Again Hobie paused briefly when his eyes landed on her. Again she was struck with the feeling he wanted to say something to her, but was holding back. Luckily the crowd was still clapping, but when the clapping ceased Hobie turned back to them, leaving Presley to wonder what was on his mind.

"I respect that about Mack Monroe. I respect any man

who understands the importance of putting people above money. Any man, or woman, who considers the impact they are having on nature and on the environment, and decides to take action to minimize that impact, ensuring our children and our children's children a healthy, happy future."

Applause as Hobie looked out across the crowd, which was full millionaires, a few billionaires, celebrities, journalists, and media people. It was also full of local merchants and builders, the Count's family members, environmental activists, and many more people she would have previously considered out of place at a party like this. The adoration was genuine from everyone in the room. Seeing the exuberant faces Presley felt a sense of camaraderie, as if she had been part of bringing them all together.

"My father is another one of those men," Hobie continued, his voice cracking ever so slightly with emotion. He turned to give Daniel Senior a heart felt smile. Her own heart warmed at the sight, as if a small candle had lit inside of her and was spreading light through her body. "I'll never forget what my father used to say to me and my brother…still does say, in fact. *It's not the money, son, it's what you do with the money…and who you help along the way.*" Cheers again and Hobie, his ease and confidence in the moment making him even more attractive in Presley's eyes, declared, "Let's have a toast!"

Waiters whisked in front of them and gave them each a glass of champagne, as they did for everyone in the crowd. As soon as everyone was ready Hobie raised his champagne glass high in the air.

"To Villa Pallotta, may it bring prosperity and joy to you, your children and your grandchildren, and to the visitors who come from near and far to enjoy its bounty."

"Cheers!" Presley's voice lifted with the others and

though she hadn't had a drop of the champagne yet, she felt giddy.

Her father turned to her, his face flushed with the success of this moment and said, "I really like that young man."

Presley almost giggled, but stopped herself. She smiled and nodded, "Yes, I do, too." The light in her heart was growing with every moment, warming her from the inside out. With pleasure she took a sip of the fizzing champagne and let it fill her mouth with bubbles.

Her father gave his head a little shake as he tsk-tsked what he was about to say, "It's too bad he's leaving."

Presley almost choked. Her throat clenched and she had to concentrate to keep the champagne from going down the wrong tube.

Finally she was able to speak, "Leaving?"

Mack Monroe nodded, explaining off handedly as his gaze swept over the room, "Yes, Daniel will be back in charge soon. I suppose Hobie wants to get back to his free roaming photography life. Danny was telling me that it's been difficult for him to settle down here and work in the business. I hear he's headed to somewhere in Asia as soon as possible."

Overtaken by a sudden queasiness, Presley stared mutely at her father. Hobie was leaving Barcom? Going to Asia? To do what? Live in some rural village and take pictures?

She blinked out over the crowd, pretending to follow her father's gaze, but actually looking for Hobie. She found him, chatting it up with a couple of the environmental activists who had become a common fixture at the Villa. As she watched them talk and laugh Presley could see how comfortable he was with them, how easily they laughed together. Peas in a pod. She tried to imagine standing with that group of people and feeling comfortable, feeling as if she belonged. She couldn't.

"Is everything all right, Pumpkin?" her father asked. He was watching her carefully.

Presley dropped her eyes and stared into her champagne for a split second before forcing a smile and looking up at her father. "I'm fine, Dad. Everything's fine."

But it wasn't fine. The warm glow of the small candle by her heart had snuffed out.

CHAPTER 42

*P*resley rested her head on the plush leather of her chair and closed her eyes. Strapped in for take off in their company jet, she could finally allow the events of the previous night to wash away. Or at least that's what she wanted to do.

Unbidden images played out in her mind's eye bringing with them a sinking feeling that exactly followed the downward spiral her heart had been in since she left the party early. Images of Hobie, handsome and confident, moving through the party with an ease she envied. Her own display of self-confidence seemed plastic, brittle, nothing more than an attempt to cover up her real feelings. Small, petty, dark feelings.

"Take a picture with me, Presley," he had reached out to her and pulled her to his side where they smiled for a photographer who was getting candid shots. "One for the society pages, you think?" Hobie teased.

Her head still spinning from the news he was leaving for Asia, she had smiled…hard. Being close to him again, in his arms again, brought up every sensation she had felt when he was holding her more intimately in the vineyard. Desire raced through her veins, but turned to ice when she thought about him leaving. A chill moved down her back and she shivered.

"Are you cold?" Hobie asked, keeping a firm hold on her waist, an adorable pucker of worry creasing his brow.

She mumbled something unintelligible, trying to ignore the way the protective look in his eyes pierced directly into her heart. After their picture was taken, he took her to a seating area in a small cove at the end of the ballroom and insisted she drink some water. He sat down next to her and watched her closely.

Her mouth screwed into a smile, "I'm not about to faint or anything."

"You sure?" He cocked his head and scrutinized her as if he was a doctor. "Because you were a little wobbly earlier, too."

Oh, that. She took another sip of water to prove her strength and dismissed his concern with a quick shake of her head. "Oh, that was nothing."

He grunted and leaned back in his chair, pushing dark curls back from his face. "I thought maybe you were still a little light headed from…" he didn't finish his thought, but gave her a secretive smile.

"Oh, *that*…" she shook her head again.

He frowned. "I hope you aren't going to say that was nothing."

"No, no, I wasn't going to say anything of the kind."

"Good," he grinned and nudged her knee with his.

A coy smile played at her lips and in one smooth move Hobie raised his arm and rested it over the back of her chair. Suddenly, she was leaning into him again. The sweet smell of the vineyard still lingered on him and mixed with his peppery cologne. Presley breathed him in and thought she might turn into a pile of mush and slide right off of her chair onto the floor.

A twinkle played in his eyes, telling her that he knew the effect he was having on her senses. The hand he had flung so cavalierly across her shoulders hung cool and loose off of the back of her chair, but his fingertips brushed her upper arm ever so slightly. In no way could anyone see that he was stroking her skin, but he was, and the light tickle of it was distracting. He leaned in close to her ear, so close she could feel his breath on her cheek. For one frightening, thrilling moment she wondered if he was going to kiss her neck.

Instead he spoke softly, "I wanted to talk to you about something, Presley."

When he said her name she had to close her eyes. The feelings her name on his lips brought up inside of her were too much to bear with her eyes open. Completely delicious. Absolutely terrifying.

"I wanted to tell you–" he started.

"That you're leaving. I know," she interrupted. She opened her eyes to see that he was taken aback by her words. She hadn't meant to say anything about what she knew. It had just spilled out. She pursed her lips together tightly.

"Yes," he said slowly. "I am leaving. I'm going to–"

"Asia, right?" She'd done it again. She bit her bottom lip to try to control the nervous outbursts.

"Yes," he gave her a questioning look. "Where did you–"

"My Dad told me," she interrupted again. This was ridiculous. What was the matter with her? She cleared her throat and tried giving him another coy smile, though it felt stiff and uneasy. "He just mentioned it to me after the toast."

"Oh," Hobie looked at her evenly. Maybe he was waiting for her to blurt out something else. When she didn't he looked away and into the rest of the people buzzing around the room. His fingers had stopped casually brushing against her arm. After a long silence he asked, "When was the last time you were in Asia?"

Eager to break the silence she said, "I went to the Maldives a few years ago."

A kind of snort escaped him, "Maldives. Figures."

"What is that supposed to mean?"

He considered her for a moment, then asked, "Have you ever been to Da Lat in Vietnam?"

The question sounded like a challenge. One that she could not win. "No…what exactly is in Da Lat?"

He turned back to her, but his eyes were not as soft, "People. There are people in Da Lat."

Her turn to snort. "Of course there are people in a city," she knew her tone was overly defensive, but she couldn't help it.

"I have friends in Da Lat."

"Oh? Anyone I know?" Again she tried the coy smile, this time it was an utter crash and burn.

Hobie readjusted in his chair, pulling his arm from behind her as he did. "I doubt it," was all he said.

Heart sinking, Presley wished she could think of something witty and marvelous to say, but she couldn't. There was only one thought racing through her mind and it had overtaken everything else. Hobie was leaving. He was leaving and something deep inside of her whispered the deeply depressing realization that she couldn't go with him. She wasn't invited.

The magical light of the ballroom seemed to darken as they sat in a gloomy silence. Hobie leaned forward and rested his elbows on his knees, his hands clasped loosely together. She couldn't see his face anymore, but it looked like he was staring at the floor in front of him, not at the crowded ballroom and the happy partygoers.

Presley's whole body was tight and brittle, like she might

shatter into a thousand pieces if someone interrupted them and tried to engage in small talk. With a fragile smile she looked around the room. The gaiety was overbearing. Taking in a breath of thick humid air, Presley was sick to her stomach, afraid she might throw up.

"You should see it," Hobie said.

His voice brought her back from the strange emotional cliff she had been teetering on, steadying her so she could speak, if just barely.

"Da Lat?" she asked weakly.

Hobie nodded, giving her a sideways smile before looking back toward the party. "The city is really beautiful, of course. It's the City of a Thousand Flowers…for honeymooners, they say." He paused and gave her a quick bashful glance before going on, "And there's waterfalls and the countryside. Agriculture like vegetables and fruit, plus all of the flowers. So many flowers."

Presley held still, afraid to comment or even move for fear she would throw her foot in her mouth once again. Say something snarky. That seemed to be her habit.

Hobie relaxed into his thoughts as he continued talking, but his mind seemed far away, "But what's really great about it is the people. They're kind and so…I don't know…gentle."

Another pause. Presley yearned to know more. She wished she could experience this place, see it through his eyes. She felt like she had lived her whole life with all of the privileges that money can buy, but had somehow missed out on something. Something organic and true. Something that Hobie Brent had in buckets, and that she, Ms. Money Bags, the first born and heir apparent of Mack Monroe's vast fortune and business empire, had never even tasted. Not one tiny drop.

"You know, there are whole systems in this world that don't even operate using money," Hobie continued, almost like he was reading her mind. But that was impossible, his gaze was still fixed on the crowded party. "They barter, they trade, they help each other with food and natural medicines." As he spoke his eyes moved slowly over the display of wealth in front of them. "They're good to each other. They live long lives. They don't have much money, but they have family and they have love," he turned his head to look at her, eyes shining. So much so that she thought he might be tearing up.

A hard knot formed at the back of her throat and she had to push hard against it to find her voice to answer, "It sounds wonderful."

His gaze locked onto hers and the intensity of it silenced any further comment. The look wasn't one of anger. Anger would have made her defensive. She didn't feel defensive. She felt connected. Drawn into his eyes, into their darkness, where all facades fell away and she could hide her soul deep inside of his.

If only she were welcome.

On the plane, a shiver flickered across her shoulders at the memory of that look. The look he had given her before they were interrupted by a business acquaintance and their last moment alone together had ended.

"Are you ready?" Jaxson sat down opposite her in the swiveling leather seat that shared a small table with her seat.

Presley emerged from her thoughts and blinked at him, "Ready for what?"

Jaxson raised one eyebrow at her and gave the tablet in his lap a meaningful look. "The construction estimates for the new office building in Denver."

"Oh, right," she pushed herself into a straighter sitting position. "Go ahead."

Jaxson studied her for a long moment, glanced down at his tablet again, then back at her. With an almost imperceptible sigh he placed his tablet upside down on the table between them. "What's the matter?"

She faltered before responding, "Nothing's the matter."

He tilted his head to the side and gave a slight shake of his head as if to say 'no'.

Presley peeked over his shoulder at Ronnie who had dozed off after her second mimosa while watching some old horror movie on the giant screen fixed to the wall at the front of the cabin. Nobody else had wanted to leave so early except her sister, who wanted to get back to work in New York as badly as Presley wanted to escape the Villa.

With Ronnie down for the count, Presley considered her options. Should she confide in Jaxson and get some of his friendly advice? He was a smart man. She trusted him with practically everything else in her life. After a brief hesitation, she decided no. She would rather forget Hobie Brent and get some work done. No need to explain her crumbling emotional state to her personal assistant.

"Jaxson, just give me the numbers," she insisted.

He shook his head 'no' again and with all of the boldness he possessed, which was a lot, he proceeded to stare her down.

It worked.

At first she opened her mouth to scold him, but found herself at a loss for words. She couldn't think of one good reason why she would rather talk about construction numbers than about what was bothering her. The biggest problem truly was she was afraid if she started talking about Hobie she might start crying. Nothing would say Out of Control Crazy Boss to a personal assistant like blubbering about her ridiculous romantic life.

Jaxson's stern look softened and his shoulders dropped. He leaned forward like a teenage girl about to share a confidence, "Look, I think I know what's going on. I just think you should talk about it instead of bottling it all up inside."

"You know?"

"Girl, everyone knows," he declared, and this honest, somewhat sassy, response was enough to push her over the edge.

Presley unloaded everything on him. As Jaxson poured her a mimosa and replenished it over and over again, she told him all about her interactions with Hobie. From how he had caught her when she fell off the veranda, to the wonderful time they'd had at their Central Park picnic, to how he had held her in his arms in the vineyard only to pull away from her after her bumbling responses to him at the party.

As she spoke, Jaxson nodded and exclaimed at the appropriate times, and basically allowed her to vent all of her feelings. Anger, embarrassment, sadness, and even the worst one, hopeless puppy love. Everything spilled out into the safe space of their private jet with only the occasional screaming of Ronnie's horror movie interrupting her flow.

By the time she was done explaining why she had bolted from the party the night before and demanded they leave for New York so early the next day, Presley was on her third, or possibly fourth, mimosa.

"I'm a mess, Jaxson. I can't stop thinking about his big, stupid face," she confessed, flopping her head back and covering her eyes dramatically with the back of her hand.

Jaxson made a comical wince. "He's got a pretty amazing face."

"I know!" she cried out dismally. Ronnie mumbled something in her sleep. Presley let her hand slip off her face and leaned in towards Jaxson, lowering her voice to a drunken whisper, "I know…and he's got an amazing body…and voice…and he's so funny and cute…ugh!" She sagged back into her chair.

"From what you've said, though, I don't see why you think this is a lost cause," he offered.

Presley screwed up her face into a scowl. "He's so nice, Jaxson!"

"And that's not good?"

"No, it's not good."

"Why?"

Presley drank down the last of her mimosa like it was a shot of whiskey, placed her champagne glass upside down on the table and said with authority, "Because he's *too* nice. And I'm *not* nice."

Jaxson laughed out loud then caught himself when he realized she was serious. "You're nice," he corrected.

Presley chuckled, but there was no humor in it. "I am most definitely not nice." She could see he was going to protest so she waved her finger at him slowly and continued, "Oh, I put on a pretty good show. I have a refined facade that might be considered nice. Sometimes I dump some of my billions of dollars on someone to get them to think I'm being nice. But deep down I'm not nice. Do you know I have never done one single solitary decent thing just for the sake of being nice? And that's the truth."

Jaxson waited soberly. He didn't seem to know how to respond. She shrugged, what difference did it make? She had already spilled her guts to him. Why not tell him everything?

Presley leaned over the table and tapped her forefinger onto its smooth surface for emphasis. Her words were a little slurred, but she wasn't going to let that keep her from telling the absolute truth. "Deep down, Jaxson...*deep* down...I'm small and selfish and wretched and–and–unworthy." Presley punctuated this admission with a hiccup.

Jaxson stared at her for a moment before he started to speak. He was immediately interrupted by the ringing of a cell phone.

"Wha–?" Ronnie sat bolt upright from where she'd been slouch sleeping in her chair. She fumbled for her cell that was blaring a techno version of Beethoven's 5th symphony and answered groggily.

Presley, meanwhile, slumped in her chair and looked at her empty upside down champagne glass with longing. Maybe she could make all of the ugly feelings go away with one more mimosa.

"Ruby!" Ronnie's phone voice was loud, but Presley ignored it and switched her stare out the plane window.

Jaxson hadn't taken his eyes off of her. She could sense his desire to continue their conversation.

"Ms. Monroe–" he started.

She waved him off with one flick of her hand. "It doesn't matter."

"But I think you may be misinterpreting–"

"No, I'm not. It's time to move on."

Unaware of the intimate nature of their conversation, Ronnie called out to them, "Ruby is delivering more of her orphan dogs in New York tomorrow. Want to meet her for dinner?"

Presley gave her a wan smile and nodded, then turned her attention back out the window. Ruby. Why couldn't she be more like Ruby? Ruby did good things all the time, every day probably. If she was more like Ruby things between her and Hobie may have worked out.

She let out a heavy sigh and leaned her head back, closing her eyes to the whole subject.

The white noise of the plane blended with Ronnie's phone conversation, the horror movie sound track, and Jaxson's stoic silence. All of this plus her four mimosas made her groggy. Just a she was about to drift into a woozy sleep, the image of Sugar Pop's funny little face formed in her mind.

Her buggy eyes looked sad and she made little breathy whining sounds. Presley remembered holding her. How it had felt to hold her tiny, wriggling body and her sweet pink tongue darting out to give her doggy kisses.

What was it Hobie had said about Sugar Pop? She was a hard one to place. That was it.

A cool liquid spilled over her heart, growing colder and colder as it moved, until it felt like it had frozen solid, tightly binding her heart so it could barely beat. She tried to swallow, but a lump at the back of her throat kept that from happening. Presley realized she was crying and if she made any attempt to stop, the lump in her throat grew ragged and painful while the ice squeezed her heart even harder.

Poor little Sugar Pop. Poor little thing. All alone, desperate to find someone to love and to be loved by.

Warm tears trickled down Presley's cheeks, but she kept her eyes closed. She could only hope Jaxson had moved on to actually working and wasn't watching her anymore.

"Oh that's really great, Ruby," Ronnie was still talking on the phone, blissfully unaware of her sister's emotional breakdown just yards away.

Thoughts of Sugar Pop and Ruby mixed together in Presley's mind as she cried silently, waiting for the ice to break her heart completely.

Suddenly, out of the dismal mess stewing inside of her soul, an idea flashed. A crazy wonderful idea. An idea that almost immediately melted the ice around her heart and made the lump in her throat disappear.

Presley opened her eyes and called out, "Sugar Pop!"

Jaxson and Ronnie looked at her in surprise.

Presley, barely able to contain her excitement, pointed at Ronnie and said, "Tell Ruby I want to adopt Sugar Pop."

A bit baffled, Ronnie did as she was asked while Presley gave Jaxson a brilliant smile.

"What is a Sugar Pop?" Jaxson asked.

"She's a sweet, dear, tragic little abandoned dog who needs me. And I'm going to adopt her."

Saying it aloud like this lifted her high into the air, which was saying a lot seeing that she was already jetting somewhere over France. She was certain that opening her home up to little Sugar Pop was a brilliant idea. No, scratch that. It was the right thing to do. It was, without a doubt, a *nice* thing to do.

All of the gloominess of her mood dissipated. Tiny flutterings of joy appeared in her heart as she imagined taking Sugar Pop out of that horrible outdated old dog rescue building and bringing her home. She could buy her all kinds of adorable little outfits and take her to lunches with Faye and the girls, even business meetings. Presley was delighted with her plan.

Ronnie nodded as she listened to Ruby then looked at her sister with a sympathetic smile that squelched Presley's exuberance even before she spoke.

"Sorry, Presley," Ronnie said. "She says Sugar Pop has already been adopted."

CHAPTER 43

*H*obie rolled over in bed, pulling the covers up over his head in frustration. It was almost five o'clock in the morning and he hadn't slept all night. He hadn't slept in days.

With a heavy sigh he threw the covers clear off so they landed with a soft plop on the floor at the end of his bed. If he wasn't going to sleep he should at least get on with his day.

He threw on some clothes and made his way through his Dad's quiet penthouse apartment without turning on any lights. No sense in waking up the whole house just because he was an insomniac.

He wasn't one. An insomniac that is. In fact, he couldn't remember the last time he had not been able to asleep in his adult life. Normally he slept unperturbed, unbothered by noises in the night or strange dreams, waking each morning rested.

That was before Presley Monroe had literally landed in his arms at Villa Pallota.

First she had invaded his head, then his heart, and ever since his botched attempt to romance her at the opening night party and her subsequent abrupt departure from Italy, thoughts of her had invaded his sleep.

The kitchen lights flipped on automatically as he entered and went to the cabinet to retrieve what he needed to make some coffee.

"Can I help you, sir?" the housekeeper, Mary, appeared suddenly in the doorway.

Hobie jumped, startled. "Whoa, Mary," he said with a laugh. "I didn't know you were up."

"I get up early most days," she answered. Fully dressed with sparse makeup and her hair pulled back into a tight bun, she definitely looked like she was ready for the day. Her eyes went to the bag of coffee he had pulled out onto the counter. "Would you like me to make some coffee, sir?"

Disappointed at the interruption, or worn out from not sleeping, Hobie didn't know which, he backed away from the counter. "Sure, sure, that's fine."

"Very good, sir," she said and started the process.

Hobie watched her with a growing feeling of discontent. He didn't need or want anyone to make him coffee. This whole lifestyle of butlers and maids and servants wasn't his comfort zone. He looked forward to getting out on his own again, out of New York. He had been looking forward to taking Presley with him, if she had wanted to go, if she hadn't shut him down at the party.

He sighed and leaned against the massive granite topped island in the middle of the kitchen. When he closed his eyes they felt scratchy and raw, and when he opened them again he caught Mary watching him curiously.

"Is there anything else you would like, sir?"

You could stop calling me 'sir', he thought, but didn't say

it out loud. It wasn't Mary's fault that he was wrapped up with an incorrigible woman. A woman he wasn't sure returned his feelings. A woman he couldn't seem to forget.

The pitter patter of dog nails on hard wood flooring gave him an out.

"No, thank you. I think we're gonna go to the dog park. I'll pass on the coffee for now."

Before she could answer he exited the kitchen and went to the foyer where they kept leashes and dog treats. He would get out of the house, get some fresh air, and come up with a new strategy.

He'd had a plan when they were in Italy. The finalizing of all of their business dealings left every possibility open for something more from he and Presley's relationship. The way she responded to him in the vineyard that night he had been so certain she felt the same way. However, that certainty had dried up and flew away by the end of the night.

"Let's go to the park," Hobie called out, the pitter patter of dog nails on hard wood down the hallway turning into a clattering of excitement at his words.

He grinned. Nothing like taking a dog for a walk. Their undying optimism was usually contagious. Maybe the lack of sleep was making him loopy, but he felt a renewed sense of purpose.

Presley was difficult, that was true, but didn't he like a challenge? Everything worthwhile took some effort. The world was full of people who failed just because they hadn't tried one more time.

Besides, he didn't feel right leaving Barcom, leaving the city, or leaving the country, without giving he and Presley another shot. If he was ever going to have a good night's sleep again he needed to try one more time.

His plan to woo her at the vineyard had flopped, but

maybe Presley needed something bigger, something more definitive, to understand how he truly felt.

"Go big or go home," he said out loud. Rocky jumped up, put his paws on Hobie's chest, and barked in agreement.

CHAPTER 44

Grace smiled politely at the two women who had braved social norms and boldly approached while she was lunching to ask for an autograph. She had grown used to this kind of attention over the decades and tried to take it in stride. Faye not so much.

"Good heavens, Grace, can't you tell them to call your agent or something?" Faye sniffed as the women retreated, huddled excitedly over her prized signature.

"It's called being generous. You should try it sometime," Grace answered, turning her attention back to her lunch companions.

Faye clicked her tongue and shook her head in disagreement. "What about maintaining an air of mystique?"

"That went away with selfies," Grace quipped. She took a sip of her sparkling wine and discreetly glanced around the dining room. Nobody else looked like they were working up the courage to ask for an autograph or a selfie, which brought on a pang of disappointment.

Grace had reached a level of superstardom in her lifetime

that exceeded her wildest dreams. Yet fame could disappear just as quickly as it arrived. She knew this from watching too many of her colleague's acting careers fizzle out. Especially after they hit 40. Especially women.

"Back to the task at hand," Ruby said.

"Yes," Ronnie chimed in. "Let's figure out how we're going to pull this off without her knowing."

The 'her' Ronnie referred to was the conspicuously absent Presley.

"I'll handle all of the birthday party details," Faye announced.

Ronnie nudged Grace under the table with her foot. Grace took the hint and suggested, "Don't you think I should do that?"

"Why shouldn't I do it?" Faye asked.

The real answer was that Faye was not the best at keeping secrets. Since they were plotting an intricate birthday surprise that required them to interact with Presley and not let the cat out of the bag, Grace's acting skills would come in handy. However, Grace decided to go with the shorter answer that wouldn't offend Faye.

"I've planned our birthday parties for years." Strangely, Grace had become their group's birthday planner. A role she fell into partly because planning a party was easier than planning a film shoot, and she had plenty of experience planning film shoots. Truth be told she had always enjoyed throwing extravagant birthday parties for her friends. Though as they grew older she sometimes wondered if birthdays held the same joy as they did when they were young, vibrant, and unwrinkled. Grace gave Faye a sympathetic look. "She might get suspicious if you do it this year."

Faye frowned. "That's true."

"Maybe you could help choose the location, Faye? And let

Grace take care of the rest?" Ronnie looked between the two of them, hoping the suggestion would ease any hard feelings.

"Marvelous," Faye said, smiling happily.

"Great," Ruby continued moving them down their checklist of to-do's. "Now, I think we need to involve Jaxson. Do you agree?"

They all nodded and murmured their approval. Nothing could happen in Presley's world without Jaxson's knowledge anyway, they may as well recruit him to their team.

"And Pete," Ronnie added. "He'll want to help if he can."

Ruby typed that piece of information into her cell phone then looked up at Ronnie, "So you'll talk to Pete?"

Ronnie nodded and said, "And Jaxson."

"Okay." Ruby nodded efficiently and scrolled through more information on her phone. She turned her attention to Grace, "And we'll wait on you to let us know when this grand event will take place."

Faye chimed in, "And I'll tell you where!"

"Will you try to keep it here? In the city? I think it would be easier given the circumstances," Ruby suggested.

"Of course," Faye said. Her elation sank a little as she continued, "Presley's been in such a state lately, I doubt she would agree to take a trip."

"Yes…" Ronnie chewed on her bottom lip, worried. "Do you think we're horrible for keeping all of this a secret? I mean she seems so miserable these days."

Silence fell over their table as they all thought about the question. Finally, Ruby answered, "It's just a short time more, a few weeks. Since we've been asked to help it's not exactly our secret to tell, is it? Anyway, I think in the end she will be thrilled. Don't you?" She looked around the table at the others and, one by one, they all agreed.

Invigorated by the fun of giving one of their dearest

something that would certainly fill her heart with joy, Grace straightened her shoulders and raised her glass. Filled with confidence at her ability to smoothly manipulate Presley into her birthday surprise, she smiled at her friends and declared, "I promise, she won't have a clue what's really going on."

CHAPTER 45

*P*resley had never considered herself someone who wallowed in self pity. Sure she had her dark moods and she could be, she knew, a little demanding, but all of that came with the territory of running a huge multi-national conglomeration. Someone had to make the hard decisions. It was simply her lot in life that much of the time that person turned out to be her. She didn't let herself dwell on it. She didn't allow dwelling on anything.

That's why she spent several weeks definitely not dwelling on the fact that she missed out on adopting her strange little soul mate, Sugar Pop.

"We have a lot of dogs that need good homes," Ruby tried to console her when they all met for dinner by offering the possibility of adopting a different dog.

Presley was having none of it. She shook her head tersely and stabbed at her crab and lemon thyme soufflé. "No, thanks. It was a momentary lapse of insanity. It worked out for the best. I don't have time for a pet."

"Agreed," Faye interjected. She beamed at Presley over her grilled salmon, "You're a powerful executive, darling.

Nobody expects you to take care of an abandoned dog, too. Besides, not everyone is cut out to have a pet."

The comment stung a little, though Presley knew Faye didn't mean it to. Faye had never been one to tolerate pets or children for that matter. Wanting no fur babies of her own, Faye meant to compliment Presley for her life choices. It just didn't feel so much like a compliment.

Presley squinted her eyes together in a debutante smile and took a sip of her cucumber water. The rest of her crab soufflé lunch would remain untouched.

Nose to the grindstone, Presley was once again all about business. She felt good in this space. Comfortable. Not dwelling on Sugar Pop and absolutely not dwelling on Hobie.

Before they landed in New York, she had realized that her little break down was over. She and Hobie had never been defined. They had never even kissed. Only almost kissed. Not the same thing. And by the time she received his text asking her why she left the Villa earlier than planned, her feet were firmly standing on the solid, concrete surface of New York City and she knew she was over him.

Work to do. No more time to waste. She had replied with a few taps on her cell phone and a flick of her wrist as she slipped it away into her purse. No response came. She was not surprised.

Presley didn't waste another moment wondering about Hobie Brent and what he might be thinking or doing or where he might be going. Their project was over and settled and she had quite literally a thousand other things to do.

"What about your birthday?" Grace wanted to know. She had a thing about birthdays, liked to make a big deal out of them. Especially her own, but also her best friend's special days.

"I'm not in the mood for a big celebration," Presley shrugged.

Grace had popped by her office after taking some big meeting with a production company about an upcoming film. She pouted her lips at Presley, "Come on, Presley. It only comes around once a year."

Presley sighed.

"I'll do all the planning if you want," Grace offered. "Ronnie will help me."

When Grace planned Faye's last birthday they had ended up in Fiji. The prospect of laughing and music and exotic drinks with little umbrellas made Presley's stomach churn. Charts and numbers and difficult meetings with bull headed executives where she could use her power and send them skittering sounded much more appealing.

"As long as I don't have to plan anything," Presley reluctantly agreed. Mostly just to get Grace to leave her alone so she could get back to work. "And no trips. I don't feel like going anywhere right now. Too much to do."

"Can I at least make it a little fun?"

"Fine. Work it out with Jaxson."

Jaxson, who knew better than to ever bring up her blubbering drunken conversation with him on the plane, was just as pragmatic as she was. She would instruct him that no umbrella drinks or any other foolishness was to be allowed at her birthday party.

"Okay, I'll get with Jaxson," Grace gave her a movie star smile and a Hollywood half-hug and went on her way.

Great. With that over, everything was back to normal.

Well, not exactly everything.

Presley, despite putting in long hours at the office and upping her workout regimen to burn off extra emotional energy, was having an exceptionally difficult time sleeping.

Laying awake, everything around her dark and silent, she could not keep her eyes closed or quiet her mind enough to fall asleep. If she did come close to dozing off a heavy weight would sink onto her and she had to focus to push it away from her. Not wanting to feel anything, she padded around her penthouse apartment and stared for hours out the massive windows with New York City sprawled in front of her, a mass of lights and movement no matter what time of night it was. If she let her guard down too long, loneliness would hit her square in the center of her chest and make it so she could not breathe.

So she did everything she could to not let her guard down, which meant no relaxation and no sleep.

Finally Jaxson got her some sleeping pills. When she took them she didn't feel the heavy weight and she didn't get up and wander, but she didn't really sleep either. Not peacefully anyway. Sleep came in fits and starts, the nerves in her legs spasmed every now and then so she would jerk awake then fall dismally back onto her pillow.

When she did sleep, she dreamed. And her dreams were far worse than staring blankly out the window all night.

In her dreams she was lost. Sometimes walking through a dark woods, sometimes through a dark town where all of the house lights were turned off and she was afraid to knock on someone's door for help. A cold wind would blow as she stumbled along, afraid that something might be following her, but mostly getting a growing sense that everything around her, the darkness, the emptiness, was all there would ever be. Nothing else existed in the world and nothing would change. She woke from each of these dreams with a sense of doom and a pressure in the room that pushed on her eardrums so her rapid breathing sounded raspy and desperate.

Then she would cry. Uncontrollably. Ragged, choking sobs so loud she would pull the pillow to her mouth and cry into it to muffle the sounds.

She decided to stop taking the pills and went back to her insomniac existence. At least it held its own kind of peace.

And so it went for several weeks, working like mad and staying up, silent and wretched every night, until her birthday.

It was the middle of summer in New York and her friends had planned an afternoon birthday celebration that was to take place at a dear friend of Faye's private gardens. Presley already didn't want to go and the idea of sitting in the sweltering heat of a garden party with Leopold and other acquaintances increased her apathy tenfold.

And yet, here she was. Dolled up in a peach Ralph Lauren linen sundress, canvas wedge shoes and the widest brimmed straw hat she could find for shade. The hat was so wide the edges of it dipped down from the weight, extending over and past her shoulders, down her back, and flopping so low over her eyes she had to tip her head back a bit to see out from underneath.

With a giant white fabric chrysanthemum as its decoration the hat was one of those fashion statements that bordered on the ridiculous, the kind that one of Ronnie's supermodels might wear, or one of Faye's old lady friends who came from money so old they were almost royalty, but Presley didn't care. She wanted shade and she wanted anonymity, even if it was her birthday party. With the help of the hat and her white rimmed Prada sunglasses she hoped to make it through the get together with minimal human interaction.

"I love it!" Ruby greeted her warmly. "Did Ronnie fix you up with that hat?"

"It's my birthday hat," Presley teased. "I picked it out myself."

Not true. Jaxson helped. She had grown closer to him after the jet plane incident, even though neither of them spoke about it. He was gentler with her than he had been before. Less crisp.

"You need this," he had told her carrying the giant hat out of her closet.

"Where did I get that?"

"You've had it and were waiting for a special occasion," he said with a grin. After she'd tried it on she looked at him doubtfully. "It's that Hepburn look you pull off so well," he said encouragingly.

She had agreed after realizing how well it hid her face and was glad for it when she got to the party.

"Happy Birthday, darling," Faye approached and gave her a side hug and air kiss.

"Thank you," Presley air kissed her back.

"Where's Ronnie?" Ruby asked.

"She and Pete are coming in a separate car," Presley said. "They tried to pretend it wasn't because they're sneaking me in some kind of present. But I think that's what they're doing."

"Of course they are…it's your birthday!" Faye linked her arm through Presley's and motioned for Ruby to link her other arm. "Now, we are supposed to take you to Grace who has something special for you right away." And they were off, walking arm-in-arm through a hidden Manhattan paradise.

So much wealth flowed through New York City that luxury was not uncommon to find. However, Leopold's garden was an unexpected delight. After entering through a 15 foot tall iron gate that reminded Presley of something from a castle in Europe, a short turning path led them into a long rectangular courtyard whose landscaping rivaled the famed Brooklyn Botanical gardens in its lush depth.

The central area was a black stone patio where the spaces between the stones contained ground cover plants, some in full white flower, some bright green. Wrought iron bistro tables filled several spaces on the patio, which was lined with luxurious flowering plants of all different varieties and heights. Ivy climbed the walls of the surrounding building and on the far end was a water feature, a waterfall to be exact, that spilled joyfully over black and white stones carefully placed to make the most delightful splashing sounds as it made its way to the small pool underneath.

A pergola of elaborately twisted iron ran along one wall and dripped with flowering climbers in yellow, orange, and pink. The foliage was so thick on the structure that it was like entering a private tunnel when you went inside. Nobody could see into the pergola from the outside and from inside the abundant plants created a magical ceiling all its own. Walking through it was like going through an enchantment, an experience that promised something wonderful once you emerged from the other side.

Gorgeous bouquets of all white blooms adorned each of the bistro tables and an arch with matching decoration had been set up over the luncheon table next to the waterfall and pool. Fat white lights strewn with white and orange ribbons would light up the garden far into the night. A guitar duo was seated discreetly in one corner of the garden to provide music for all of the guests. About 40 people were milling about and being courteously attended by half a dozen neatly turned out serving staff.

It was lovely. Truly lovely. Still, the dull drone of depression suppressed any joy Presley may have normally felt.

Two pure white Bichon Frise, fluffed to the nines, raced to meet them as they entered the garden, followed closely by Leopold himself.

"You're here," he panted as he weaved through the small crowd and tried to keep up with the dogs. "Lenny! Baxter! Leave the birthday girl alone."

The Bichon's hopped happily around Presley's feet and

she let go of Ruby and Faye to reach down and pet their impossibly soft fuzzy heads.

"It's all right," she told Leopold, who was overly concerned with any damage the dogs might cause to her shoes. "I love dogs." The words popped out and took her a little off guard. Ruby and Faye exchanged a look and Presley knew they had found it an odd statement. At least coming from her lips.

Leopold scooped up one Bichon in each arm, scolding them mildly as they licked his face, and led the way to the white flowered arch. As their small procession progressed through the other guests they greeted her with side hugs and air kisses and all the best birthday wishes.

"Happy Birthday!" Grace exclaimed. She stood in front of a long table laden with food in shining silver dishes. In the center of the table was another lavish bouquet of white flowers, this one quite a bit taller than the others. Really tall in fact. Grace saw Presley admiring it and clapped her hands together like a little girl. "That's your cake!"

"What?" Presley looked again, disbelieving.

"Isn't it gorgeous?" Grace asked without needing to have an answer.

Presley stepped closer and peered at the intricate frosting design that looked uncannily real. White roses, lilies, and hydrangeas cascading over and around each other. She turned to Grace to tell her how amazing this cake was and ask her how they were going to cut into it, but stopped short when she saw what Grace was holding.

"This is for you, too," Grace held up a white satin sash with the words "Birthday Girl" blazing in glittering gold across the front.

Presley blinked, looked up into Grace's big green eyes full of delight and said, "No."

Faye and Ruby giggled like school girls on either side of her as Grace pouted her lips in an exaggerated response.

"Ronnie said you would love it," Grace said.

"Ronnie lied," Presley quipped.

"Come on, Presley, it's your birthday!" Ruby took the sash and held it up so they could get a better look. "You only get one a year."

After a round of good natured teasing and cajoling by all of her friends, Presley reluctantly put on the sash. What did it matter anyway, it's not like they were out in public where just anyone could see her.

"Now," Leopold took her to the side of the table so they were standing in the relative quiet at one end of the flower covered pergola. He was still holding Lenny...or maybe it was Baxter. The two dogs were impossible to tell apart. "I've been wanting to talk to you about something Steven and I have been working on."

Presley listened politely at first, then with deepening interest as Leopold described a new program he and his husband were putting their significant money and resources behind. It was a non-profit that hoped to help transform the roughly 40,000 acres of New York's rooftops into green roofs.

"We're addicted to gardening," Leopold laughed as he swept his arm toward the gorgeousness around them. "We thought we could take that passion and do something important with it."

"That's wonderful, Leopold," Presley told him, truly happy at this idea.

"As you know, green roofs are not only beautiful, they cut carbon emissions, insulate the building so it uses less energy, and they absorb rain water–

"And they help control storm runoff plus provide space for wildlife," Steven stepped into their conversation holding the other Bichon. "And you know how we love the birds and the bees, sweetie."

Presley chuckled, "It sound great, how did you get involved?"

"Well, that's what we wanted to thank you for," Leopold reached out and squeezed her arm warmly. "We heard all about what you were doing with Villa Pallotta."

"You know how Faye can talk. She told us everything," Steven said.

"How you and Mack were turning your business interests towards sustainability and..." Leopold blinked back tears. "Well...we were inspired."

Surprised, Presley asked, "Inspired?"

"Yes, sweetie. You're an inspiration!" Steven exclaimed, the thrill in his voice sending Baxter and Lenny into wriggling fits.

She stared at the two men for a long moment as a warm fuzzy sensation swelled in her chest.

Inspired? By her?

Leopold and Steven shared a kind smile then turned their loving gazes back to her. Leopold was her same height and when he leaned in to speak softly to her, the Bichon's soft white fur tickled her chin.

"Don't look so shocked, Presley. You're changing the world. You should be proud of yourself."

Tears welled up in her eyes as all of the shame and guilt she had been wrestling with came to the surface and was met with a brand new truth. She had done something nice for the world. It wasn't the biggest contribution that she could make, but it was only the first. She could do more. She would do more. She would *be* more.

Presley let out a small choking laugh and took Steven's hand that he was offering for comfort.

"Thank you," she said. And she meant it, she truly did.

"I'm so–" her thought was cut short by a loud disruption at the entrance to the garden.

A woman's surprised squeal. The clatter of a chair tumbling. The jingling of dog tags. A man's voice calling out, "Rocky, no!"

Presley turned toward the noise. Even as she recoiled in surprise from the giant brown blur running at her, a thrill she could not control exploded inside of her heart.

CHAPTER 46

*P*eople scattered in all directions yet Presley's feet stayed stuck to the ebony stones. With her head tilted back so she could see out from under the rim of her giant hat, the only sound she heard besides the violent yipping of the Bichons was Hobie's voice.

"Rocky, leave it!"

Less than two feet in front of her, a hairy, panting powerhouse of animal playfulness stopped his forward motion mid-air and plopped his butt down on the ground obediently. Rocky looked back at Hobie who was just a few steps behind him, a broken leash in one hand. Hobie lunged forward and took hold of the big dog's collar before he decided to disobey then looked in her direction with wide eyes. But he wasn't looking at Presley. Something behind her held Hobie's attention and from the expression on his face it was something awful.

She turned, jamming her hip into the buffet table. She must have stepped backwards and bumped into the table as Rocky approached. A few candles were knocked over. Several rolls had toppled off the top of very full baskets. But it only took an instant for Presley to see what held Hobie's horrified attention.

The cake.

Her beautiful white flower cake that towered over the rest of the food like a pyramid built for Aphrodite was wobbling. Not just wobbling. Swaying. Undulating from the base up like a belly dancer about to leap off of the table. It seemed alive.

Everyone froze, watching in alarm, aghast at what was obviously about to happen. All of the guests were strewn around the garden as if a tornado had flung them aside. Too far away or too confused to do anything. Utterly unable to stop the disaster taking place in front of their eyes.

Presley gasped and reached for the cake, but she was unstable on her feet because of her twisted position and recent shock of being nearly mauled with slobbery dog kisses. A hand grabbed the back of her arm, steadying her. Hobie, she knew from her visceral reaction to his touch.

Leopold's lone voice rose up like he was shouting in slow motion, "The caaaaake!"

He shoved Baxter or Lenny into Steven's arms and bolted toward the unstable pastry, arms outstretched. He was determined, red faced with effort, but it was obvious to Presley he was never going to make it in time. Everyone could tell by the tilt of the giant cake that it was about to go over and they raised a collective gasp.

From somewhere on the back side of the table, two hands reached around the middle of the cake and smooshed into its sides, stabilizing it, but not without damage. White frosting flowers crumbled under their fingers making deep gouges and squishing layers of cake from underneath all over their hands.

Though the damage was severe, it was restricted only to the two sides where the hands had taken hold. The good news was the rest of the cake stopped moving. Grace's lovely face popped around the side of the cake, awash with astonished delight.

"Grace!" Faye called out from where she had stumbled and been saved by a handsome young waiter, "You saved the day!"

Cheers lifted from the partygoers as they regained their composure. Grace raised one frosting covered hand to give a wave of triumph. Dismayed at the ruined spots on the cake she looked at Presley.

"I'm sorry, Pres," she said.

"No, I'm sorry," Hobie said. He was still holding the back of Presley's arm. She turned to see him better, but was blocked by her hat. "Brand new leash, he goes through them quickly, but not usually until they're a little worn out."

"No harm, no foul," Leopold declared. He was inspecting the remaining floral design on the cake. "It's still standing!" More cheers from the guests.

"I'm so sorry, Presley," Hobie's voice was nearer, as if he was leaning into her.

Presley used one hand to push up the rim of her hat so she could see him. His head was tilted sideways so he could look into her eyes. With her hat blocking out everything else it was like they were in their own little bubble. Just the look of him, his strong jaw, short cut beard, and the unbearably attractive wrinkle of worry on his brow took her breath away.

"I don't know what gets into this dog when he sees you," he said quietly. Despite the fact that this was an apology for a near fiasco, there was a twinkle in his eyes. "He goes a little nuts."

She blushed. Fiercely. Her giant white flower cake may have stopped wobbling, but her heart was wobbling like crazy.

The entire garden party was in a tizzy. Their narrow escape from catastrophe seemed to have raised everyone's vibration, creating boisterous conversations and bursts of laughter from all directions. Some of the waiters set the food table back to rights and some rushed off to bring new rounds of drinks at Leopold's request.

Presley couldn't tear her eyes from Hobie. In a white cotton long sleeve shirt and a pair of worn blue jeans he could have been any handsome guy at a coffee shop or grabbing a hot dog from a street vendor or meandering through a museum on a Saturday afternoon. But he wasn't just any handsome guy. He was her handsome guy. The handsome guy she was in love with.

This thought hit like a bucket of ice water dumped over her head. She sucked in her breath and could not exhale. Goosebumps raced across her arms and she was frozen in place, gawking at him as if she had never laid eyes on him before, yet certain she had known him since the beginning of time.

All of the wrenching pain and suffering since she last saw him in Italy rushed down through her chest into the pit of her stomach where it churned like lava. Nauseated, she knew she had to breathe before she fainted, but breathing was a struggle. She gripped her Birthday Girl sash with both hands, managing to inhale shakily, but was only overcome with the smell of his cologne. Dizzying.

The twinkle in Hobie's eyes dwindled, "Are you all right?"

She tried to smile and answer him, but her mouth only twisted awkwardly. A sound emitted from her throat, a high pitched squeak that barely formed the word, "Okay".

"Here," he slipped his arm around hers while also getting a firm grip on the short broken leash still attached to Rocky, leading them both into the quiet shade of the flower covered pergola. The cooler air helped Presley regain her ability to breathe, but Hobie did not let go of her arm. No doubt he was afraid she was about to faint.

"I'm fine," she tried to sound strong and reassuring.

Hobie gave her a shrewd look.

"No, really, I just got off balance…" her voice trailed off as she gazed at him, tipping her head back slightly so she could see all of him from underneath her hat. How could anyone look so amazing in jeans and a plain white shirt? Astonishing.

The concern in his eyes shifted as his own gaze wandered down to her sash and back up to the giant white chrysanthemum on her hat. He grinned. A sideways sexy grin that made her knees weak.

"Nice hat."

She dipped her chin and looked down at her feet. Her heart beat wildly. Being so close to him again, hearing his voice, the sparkle in his eyes, it was so much to take in. How could she manage a conversation? How could she tell him what she was feeling? How could she ever live without him? Her mind raced with questions and before she could regain control she began to cry.

Rocky whined and cocked his great furry head. She had a perfect view of him through the tunnel that her hat provided. Thankfully, the same tunnel was blocking Hobie from seeing her blubbering. All she could see were his shoes and the bottom of his jeans.

"Presley?"

Sniffling, she did her best to sound normal, "Yes?"

"Are you crying?"

She shook her head, sending her hat brim flopping. Hobie ducked down. She turned her head so he couldn't see underneath the brim, but he shifted his body with her every move so eventually she had to look at him. Either that or turn and walk away, and she couldn't bring herself to do that.

When he finally got a good look at her, red eyes wet with tears, his face fell. Instinctively, he placed two fingers under her chin and tilted her face up towards him so neither of them were ducking or bending anymore. Rocky made another sorrowful noise.

"I'm sorry we busted into your birthday party like that," Hobie said, genuinely distressed.

Presley coughed out a laugh, which thoroughly confused him. His bewildered expression sent her into a sporadic fit of giggles. He thought this was about the cake. That was adorable. And awful. Tears streamed down her cheeks as she tried to stop laughing. Was this what being hysterical felt like?

"It's not that," she finally said, waving her hand toward the cake that was standing somewhere on the other side of the wall of flowers.

"What is it then?"

His tone interrupted her bizarre laughing-crying and she stopped suddenly, a tiny hiccup escaping her throat. She peered at him from under her hat, seeing for the first time the fatigue in his eyes. His face was thinner and paler than Italy. A sharp stab of fear hit her heart. Could he be ill?

Presley reached out and touched his forearm. Too late, she realized this was a wildly reckless thing to do if she wanted to keep her feelings unknown. But she did it without thinking, only wanting to comfort him, to wipe the sadness that had crept into his eyes away.

"It's something...else..." she tried to think of a way to assure him that he and Rocky had not made her cry, not exactly anyway. If only his arm wasn't so strong underneath the cotton shirt. If only she could take her eyes away from his. If only she could tame her heart and convince him her outburst was nothing. That they were nothing.

So sensitive were her fingers to the sensation of him that

she felt his forearm flex underneath the thin white material of his shirt an instant before he moved. Even with that warning she was unprepared for the speed in which he slipped out of her grip, pulled his arm back, and caught her hand in his. When he lifted her hand to his mouth and brushed his lips across her bent fingers, her breath caught in her throat.

"Won't you tell me what's wrong? I hate to see you upset," he asked, still holding her hand in his, having moved it so he was holding it against his chest. Then with a shrug and a grin, "It's your birthday. You should be having fun on your birthday."

Torture and paradise. That's what Hobie holding her hand to his chest did to her senses. It was too much to bear, but everything she had ever wanted.

"Um…I'm a little more worried about you than my birthday," she said, crinkling her brow as she sniffled.

"Me?"

"You look tired…is everything okay? You're not sick are you?" The question popped out of her mouth too quickly to censor. She hoped it didn't sound too motherly.

He looked into her eyes for a long moment and she watched with growing excitement as the sparkle returned to them. His lips twitched, amused, as he glanced at the ground and back up again, catching her in that sparkle and not letting her go.

"I'm fine. I haven't been sleeping well…lately," his voice was tender yet scratched with an unspoken wretchedness she understood. Had he been suffering the same insomnia she had since Italy?

Almost all of the moisture left her mouth as she attempted to answer, "I–I haven't been sleeping well either."

Hobie raised one eyebrow, "Really?" He let his eyes wander over her cheeks, her lips, and down her neck, before lifting them again. "You don't look any worse for wear."

It was her turn to smile. "No?"

"Well, you're always well put together, Ms. Monroe."

Hobie squeezed her hand and her heart melted a little bit. All she wanted to do was run her fingers along his chest and wrap her arms around his neck, letting him pull her close like he had in Italy. If he would only do that everything would be fine.

"I want to…I need to talk to you–" he was interrupted by a loud, rough bark from Rocky. Presley jumped, startled from the sudden noise. Hobie frowned at his dog and said, "Rocky, that's enough."

"There they are!" Faye's voice floated down the long tunnel of flowers and both Presley and Hobie turned toward the sound. To Presley's great disappointment, Faye, Grace, Ruby, Ronnie, Pete and Jaxson all crowded around the corner and into the flower tunnel to join them.

CHAPTER 47

She liked the tall one. The one with long black hair who smelled like pepper and had a deep soft voice. He spoke to her with kind words, though she did not understand what he said.

The brown fuzzy one was bossy. Very bossy. He liked to tumble when he played and hopped dangerously around her with giant clumsy paws. She didn't like him as much as she liked the tall one, but sometimes, when he was sleepy, the brown fuzzy one curled up next to her on the big soft pillow near the window and she liked to sleep there with him.

The others were kind. They had many smells and she remembered the calm one with the warm brown eyes who had given her a place to sleep and eat when she had none of those. She liked the calm one.

The calm one was here now, but she was not holding her. The one with many treats was holding her, or trying to hold her, but she could not be still in his arms. Not for all the treats in the world. Because she smelled the tall one and the brown fuzzy one and someone else. Someone she had only smelled once, but had never forgotten.

Her favorite.

Her favorite was here, now! She could smell her scent on the breeze, above the scent of food and flowers and all who were present. She would never forget the way her favorite smelled. It was definitely her. If her favorite was here she had to find her, see her, be next to her.

She had to tell her favorite not to leave again. She had to tell her favorite that they were supposed to stay together. Surely her favorite would understand this time and keep her forever.

CHAPTER 48

*B*efore she could call out for them all to stop, turn around, and leave her and Hobie in peace, Presley noticed something squirming in Jaxson's arms. Something black and furry, skinny and odd looking, with a glint of gold. When the something caught her eye it yipped. Tiny, excited, desperate little yips.

Presley's mouth dropped open in surprise. "Sugar Pop?"

Hobie turned back to her, his smile beaming ten thousand volts strong. "Happy birthday!"

The sentiment was echoed by the whole gang as they joined them. Rocky and Sugar Pop punctuated the human's celebration with their own excited barking.

"Oh, Sugar Pop," Presley reached out to the funny little dog who was struggling against Jaxson's hold to get to her. Someone, Jaxson she suspected, had dressed her in a glittering gold doggie dress and stuck a matching doggie tiara to her head. This accentuated the fact that she only had one silly looking ear.

Still, Presley eagerly took the little bundle from Jaxson and held her up to her face. Sugar Pop emitted so many violent squeaking sounds of happiness that Presley wondered if she was going to pee from excitement.

Jaxson read her mind, "We just took her for a wee-wee so you should be fine."

"Yes, we don't want a repeat of the last time you held her," Ruby laughed.

"I don't understand..." Presley nuzzled her nose into Sugar Pop's barely fuzzy neck.

"Read her dress," Ronnie pulled out the stretchy material of the dress so she could see the words.

My Mommy's the Birthday Girl!

Presley laughed out loud. "What? How?"

She looked at all of her friends for an explanation. They were delighted with her reaction to her birthday gift. And all of them, especially Jaxson, glanced meaningfully at Hobie.

She turned to him, "You did this?"

He shrugged bashfully and gestured at all of her friends. "They all helped."

"But I thought she'd been adopted!"

He nodded, "She was, by me." When he saw she was still confused he continued. "Nobody was adopting her and I was worried she would never be chosen." He reached out and carefully rubbed Sugar Pop behind her one good ear, who rewarded him with a bout of spastic licks. "So I got it all organized before we went to Italy..." He shifted a little uncomfortably on his feet and his face reddened. She knew he was thinking about their intimate moments in the vineyard and the subsequent break off of all communications.

"Then I told him you had asked about Sugar Pop and he insisted on giving her to you instead," Ruby added.

"And he wanted to do it for your birthday," Ronnie said.

"It seemed like perfect timing," Grace interjected.

"It was perfect," Faye said with a wide smile. "Just look at her face. She's so ecstatic she's crying!"

Presley didn't know what to say. She was bursting with emotion and if the past few months had proven anything to her it was that she wasn't that great with expressing emotion. Hobie and all of her friends were enjoying her wonderful surprise almost as much as she was and she knew that she was utterly blessed.

"Thank you," she said. "Thank you so much." She had never been so grateful for a gift or a show of love like she was in this moment.

Baxter and Lenny, drawn by all of the noise, bounded into the pergola to investigate, followed quickly by Leopold and Steven. The crowd was too much for the tunnel of flowers and they all moved into the main garden where Presley showed off Sugar Pop to the world.

There were champagne toasts and she had to cut the slightly damaged flower cake. It was delicious, of course. To Presley's surprise she found that she was enjoying her birthday, introducing Sugar Pop to her friends and acquaintances, and chatting.

Hobie didn't leave her side. He and Rocky dutifully stayed with her and her little bundle of joy as she mingled and moved through the party. Hobie stayed so close to her that their bodies brushed against each other now and then. Presley didn't mind.

A few times, in especially crowded moments, he put his hand on the small of her back to guide her, much like they were on a date. Warm and fluttery, inexplicably content, Presley allowed her mind to wander and where it ended up was mildly amazing.

They were a couple. At least, that's the way this felt. Mingling together, Rocky dutifully in tow, Sugar Pop happy in her arms, Presley hadn't felt this much like a couple in her whole life. Not even when she was married.

Flushed. Talkative. Riding on a wave of domestic bliss, real or imagined, she never wanted this day to end.

But end it must, as all things do.

Jaxson appeared out of nowhere and announced, "I'll take these two for a wee walk." He gathered Sugar Pop from Presley's arms and took Rocky's short broken leash firmly in hand. Just before he turned to go he looked at Hobie and ever so slightly jerked his chin toward the pergola. Hobie gave him a barely perceptible nod.

What were they up to?

Before she had a chance to open her mouth and demand to know what else was going on, Hobie pressed his hand firmly into the small of her back and said quietly, "Come with me."

The guitar duo started a new song, Moon River, as he led her into the pergola again. Their carriage ride song. Presley looked to see if Hobie noticed, if the song held the same meaning to him as it did to her. She couldn't tell because he seemed focused on getting them to their destination with as little fuss as possible.

Surprisingly, the pergola was completely empty. For such a glorious space to be empty during a garden party seemed strange, but she was distracted with Hobie so close and the silent tunnel of flowers around them. Besides she didn't mind being alone with him and she reminded herself that she didn't need to always question everything. She needed to learn how to experience life as it came and stop trying to control everything.

He turned her to him, letting his hand slide from her back to her waist before taking her hand in his and smiling down at her. Butterflies filled her stomach then her chest and then her whole body. Their song floated on the warm, sweet smelling air.

"Thank you so much for Sugar Pop. I love her," she said.

"I'm glad. She loves you, too, I think." His eyes twinkled.

Her heart warmed and she smiled, biting her lip to keep from responding. The best way to not ruin the moment by blurting out something strange or awkward was to remain as quiet as possible.

Hobie, still holding her one hand, reached out and took the other. He ducked his head and cleared his throat, then said, "You know I'm leaving in a few days."

"Right...I know...where in Asia are you going?" She bit her lip again, stopping the flow of superficial conversation that wanted to rear its boring head.

He dismissed the question with a shake of his head, "No. That's not what I wanted to talk about." He looked up and his dark eyes pierced hers so intensely a piece of her soul was drawn into him. "I want to talk to you about something. I don't want to leave without saying...without telling you... without you knowing..."

She waited, her heart pounding so loud she was afraid she may not hear him when he did speak. Yet she only dared stand perfectly still. Trembling. Mute. Terrified.

"Presley, I think you should know that...that I've fallen in love with you."

The words hung between them. She could hardly believe she had heard him correctly. He squeezed her hands in his and took one step closer. The warmth of his body drifted across the inches between them and made her tingle. She thought her heart might explode with joy.

"I think I've been in love with you since we were kids, really," he continued. "When I saw you again after all those years the old feelings came back."

Presley stared at him and kept her lips firmly pressed together. Afraid to talk, but also afraid she might start crying again.

He shifted on his feet, but didn't let go of her hands as he kept on, "Maybe these past few months haven't meant the same to you, maybe it was just work. But it wasn't just work for me. Working with you, being around you, seeing you, standing next to you, it's…I've come to realize that those moments with you are everything to me." He let out a laugh. "Even when we aren't getting along. When we don't see eye to eye. I love those moments, too, Presley." He sighed with relief, the relief of someone who has been holding something in for too long. "The thing is, I don't ever want to be away from you again."

Stunned, her breath came fast and shallow. His face, his dear, handsome face, was taunt with emotion as he waited for her to respond. After a few moments in silence, she watched as the hope and intensity retracted from his eyes. They darkened and she felt his hands loosen on hers.

No! She wanted to shout at him. Don't leave me. Don't pull away! But no sound came. All of her love for him, all of her insecurity and fear, tangled together at the back of her throat and she could not answer.

He searched her eyes and she saw the questions and the pain rising in his. Leaning closer to her, whispering gruffly, he said, "Say something. Anything. Can you honestly say you feel nothing for me?"

The lump in the back of her throat hurt, but the look on his face was worse than the pain. Just as his hands began to drop, just as he was about to pull away, she managed to cry out.

"Yes!" The word sprung from her throat mixed with a choking sob.

His brow furrowed. "Yes, you feel nothing for me?"

"No!" she was sobbing now, uncontrollable happy sobs.

He studied her as she sniveled several unintelligible words. "Presley," he said with finality. "I don't know what you're saying."

She took a deep, shuddering breath and tried to compose herself. Then, when she thought she was ready, she blurted out, "I'm trying to say I love you, too." Immediately her face screwed into an ugly cry and she covered her mouth with her hand.

All of the tension and pain left Hobie in an instant. He stood, dumbfounded, for a few moments before saying, "Wait. You do?"

She nodded, still crying into her hand.

"You love me?" he asked, this time more sure of her answer as he pulled her into his arms.

She nodded and said, "I do!" It came out as a wail.

He deftly wrapped his arms around her and bent her hat brim back so her cheek could rest lightly on his chest. The firm warmth of his muscles and the sound of his heart beating strong and bold calmed her down. She was trembling all over and he stroked her back and arms, making shushing sounds until she stopped crying completely.

When she sighed contentedly and was fully relaxed into him, his chest rumbled with a low chuckle.

She tilted her head back and looked up at him, "What's funny?"

Hobie Brent, her dearest love, looked down into her eyes and grinned. "I don't know if you know this, but you're not the easiest person in the world to read."

This made her chuckle, too, but she didn't laugh long, because the next moment Hobie's hand cupped her chin and he tilted her lips up to his for their very first kiss. Firm and tender, it was pure bliss and Presley's heart lifted out of her body so she felt as if she was floating through the tunnel of flowers on her way to heaven.

The notes of Moon River danced around them and every other thought left her mind. There was only Hobie holding her tightly, kissing her gently with a hint of intense passion barely controlled in his touch, murmuring into her hair, running his fingers up and down her back, whispering his love into the small of her neck.

Just when she thought she would never be able to return to the party, a clip-clopping of horse's hooves interrupted their embrace. The sound grew louder and Presley's curiosity overcame her.

She pulled away from Hobie and cocked her ear to listen. "Do you hear horse hooves?"

His smile gave him away and she knew that he had more magic in store for her birthday.

"Your carriage awaits," he said with a bow.

Minutes later they were in the carriage. Rocky at their feet, Sugar Pop tucked between them, riding through the streets of New York City.

"So we're going to finally finish our carriage date?" she asked with delight.

"Oh, no, Ms. Monroe, we aren't finishing anything. This is just the beginning," he said.

"Is that a promise?"

Hobie flashed her his shining smile, "It's a guarantee."

And as she had come to expect, he was true to his word.

The End

EPILOGUE

The first thing he did was whisk her away to
Vietnam. To Da Lat, the most romantic city in
Vietnam and one of the most enchanting places she had ever
seen.

The Ana Mandara Villas was considered one of the most
romantic hotels in Vietnam and Presley found they lived up
to their reputation. Built on the side of a hill surrounded by
deep green foliage and extensive gardens with elegant landscaping the hotel had an Eden-like feeling. Slow buzzing
insects and long stemmed flowers bending in the gentle
breeze soothed her mind. Pure serenity.

The buildings had been built in the 1920's in the French
style. Rich hard wood floors underfoot and dark wood
framed beds with soft white comforters provided a peaceful
place to nap after long mornings of sight seeing. Slender
French doors opened onto a private patio. A sweet table and
two chairs sat on the patio, which looked out over one of the
quietest sections of the garden. They even had their own
stone steps leading off the patio to a private path that led to a
hidden gazebo.

Presley stood next to the bed where Hobie still slept. The afternoon air was warm and heavy with humidity. A white canopy of paper thin material stirred gracefully under the whirling ceiling fan above. They had spent the morning visiting the fields of hydrangeas and buckwheat so Hobie could take pictures and had returned exhausted.

To her surprise, Presley found the buckwheat to be her favorite of all the flowers they had seen in this City of Flowers. Tall and rustic with white and pink puffs of petals along narrow stems, reaching for the sky and waving daintily in the wind, as far as the eye could see. Acres and acres of them. They had made her want to run and skip through the field, which admittedly she did a little bit so Hobie could take her picture, but not so much it would damage the flowers.

"You look like a flower fairy," he'd said as his camera clicked and whirred.

Presley laughed, "Are you saying I'm a buckwheat fairy?"

"I'm saying you're breathtaking."

She paused and pretended to ponder his compliment before answering, "I'll take it."

He lowered his camera and gave her a full dimpled smile, "Good."

Their morning adventure eventually brought them back to their room. Hobie stripped off his shirt because of the heat and they cooled off stretched out on the bed under the ceiling fan, holding hands and talking about all the different fields of flowers and all of the butterflies they had encountered before eventually drifting off to sleep.

He still slept. Presley, on the other hand, had woken well rested and was curious if their attendant had placed the afternoon tea on the patio as had been the custom since they checked in. She got out of bed as quietly as she could so as not to wake him, but she couldn't bring herself to leave the side of the bed.

Enchanted by his sleeping form, long and lean, muscled chest and abs, arms that twitched and flexed occasionally as he dreamed, gorgeous legs that she had only recently been introduced to after they arrived in Vietnam and she saw him in shorts for the very first time, and the dark curls falling into his chiseled handsome face, all of this held her in a kind of trance. Just looking at him brought on so much love and passion she wasn't sure she could eat anyway.

He filled her up completely. That was the truth of it. Since her birthday they had been inseparable and so happy. Not a giddy kind of happiness, more calm and harmonious. But a new level of happiness for her.

They spent their first week in Vietnam at the small village he was always talking about where his friend the Vegan Cowboy lived. All concerns Presley had of fitting in with the humble farming families he thought so much of were washed away when she met them. Kind, gentle, welcoming, funny, they were absolutely delightful. Everything he had told her they would be and more. And the more time she spent with them, with him, in this exotic and wonderful place, the more she realized how much he had opened her up to the world. For the first time in a very long time Presley was excited to explore and see everything she had been ignoring for so long. To see it and to do whatever she could to make it better.

That's what Hobie had brought into her life, openness and harmony and a desire to do for others. She would be forever grateful to him for that, and forever in love with him, of this she was certain.

Presley reached down and pushed a rogue lock of hair off of his brow so she could see his face better.

"Perfect," she said under her breath.

Light sounds of clinking dishes filtered through the French doors and the thought of buttery scones and the hotel's special artichoke tea, which she adored, won her over.

Presley padded in bare feet across the floor and pushed open the French doors just in time to thank the attendant graciously as he disappeared down the stairs.

The food smelled delicious and her stomach growled. In addition to scones there were small sandwiches and tiny little bite sized pastries. Reaching out and breaking off the corner of a scone, Presley was about to pop it in her mouth when she felt Hobie's strong arms slip around her waist from behind.

She sighed contentedly as he kissed her on the ear. He mumbled sleepily, "Is it tea time already?"

"It is," she smiled.

He squeezed her back side into his stomach and lowered his mouth to kiss her on the neck. He was still groggy, sleepy, sexy.

"What are you thinking about?" he asked.

"Oh, I was just thinking about the wonderful things you've shown me here."

He grunted with satisfaction, still nuzzling into her neck. With a half yawn he said, "I have so many things I want to show you. It's a good thing we have our whole lives together ahead of us."

A wave of love and happiness moved through her heart. "We do?" she asked coyly, enjoying his attentions here on their private patio.

"Yes we do. I'm marrying you someday, somehow, Ms. Monroe. There's no doubt about that."

Another wave of joy rose up in her and she leaned back into him, looking across the beautiful green hills of Da Lat and believing him completely. Letting his words sink into her soul they became a part of her.

She was certain that Hobie Brent was the man she was meant to marry and nothing could ever make her any happier than she was in this moment.

A warm breeze came across the garden and brushed against their cheeks and it was as if the ancient countryside was sending them a message of their destiny together. A life of tenderness, giving, curiosity, and love was in store for her and Hobie.

They would grow old together, yes, but their future was still a thrilling mystery. Where would they go? Where would they live? What would they choose to do to make their special mark on the world? Would they have children? That was a question Presley hadn't allowed herself to consider since she was a young woman. Until now.

The specifics were yet to come, and that was okay. The uncertainty was kind of exciting. Knowing only that Hobie would be by her side the whole time was all she was certain of, and that was enough.

Well, maybe she was certain of one other thing.

There was one detail of their future she knew without a doubt would happen, but she hadn't talked to Hobie about it yet. She would, in time. Something told her that he would be all for it. It had come to her in a flash as they sat around a campfire with the Vegan Cowboy and his family drinking hot tea and watching the sun come up over the deep green fields.

That one detail was this—when the time did come for them to get married, to join together as man and wife, they would forgo the expensive wedding, grand reception, and lengthy jet setting honeymoon. No, that wasn't for them. When she and Hobie did get married Presley knew without a doubt that they would elope.

The Final End

For more books by Darci Balogh go to
www.knowheremedia.com/books

ABOUT THE AUTHOR

Darci Balogh is a writer and indie filmmaker from Denver. She grew up in the beautiful mountains of Colorado and has lived in several areas of the state over her lifetime. She currently resides in Denver where she raised her two glorious, intelligent daughters to functioning adulthood. This is, by far, one of her highest achievements.

She has a love-hate relationship with gardening, probably should dust more, adores dogs and is allergic to cats. She has been a writer since she was a child and enjoys crafting stories into novels and screenplays.

Big surprise, some of her favorite pastimes are reading and watching movies. Classic British TV is high on her 'Like' list, along with quietly depressing detective series and coffee with heavy cream.